The Lonely Life
of a
Pornographer's
Wife

By

J. Carol Johnson

Third Paperback Edition
June 2021

PROLOGUE

This story concerns family members, namely the wives, who unwittingly became involved in the pornography business through their men. From the background, these loving women saw the changes money made in their spouses and how that way of life consumed them. And their married lives were also affected.

Pornographic movies could make many millions of dollars for those who would direct, produce, and distribute their films. That much money lead to greed for more money and greater power. Like the Good Book says, "The *love* of money is the root of all evil." However, evil stepped in.

Organized crime became involved when the pornography business flourished during the 1970s. With that, there came stronger greed for more money, power, and ways to attain and maintain them. That could be through threats, physical harm, destruction, and sometimes murder.

No matter, somewhere down the line, someone figured out that sex sells, and it's here to stay... unfortunately for some, such as Carla Martin.

Please, do read on.

Chapter One

COMING HOME

March 1973

1973 was the year of the Ox. In *The Exorcist*, a young girl levitated as viewers sat at the edge of their seats. That year the Vietnam War was cooling down while Watergate was heating up, and Carla Martin was coming back home.

She closed her eyes, leaning back to rest from looking through her many drawings during the long flight. Carla had acquired the education, experience, and knowledge to be a great interior decorator. Now, if she could become established in Portland sooner than possible

That's *if* she could. This small word holds wonder, mystery, hope, intrigue, power, fear, danger, and perhaps even mayhem. It was far beyond Carla's vast imagination that coming home again would cause her to wander down a darkened path into the clutches of the West Coast's most powerful mafia. However, she knew that her first feat would be dealing with her interfering parents.

After leading her high school honor roll, Carla was awarded a four-year college scholarship plus an additional six months of all-expense-paid field study in Europe. However, her scholarship time had now expired.

Having no other choice, she was returning home to her blue-collar parents. They invited Carla to stay with them until she could support herself. For her, that would be no longer than necessary. The Martins were more than content to work at a factory job until retirement and thought she should do the same.

While growing up, her mother had taught her to be grateful that God blessed her with beauty. However, He gave her a far more precious gift, her intelligence, which held precedence over appearance. Eddie, her younger brother by two years, also carried top grades, although he lacked looks in comparison.

When Carla began her new career in Europe, Eddie was fresh out of high school. He enlisted in the Marines to start a new life by getting away from his parents.

By the time the Vietnam War ended, Corporal Edward Martin had received an honorable discharge from the Marines and then was sent to the Veterans Memorial Hospital for a two-month recovery stay because of severe depression and fatigue. At six-foot and one inch, Eddie's robust and muscular body dwindled from two-hundred and twenty pounds to nearly one-hundred seventy-five.

After he regained some strength and appetite, he went to live with his parents. Mom's home cooking readily brought his weight back up to near normal.

It was announced that the plane would soon be descending. Carla flipped her long, auburn hair away from her neck and leaned back again. While thinking of Senator Peter and Beth Nichols being there to meet her, a tranquil smile came across her lips.

Dear Peter Nichols. He was her closest male friend from college, and now he's the youngest Oregon State senator. Carla had introduced him to her dear friend, Bethany, who was studying to become a paralegal. It wasn't long before their friendship turned into love as they became partners in business and then in marriage. Carla and Beth were the reasons Peter exalted himself into a partnership with his family's law firm. With their steadfast encouragement, he proved his worth as a prominent attorney in the political field, as were his father and grandfather.

However, even with his immense knowledge, he never thought that he and Beth would be the salvation of Carla's very sanity in the near future.

During the twenty-minute drive to her hometown of Trenton, Carla had ample time to discuss recent happenings with Peter and Beth.

He said, "There isn't any difference on the home front. Your parents still think you should forget about this "foolish career stuff" and work in the same factory as themselves."

"Apparently, she isn't ever going to change. My brother doesn't have much choice except to stay there for now. But if he stays too long, he'll be right back in the mental ward."

As Peter drove, Carla looked around the landscape. Mount Hood majestically reigned over the lush, fertile valleys and cascading rivers. Those waters housed the critters for which Oregon was nicknamed "The Beaver State". As they approached her parents' home, this familiar area felt strange to Carla for having lived in a culture centuries older.

Peter reminded her of the party the following Saturday evening. "I've invited many well-to-do guests, including some available men who'll want to be meet you. We'll see that you get a career started really soon. Then you can move into Portland."

Beth said, "And I know you'll look spectacular as always. Oh, and Peter asked Eddie to escort you in his dress uniform, with all his ribbons. We think it would help renew his self-esteem."

Carla's attitude perk-up in that she was going to meet new people. People who had careers, not just jobs. People with status, sophistication, and education. People who had traveled, who had seen the Eiffel Tower, who smiled back at the Mona Lisa and cheered for the bulls in Madrid. Yes, someone with whom she could intelligently converse out of her experiences.

Eddie greeted his sister with a warm, welcoming hug. However, their parents were more interested in striking up a conversation with the senator. It was apparent that his presence was more important to the Martins than their daughter. After the Nichols hurriedly excused themselves, Mrs. Martin got Carla settled into her former upstairs bedroom.

In the following few days, she showed Carla a list of jobs she had found that paid well. Mr. Martin mentioned the union's medical insurance and sick-leave benefits.

"Mother, I'm an interior decorator. What I can make for doing just one room will be more that I can make working three forty-hour weeks. And I'll love what I do, not just go to work and do the same hum-drum job day in and day out." Carla nearly bit her tongue for having said that. Now here comes the lecture.

"Well, it fed you and your brother all of your lives and put a roof over your heads. That job your dad and I go to every day, day in and day out, paid for this house and the car we drive. We didn't bring you up to be ungrateful to your elders. If that's the way people do things in London and Paris, then I'll tell you what, young lady, that is *not* the way you will talk when you sit at my table and eat the food I cooked from the money I earned at a job that I am very proud of. Now, what do you have to say about that, Miss *Fancy-Pants?"*

Carla looked at her mother's stern, red face and then at her father. She thought her brother would say nothing, knowing well that the following spiel would be to him. However, he surprised her.

"That's enough! I have to put up with all of this crap from you two, but you have *no* reason to talk to my sister like this. She's twenty-three years old, and you act like she's still in high school. Just knock it off!" Eddie marched out the back door.

"Now see what you've done? You upset your brother," her father snapped. "He's bad off enough as it is without your coming home from your big Europe trip acting all highfalutin' and upsetting everyone. The Good Lord knows we're doing all we can to help your poor brother along. Now you've gone and upset him."

Carla calmly rebuffed her parents, "No, I didn't upset him. You and mother do that every day that he's here. You remind him that he's not well. Eddie had to fight in some stupid war and kill other human beings. He had to watch his buddies get blown up before his very eyes. That's what upsets him. When did you two tell Eddie that you love him no matter what?"

Carla held her temper back enough to leave the table gracefully. And then she comforted her brother as he sat on the patio swing.

"Look, Sis, don't worry about me. I just let them rattle on or suddenly get one of my 'headaches' and go off by myself. I'll be okay."

Carla reminded him of the party. "I'll be so proud to walk in there on your arm. I'll bet you can meet someone to hire you. You have your construction license through the service and all that. You're just terrific at building buildings. And you've always had great ideas for stuff to build, even as a young kid. Eddie, you served our country. These people owe you. We owe you. Now let's go look at that uniform."

Eddie saw the esteem on her face. His strength and being were renewed through her. He put on the uniform he had worn with pride while Carla anxiously waited in her room.

In presenting himself, he stood at attention to see a glow on her face. Then tears stung her eyes. "Oh, Eddie, you are absolutely stunning."

Hearing a rustle, they turned to see their snoopy parents watching through the open door. Their mother gasped, demanding to know why he was in his uniform.

"The senator and his wife are giving a party Saturday evening to honor my sister. I'm going to be her escort."

He wasn't asking permission; that was a statement. It was an affirmation that he would do this of his volition, and indeed, with or without their consent.

"And I'll need to use your car."

"My car?" Mr. Martin looked at his wife, who was stymied by the handsome young man standing before her. She nodded.

"Well, yes, I... I guess that would be alright, son."

A number of guests had already arrived when they reached the senator's grand home. The gaiety of laughter and conversation inside was heard as Eddie rang the doorbell. The hosts warmly greeted the couple with embraces before announcing the guest of honor. And then Peter proudly introduced Eddie.

Carla and Eddie met several of Peter's friends and colleagues. After a time of cocktails, hors d'oeuvres and small talk, Eddie noticed someone who might be interested in his sister.

"Look over my right shoulder at the dark-haired guy with the beard. He's about six feet tall and maybe two hundred pounds.

"Yes, I noticed him looking this way twice before. He has beautiful thick hair. Must pay his barber a small fortune. And it looks like he's used to wearing a tux. Have you talked to anyone worthwhile yet?"

"Yeah. For one, Peter's uncle is a retired Marine and likes to make stuff. He needs my help with building something. Oh, the big guy's coming over here."

"Corporal Martin of the United States Marines, is it?"

"Yes, sir." As Eddie stood at attention, the man smiled with his hand extended. Eddie shook it.

"Oh, relax, I'm Roy Jacobs, a friend of Peter's. It's good to see a serviceman who's on duty. You're not only protecting our country but apparently, our guest of honor as well."

"May I present my sister, Ms. Carla Martin? Carla, this is Roy Jacobs, a friend of the senator."

She nodded, "Hello."

"I understand that you're into interior decoration and may have some remodeling ideas?" Roy asked.

"That's correct."

"Well, I have some movie theaters that are well past the need for a fresh look; they're decades behind in decoration. I didn't know if this was your forte or if you worked primarily with homes."

"The interior of a movie theater *is* like a home. Its many guests enjoy being surrounded by comfort and beauty as much as they would in their own home."

Roy's eyes widened, as did his smile. "That's a good analogy. I want to think my patrons are comfortable and pleased enough to want to come back repeatedly. Have you worked with anything as large as a movie theater before?"

"Well, no, but the only difference between a living room and a theater is the size. That would just take more time and work than a home." Carla spoke with immense confidence, wondering if this might be an unusual opportunity to prove herself or if he was interested in more than her decorating qualities.

"Oh, I see you two have already met," Peter said as he approached them. "I told Roy you're an interior decorator. He has some movie theaters that badly need your help, Carla."

She smiled with relief. "We were just discussing that."

"Great. Because I know Roy's been putting it off for way too long now. He has two theaters here in Portland and four more where he lives in Salem. These places are like landmarks in both cities, but they're very outdated in decors. They need far more than just fresh paint. Roy, Carla has fantastic ideas. Even your father will love them."

He turned to Carla and Eddie. "His grandfather and dad built the two theaters in Portland during the late forties, and they've always been wonderful movie houses, you know, on the luxurious side. People always love to go there for a movie, then go out to dinner." He looked at Roy again, "Or is that dinner and then a movie? I should get out more often," he laughed. "Okay, I'll leave you folks to chat."

Eddie asked about the age and structure of his buildings, their foundations, main joists, and the possibility of any mold.

Roy hesitated. "I don't have any idea. I'd have to check into that. Why do you ask?"

"If there are any problems with these, they'd need to be addressed before any cosmetic work is done. I assume you want to have quality buildings that will last. And how are the roofs? Have they been inspected recently?" Eddie saw Jacob's smile.

"You sure seem to know your way around construction."

"I'm a licensed builder. And I take a special interest in helping Carla." Roy certainly understood that message.

"Perhaps we can get together to look them over and see if you're interested in doing something with them." He reached into his jacket for a business card. "You can call me anytime, and if I'm not in, just leave a message, I'll call you back as soon as I can."

"I will do that, Mr. Jacobs."

He nodded and then turned toward the bar as Carla put the card in her purse.

Even though Jacobs seemed at ease and self-assured around the many guests, she needed to speak to Peter further about him. The senator assured her that Roy was a profitable business owner.

"He runs a tight ship which is why he's worth at least a couple of million. He doesn't date much. His theaters are his love."

Later in the evening, Roy approached Carla a second time to ask about her European escapade. She was more at ease now in conversing with him. As they spoke, he offered his opinions on several foreign cities, and even their architecture, allowing her to deduce that he was well-educated and had traveled. This relaxed her opinion of him as they sipped cocktails and chatted.

However, doubts still entered her mind. Carla needed to know much more about Mr. Jacobs before things went any further. She looked around the room for Peter.

Chapter Two

THE DIRTY MOUTH

The mafia Family business meetings were held in the secure mansion office of Don David Levine. These meetings could involve the Levine Film Corporation, the Families' interests in their movie theaters, the making and distribution of pornography movies, or other topics such as rival gangs or turf invasion.

CEO Levine sat at the head of the eight-foot-long, dark walnut conference table while the other members took their seats. Drinking wine or liquor before or during meetings was not allowed. The men needed to have a clear head for these discussions, so each were given an empty glass. Pictures of water were at either end where they could serve themselves. Notepads or writing utensils were obviously absent since their written words could be traced.

Due to slim but possible wire tampering or bugging devices of the Levine Family meetings, Harry Philips, the corporate attorney, strongly suggested the members speak in erroneous or vague terms. This way, nothing could be proven in a court of law that any actual events or situations were mentioned or known by these members. For instance, if a person was dead, they'd be "sleeping" or "asleep", and their theaters were called "stores." This also gave the men an opportunity to challenge one another as to their eloquence of speech. In doing so, it added a bit of enjoyable flair to these meetings.

Saying nothing, most of the men realized he was uncomfortable about having the "outsider" at the table, even though he had come highly recommended by their former partner, now near death in the clutches of cancer.

This man seemed to have had a cocky attitude, although, he was quiet in the meetings. He dressed well yet was unkempt and with dirty fingernails. That caused Levine to have further doubts about him. After this third meeting, the executive board would determine in which position he would be placed.

When all necessary matters had been discussed, Don Levine asked if there were any new topics to cover.

Philips, the first partner and adviser, said videocassette recorders were becoming prevalent on the market.

"They're calling them VCRs. With these new recorders, all kinds of movies can be rented to show on TV sets. Several manufacturers sell the VCRs but they can also be rented at stores called video markets."

"These new gadgets, these new recorders, will they become a threat to our business and our livelihood?" asked Levine.

"Are you shittin' me?! These goddamn things are gonna eat us outta' house and home," spouted the new man. "They're gonna get so fuckin' big that they're gonna put this industry right down the toilet. You're goddamn right we gotta watch out for them. I'll betcha that pretty soon somebody is gonna' sell 'em cheap enough that every asshole on the street will be able to buy one."

The man's language annoyed Levine considerably, however, he let him continue.

"You'll see porn on them things left and right, and there goes your porno movie industry, *and* your goddam theaters too! Men won't pay to go to a theater to watch that shit when they can stay home an' jack off an' watch it for almost free. "

He looked around the table at the men who were either looking down or away. No one spoke.

"What the hell's the matter with alla' you guys. Cat got your goddam tongue?"

Richard Hirsh spoke for the rest of the men. He was the second partner, also known as the Family 'enforcer', who readily saw that matters were taken care of and often first-hand.

"We do not use that kind of abusive language at our meetings."

"What? You guys a bunch of pussies or something?"

"We are gentlemen, and we speak as such at our meetings. And we show our respect to Don Levine in doing so. There are too many words in the English language than to use the expletives you did."

Levine motioned for him to go on.

"Do you recall the tablets that Moses gave his people?"

"Well, yeah. They was the ten commandments."

"And what was the first commandment?"

"Uh, well..." He knew he had better answer this question correctly. "I'm God, and you can't have no more gods around me."

"And then what?"

The man in question looked at the faces glaring back at him. He saw what now seemed like a death squad. "Um, you ain't supposed to use God's name in a bad way."

"Did you not just break that commandment before these witnesses?"

"Uh... yeah, I guess I did. I apologize for that, I'm sorry. I didn't mean to offend Mr. Levine, or any of you... or God, for that matter." He looked upward, "I'm sorry God, I didn't mean to offend you either, I guess... I guess I just didn't think." The he bowed his head.

Most of the men looked at Levine, who nodded slightly to Samuel Blum and then glanced at the door. This enormous, quiet-spoken black man was the bodyguard and protector of all the Family men, their wives, and children. He would instantly lay his life down for Don David Levine.

Blum quietly stood up and walked over to the man. "Let me escort you to your car, sir."

Levine's eyes flashed at Hirsh who joined the other two as they left the room. He and Blum returned shorty.

"The gentleman sends regrets that he has to leave town and won't be able to attend any future meetings with us," Hirsh reported. "However, he did voice an interest in learning more about the scriptures... burning in hell, in particular.

Levine nodded, "Some things are best learned first-hand. Too much knowledge is a dangerous thing. Are there any further comments on this recorder issue?" The other men subtly shook their heads. "Is there anything else to discuss today?"

Hirsh spoke up. "There is one thing that I'd like to cover briefly, sir. It's about a young man from Salem, Oregon. I understand that he's taken over his father' two Portland theaters, which his grandfather established. He also has four of his own in Salem. These establishments have merited him a vast income. I was told the grandson might show porno films in his establishments. He seems to have the ambition that would interest us."

Hirsh organized and allocated specific Family duties. His opinions were regarded as having had thoroughly considered all sides of an issue.

Levine said, "That may be something to investigate. Tell us more about him and what his ambitions might be."

"His name is Roy Jacobs, twenty-nine years old with a college degree in business administration and management. Some noted that he dresses particularly well and drives a new model Town Car. He's single, lives alone, and doesn't date anyone in particular."

Levine raised his eyebrows. Leaning back in his well-padded, black leather office chair, he said, "I think this young man sounds to be of interest to us. Perhaps you can take a brief trip to visit the area. He may be available to show you around town. What do you think, Richard?"

"I'd certainly like that. I haven't been to Salem or Portland for a while. If this young man *is* rather ambitious, it would be a good thing to invite him to be a part of our Family before Perez or Gorvetti persuade him to join theirs. These two so-called 'Families' deal in prositution and get school kids hooked on their drugs. Then they're worthless after that. It would be a shame to have them influence someone like this Jacobs man."

With that said, Levine turned to Blum. "I want you and your men to see that these Perez and Gorvetti outlaws do not infiltrate our area at any cost. We know only too well their ways of persuasion."

Levine looked at the partners, "I think that in using our more gentle approach, this young Portland man may be interested in joining us. I understand that the Salem area is less prone to Mexicans than Los Angeles, but not so with Italians. If there is nothing else, we can adjourn now.

Samuel Blum was a soft-spoken, gentle black man whose mother taught him that his enormous size would always invite trouble; he should be gentle to all creatures, large or small, treat women with respect, children with kindness, and always be polite. He also had great admiration and respect for Don David Levine from his neighborhood of many years.

There was a day when he saw someone who did not have that regard, it seemed, for any other one but himself. That man stepped in front of Mrs. Levine as her husband opened the restaurant door. He barged past other awaiting customers to demand a table for himself.

Blum was a dishwasher who saw this when he set out a tray of clean glasses. Still wearing his work apron, he gently excused himself to address the "gentleman" in question.

"I believe you owe Mr. Levine and his wife an apology, sir."

The blowhard looked Blum over and then spat on him. "Get the hell back in your kitchen, *boy*!" He then turned his back to him.

"I think you should leave this fine establishment now, sir," Blum answered quietly. His enormous, muscular hand engulfed the man's neck and turned him around toward the door. The bully was unable to breathe, let alone speak. Blum released his grip enough for the man to gasp for air when they reached the Levines.

"Now apologize to this fine lady and gentleman, sir."

Levine acknowledged that he understood the garbled message.

Outside, Blum threw the man down onto the sidewalk, twice slamming his size thirteen shoe into his belly hard enough that blood spewed out of the man's mouth and again to his chest as onlookers cringed to hear his ribs crack.

"Don't ever show no disrespect to the Don of this neighborhood again. That was just a 'love tap' you got today, mister," Blum said adamantly.

When he went back inside to finish putting away the tray of glasses, there was a note offering him a better job. It was signed, "With appreciation, Don Levine."

David Levine and Harry Philips were childhood friends from the same neighborhood. However, they became separated after the Korean War. Harry had served with Richard Hirsh, the son of a much-respected furrier. Hirsh senior was renowned for his fine garments of rich sable, Canadian mink, fox, and many other furs.

Richard apprenticed in his father's business with the same love of furs, and Harry studied law extensively, hoping to work beside his renowned father as a partner in his prestigious law firm.

David's father, Herbert Levine, provided well for his Family from the latter days of vaudeville when he noticed the popularity of burlesque.

Young ladies with exquisite, curvaceous bodies enjoyed the generous tips and cheers from gentlemen who patronized the private, all-male nightclubs. And by earning extra income as personal escorts, these tempting and tantalizing teasers could afford finer garments for their titillating on-stage performances. Soon, there was an enormous growth in Levine's business.

Many dancers learned that by giving very "special" attention to these gentlemen, especially the older, more established ones, they received very special gifts. Hirsh occasionally favored them with an elegant fur, or a lovely piece of jewelry came from Mr. Kaplin, one of Levine's business friends.

Another close friend, Sylvan Fraiser, was becoming renowned for his real estate savvy and construction business. He offered the land and built Levine's casinos on it for quite a fair price. For this, both men's businesses grew immensely.

These casinos sheltered prostitution brought about by the unique on-stage dancing girls who were on musical display for the male customers. A gentleman would merely give the waiter a number, and a generous tip, for the manager to arrange a "meeting" with that customer and the particular cute dance number.

When two over-sized men approached him for employment, Levine thought they could be of good use as guards at the front of his establishments. They would defer any less-than-reputable clients and give security to those whom they welcomed.

This man learned well from wise adages, sages, and personal experience that treating his customers as gentlemen and with high regard would return their respect. Those men were welcomed and shown much courtesy by employees who appreciated their lavish gratuity.

The townsfolk referred to him as the *Don* Hubert Levine, which is a way of addressing a man of honor and respect in an organization or community. For this, he reciprocated by offering employment to his community and giving generously to charities for the needy.

Eight-millimeter films shown in private dens brought an enormous surge in popularity. His interest in the film business led Levine to pursue that field, so Levine became educated and then productive in the film industry. He earned a vast income in making and showing "indecent" movies in the theaters.

And Levine knew if he owned these establishments in which to show his films, his income would be that much more significant as his 'Family' grew larger

Herbert Levine approached one theater owner to sell his movie house for a reasonable offer. He refused, knowing what kind of "filth" would be shown, even though Levine explained that these were educational movies. The owner failed to see the true meaning of this kind of learning until Levine asked two of his associates to explain it to him. Upon regaining consciousness in the hospital, the owner could fully understand that it was indeed a good idea to sell Levine his theater.

With that, an adage from his grandmother was applied to the movie house; "A little love and a little paint makes a home look like what it ain't." The attendance was increased by those who enjoyed these 'specialty' films being shown in a more lovely and comfortable setting.

For this, Sylvan Fraiser provided Levine with the property and construction of more theaters.

Levine passed this wisdom, knowledge, and advice on to his son, David, who was now old enough to learn this business and interested enough to apply his father's education. His fascination with the beautiful ladies further stimulated his ambition.

One day, David Levine entered a restaurant where Harry Phillips and Richard Hirsh were dining. After joining them, the three became like-minded and as one during the lengthy conversation. Each understood that by combining their fields of endeavor, they could be of greater strength in giving service to those who came to them for needs, help, advice, or problems that they alone could not solve.

Since Don Herbert Levine had established repertoire through his business of vice, illicit movies, and prostitution in the community, his son David came to earn that same status. As the elder and more worldly of the three, Harry Phillips and Richard Hirsh gave him the honor to act as commander and chief in having the final decision in all authoritative matters of this small group. They joined in brotherhood to become as one, and thus David Levine became the Don of this Family, as was his father over his Family.

Throughout the following years, this Family grew not only great in number but in strength, power, and money enough to merit respect and admiration, although, sometimes fear, if others were foolish enough to cross that line between honor and distrust.

Chapter Three

THE GRAND OPENING

When they viewed the theater buildings, Carla offered Roy several immediate suggestions. He was impressed in her ability to look past the walls and vision what could be done. In their next rendezvous she presented several options rendered through her sketches. Upon his picking a theme, Carla offered figures of overall costs, which included Eddie's work.

Roy was pleased that she selected materials and furnishings at much less a cost than offers previously submitted by other builders. That fascinated him. *A beautiful woman with a good head for business to boot, I like that.*

"You just got yourself a job."

Roy showed them the charming two-bedroom apartment above the main lobby. It was completely furnished, including the kitchen. He offered this rent-free. Carla could use the second bedroom as her office. She'd have use of a company car since refurbishing the whole theater would be a long project for the two. She accepted the offer insisting this would be included in the employment contract.

In no time, supplies, contractors, painters, and materials were ordered. Within two months. Carla saw her vision come to life. Roy occasionally stopped in from his hometown of Salem, where he was tending to his other theaters. He was taken aback to see how well and how fast the remodel was coming along, assuring himself that he had made the right decision in hiring her.

Upon his arrival to the Majestic one day, Roy was immensely pleased that the remodel was nearly finished.

He marveled at the major differences to the theater. The colors were pleasing, the furnishings were elegant, the wallpaper was enchanting, and the was carpet practical, yet attractive. The cost was below budget, which further impressed him. Carla informed him of the exact finish date. Then Roy arranged to have a grand re-opening as soon as the work was completed.

Amid the many various stores and shops displaying their fine clothing, precious jewelry, custom-made furs, and hand-crafted gifts, now stood the Majestic movie theater in all its glory. It was transformed into the luxury of kings and queens, lords and ladies from jolly old England of yore.

Roy appreciated the glass ticket sales booth which boasted a large, gold ornately framed mirror at the back wall. This reflected the patron's images. The salesperson sat on a gold, throne-like chair upholstered in red velvet.

The theater's front was all glass to exhibit the elaborate lobby that had a golden center fountain. It gave guests an opportunity to make a wish and then toss coins into the cherub's purse. An imposing staircase lead to the restrooms which were finished in red and gold with ornately framed mirrors, deeply cushioned settees, and shining marbled floors.

The concession area was well-lit by several small crystal chandeliers. Their light reflected on the glass display shelves below which held a grand selection of confections. Behind that were the drinks and ever-popping corn to give off its inviting aroma. The servants were dressed like... well, like servants.

On grand opening night, complete with klieg lights, Roy dressed in kingly garb to escort "Queen Carla", wearing an exquisite gown of the era. The gala event was attended by Senator and Mrs. Nichols, who cut the ribbon. They guided the gathering into the finely decorated theater, complete with newly re-upholstered seats for greater comfort of the customers. The townsfolk celebrated the oldest and now the finest theater in Portland.

After a day's rest from the excitement, Carla was surprised by a visit from Roy with a bonus check. He asked that she'd set aside any possible work plans to refurbish the Regency Theater in likewise fashion and then to move down to Salem to re-work those four theaters. Stymied but thrilled for steady work with the same employer, Carla conferred with her brother. They accepted his offer.

The Regency became as spectacular as was the Majestic. Carla used the French Provisional era to be the theme in the same elegance and glory. Again, the opening was spectacular.

In French attire of the day, "King Louie and Queen Antoinette" lead the gala procession in the same pomp and glory as was the Majestic grand opening. Once again, Senator Nichols cut the ribbon as camera lights flashed.

Now it was off to Salem. Carla suggested using the identical themes of the Portland theaters, changing those names to the 'Majestic' and 'Regency'. The same contacts for the materials were used so this remodeling went much faster and saved Roy a vast amount of money.

He offered her the three-bedroom, two-bath apartment above the larger theater, and again she accepted. Her brother would use the third bedroom during their employment.

Eddie and Carla began working as soon as Roy approved of her design suggestions and cost estimate. He asked that she made that office in the Majestic Theater more comfortable in that he'd be conducting most of his business there. In a short time, he was elated to see a near-duplication of the Portland theater.

One day, Roy received a phone call from Harry Phillips.

"I'm David Levine's attorney," he announced. Roy recognized that name. He was *the* man of the West Coast pornography industry.

"Yes, what can I do for you, sir?"

"I understand you've been doing some excellent remodeling work. We have some theaters that need a good going-over and would like to see what you've had done. I'd like to send one of my partners up to see it. And perhaps you can recommend your designer to us."

Roy wondered how Levine's attorney learned about his theaters. "I would be happy to show him around. My two in Portland are completely re-finished. He can see what we've done with those," Roy suggested.

Since there was more work in progress on the Salem movie theaters, this inferred that Jacobs had more money than suspected.

"He can fit that into his schedule. Would Friday be convenient for you?"

"Certainly, I can pick the gentleman up. What is his name?

"Richard Hirsh. I'll have him use Alaska Airlines. There's one that would arrive in Portland at ten-twenty A.M., unless that's not convenient for you."

No, but I don't dare say that. "Certainly, I need to be in Portland that weekend, anyway." Roy surprised himself with that quick lie, although, it was necessary.

Philips went on to describe Hirsh, who sounded like a typical Jewish businessman.

"I'll be sure to pick him up then. Goodbye." *Damn, they already had this planed. So what's really going on?*

Roy knew that he had to play this game well. He also knew the prestige Levine carried in the porno business, but how did he come to be interested him, his theaters, and where did Phillips get the information? This was truly flattering but also rather scary. Roy sat in his office chair to ponder the situation.

He picked up the phone again to call his attorney. This man could be a little underhanded, however, he was very knowledgeable as he had proven to Jacobs in the past. Larry Cross had been a high school chum who befriended the Jewish Roy when other kids bullied him because of his heritage.

In keeping to their own communities the immigrants stayed strong and supportive of one another until the integration of education separated the children from their families. Many a child weakened in their togetherness to join the "accepted" white kids' traditional lives, thus falling away from the parental stronghold. Having known want and hunger himself, Cross offered some clients a lesser fee than other attorneys. In doing so, he garnered respect as a lawyer and in the community. At thirty years of age, his responsibilities included providing for his wife, their two children, and a mortgaged home.

Upon explanation of the phone call, Roy awaited an answer. He knew if Cross pondered a while, it was because he seriously considered all sides of the issue.

"What do you know about this Philips guy?" Cross asked.

"Never heard of him before."

"I'll start there, and his partner will be next. It shouldn't be a problem if he's listed in the attorneys' directory as such. Not all of them passed the board, though. But they could have just enough education to be used by someone like Levine. Or perhaps his boss bought off a formerly 'good' lawyer to do his job just inside the lines. You say his attitude was kind of mafia-like, or have you been watching too many movies?" Cross laughed.

"Maybe *he* has, but yes, I've dealt with men like that before. And it isn't a put-on. He had the right attitude and all that."

"Alright Roy, I'll get back to as soon as I get anything. By the way, is this a one-time job or will you be putting me on a retainer?" The question was amiable but serious.

"It may come to a retainer. Let's see what you can find out."

"Good enough. I see that you're still being evasive, so I'll do my best to help you out," Larry answered.

"Looks who's being evasive now?" Roy laughed. *He's going to work for me, at least I can trust him.*

Larry later had some good news and some bad.

"Philips is on the bar with excellent grades in school and knows his stuff."

"And the bad news?"

"That was the bad news. He's worked with Levine most of his business life, and he's a younger brother to him of sorts. You know, a shirt-tail relative or something. This guy has a good law business and knows everything David Levine knows, but not everybody else around knows that. Except for his wife, Jada. She's quite the beautiful socialite. And they just bought the old Metzler mansion."

"What? The movie producer, Harold Metzler?"

"One and the same. So, we know that Levine is stepping up in the world. Now I haven't found out if he's still doing porno or if he's going legit. I have feelers out on that, but either way, I'll bet he's going to need a damned good interior decorator for that mansion. And Mrs. Levine seems to take the best talents under her wing. Fancy that."

"You just got yourself a retainer, pal! Now, I need to clue Carla in on that. She's got a really good business head, extremely talented,and attractive."

"Oh, beauty and the beast, huh?"

"Thanks, pal. Like I said, she's business first, but a real lady who has her own bodyguard. Well, two of them. Her younger brother watches out for her; he does her construction and all that. The other one is a college pal, and get this, he's Senator Peter Nichols. It seems that they've been pretty tight for several years."

"No kidding? Wow, that's a good one to have in her pocket. How'd ya' meet her?"

"The senator gave her a big homecoming party when she got back from Europe. I was probably invited because I'm close to her age and single with money. But I don't mean to stay that way forever. You'll really like her, Larry."

"Sounds like you sure do. Okay, I'll get on it and see what else I can learn. Just play it cool and wise with this Hirsh character. Oh, by the way, you might want to brush up on your Jew background because this outfit is all *Heebs*."

"Now, now Larry, that's not nice. We are *Jewish* folks," laughed Roy.

"Alright, some more than others. And this guy just might want to meet Carla. If she's all *that* good he can pass the word on to the Don."

"The who?"

"The Don."

"You mean as in godfather?"

"Sure do. The *Don* David Levine."

"Oh, shit. Yeah, thanks for the heads up on that! Catch ya later."

Roy Jacobs leaned back in his chair trying to think of how it would be to meet this 'Don' character. He had to "think himself into the proper shoes to wear," as his college drama class coach would say.

Roy chuckled to himself when he recalled the overheard conversation between his parents. His wise father wanted him to take the drama class to build up his self-esteem and confidence in dealing with other businessmen. His mother thought that class would make a sissy out of him.

"No, mother, it will make a man out of him, so he can learn to stand up to his competition with confidence. Usually a man learns this by being around women and learning about manhood that way. Our son? So, where are the girls? Sure, he doesn't look bad if he keeps his stomach trim. But he has no backside and no biceps. That's what a girl looks at when she isn't looking at his zipper wondering what he has in there."

"Oh, Papa! Watch your tongue."

"Now Mother, I know you did some looking at me yourself when we were young, so don't 'oh Papa' me. But I liked to see you look."

His mother giggled. "I thought you were a handsome boy, too."

"I still am," he laughed, "but look at our son. At least the good Lord gave him a brain, but a face?"

"Oh, now Roy is not ugly."

"Well, no, it's just that he's not *not* ugly. Maybe he can just grow a beard. He has to build up his mind and think strong.

One day he can take over this business, just like I took over my papa's business."

Roy grew that beard and wore slightly tinted glasses. They became like a disguise for him. People couldn't read his facial expressions if they couldn't see them. Now he needed to focus on someone like Charlton Heston, Burt Lancaster, or Kirk Douglas. They were a *man's* man. In the bathroom mirror, he practiced his best performances until he was "wearing their shoes".

He suddenly thought of contacting Carla. Hirsh would want to meet the decorator too.

She was impressed wih the upcoming meeting for Roy, but not in her meeting Hirsh. "I don't think you really want me to meet someone like that. I'm not at all known. He'll want a big-name decorator, you know how it is. They brag about having the best and biggest, the most exclusive ones."

"You *are* one of those. With the work you've done for me, I'm sure they'll want to hire you. For as many theaters they must own you'll have work for many years to come."

Carla took a deep breath and let the air out slowly while Roy kept his eyes on her. She shrugged and then turned around with a sigh.

"Okay, you convinced me. But I sure don't want to decorate movie theaters for the rest of my life. I was taught to do homes."

"Oh, but the interior of a movie theater is just like a home, only much larger. And don't you want your guests to be surrounded by beauty and...."

They laughed when Carla recognized her words said with a twist. "Alright, I'll meet the man, but I don't want to get into any long talks or conversations with him."

Roy recognized Richard Hirsh when he arrived. He was a rather pleasant man who was highly impressed with the new Majestic Theater. It was his understanding that his grandfather had built it. Hirsh had done his homework in knowing this was still in his father's name, which would make it difficult for his mafia people to take it over.

Reaching into his sport coat pocket, Richard withdrew a small disc camera. "Would you mind if I take some pictures for the Levines? I know that Jada will enjoy seeing this fountain, and especially the concession area with those lights above it."

"Oh, certainly you may, and the Regency theater too, if you wish. I'm very proud to show off my decorator's work."

Hirsh was equally impressed to see the Regency and was interested in meeting its decorator. Roy called her to the lobby. Carla noticed the smile and widened eyes of Mr. Hirsh as she offered her hand with a smile in return. Roy was sure to mention that her brother was the one who headed up all construction issues.

"It's good to keep matters in the family and not have to depend on outside help that may not accept your authority as a woman. I defiantly admire what you have done in your work here. Probably not as much as Roy does, though. I understand that you were trained in Europe. What was your favorite city?" asked Richard.

Roy tried not to flinch in the realization that this man had done a background check on her.

"Oh, I believe I was most impressed with Rome, but my heart is still in London."

"I can certainly see the English and French influence in your work. It's quite true to the old-world culture."

Richard held up the camera. "May I take your picture? I'm quite sure that Mrs. Levine would like to see what you look like and that the Don Levine would appreciate your beauty."

With a blush, Carla gave her approval and then turned to show her better side to the camera.

Chapter Four

THE PROPOSAL

After considerable time working together, Roy cautiously made his good intentions noticeable toward Carla, although wordlessly. His presence, voice, and attitude softened. For a man to show Carla deserving respect, that he'd keep his private thoughts in check, impressed her immensely.

When Eddie finally finished his work, there was no longer a need for him to stay in the apartment. Carla looked forward to Roy's visits, which sometimes led into a late evening not always on the sleeper couch.

Roy's caresses were tender. As his words softened, he filled them with care and love, a love that she could now recognize. His infrequent lovemaking was gentle with much tenderness, although, inexperienced and somewhat inept. Nevertheless, it was filled with love.

Carla understood that this was a man of the world; just not the world she had known; that of her being attractive to men because of her beauty and sex appeal far more than her mind. Roy's experience was with business more than women, partly due to his appearance. Although, his financial prowess attracted the ladies.

For now, neither was in a rush to develop a full sexual relationship. Carla had proven herself to Roy as an independent, financially secure woman of remarkable insight, with a stable sense of business and integrity. How could he not fall deeply in love with her? For her to return that emotion was truly sublime for him.

One day, Roy asked Carla to see a house he was interested in buying, a little way out of the city. It was reasonably large with three bedrooms and a two-car attached garage. The sizeable backyard had a full deck and patio for barbecues. The front yard was smaller and definitely needed her attention.

The polished stone entry led to the massive living room. It had a cathedral beamed ceiling and one entire wall of glass windows facing the street. At one end stood a commanding stone fireplace and mantel. The opposite wall was barren. That led to a large kitchen with an island counter and then to a formal dining room.

Roy smiled with knowing pride as he watched the woman's facial expressions and body language change with ideas on how she could redecorate this home. He escorted her down the hallway to a large master bedroom that could easily accommodate king-size furniture. She marveled even more to see that the en suite bathroom sported a large whirlpool tub, separate shower, double sink vanity, and a walk-in closet. In the hallway, she noticed the full-size guest bathroom.

"There are two smaller bedrooms with baths further on, one could be an office, or you can put one in down here." Roy led her to the semi-finished basement room off the garage. Carla saw it could be made into another den or office. Her face lit with ideas.

"Roy, I can make this into a glorious den so you can have your business meetings here. I can do wonders with it for you." Carla looked at Roy, who was smiling with warmth.

"Not me, it's for us." Her face sobered as she looked around the empty room.

She was confused. "Us?"

"I mean that I want to marry you." Carla continued to look into his eyes that were filled with sincerity. "Will you marry me?"

"Oh, my gosh...yes." As he embraced her, Carla said, "Yes, Roy, I will."

Since Carla had nearly completed his theaters, Roy purchased the house for her to move in and start changing it into the home of her dreams. Roy gave her credit cards to use as she pleased. He continued to live in his own home while the redecorating was in progress.

Soon, Roy received a call from Richard Hirsh inviting him to meet with himself, Mr. Levine, and their wives for dinner in Los Angeles. This invitation was not one to be turned down.

An airport hotel room had been reserved for him near the luxurious restaurant. The awaiting group was just into their first cocktails. To Roy's mild surprise, the Don was not a fat, bald, old man as he had imagined. Instead, a medium-built man with a slight paunch, a full head of dark hair, and in his late fifties. Mrs. Levine was a stately, trim, and beautiful woman who was exquisitely dressed and about the same age as her husband of many years. Sharon Hirsh was more curvaceous, although, just as lovely and attractively dressed. In their company, Roy felt at ease.

As dinner progressed, so did the subjects they discussed. The stupendous remodel of Roy's theaters was a top subject. The inquisitive Sharon and Jada asked impertinent questions about the designer. Roy concluded that this was concerning their purchase of the Metzler mansion; they would need an interior decorator. He informed them of his recent betrothal to the fantastic designer and was very involved in redoing their new home-to-be.

After congratulations were said, Jada sat back with a sigh of relief. "I was terribly concerned that she might find other work and that I couldn't retain her because we're not ready yet."

Oh, their minds had already been set on Carla. "Wouldn't you want to meet her first?" Roy asked.

"Why don't you see what she has to say? Then we can make plans for both of you to come down for a visit. You can stay at our guest house," Jada suggested.

When dessert and coffee were served, David said something that caught Roy off guard.

"I understand that you're considering showing more graphic movies in some of your Salem houses."

"Yes, I've been thinking of going that route, a little at a time. I'm not too sure how downtown will take to it, so I'd show that in one of my outlying theaters."

David smiled, "When it comes time, perhaps you will contact us. I have some outstanding films that you might be interested in showing to your community."

"Why, thank you very much for the offer, sir. Yes, I wouldn't show anything other than your excellent movies to my customers. I have learned long ago to listen to their input. Their return visits are much appreciated." *It wasn't just Carla. He's been checking on me too.*

On the flight back, Roy considered the proposition carefully. Perhaps the Levine Family wanted to expand their territory. With them, Roy would have excellent protection from any advances by the notorious Gorvetti and Perez Families.

He needed to consult Larry Cross about the Don's proposition.

"Yeah, I think Levine wants to make a move up north before the other so-called '*families*' try to get their foot in the door," Larry said. "At least the Levine Family is upfront and out in the open with everyone. They look to be within the law, and with them, you'll have good protection. They don't shake anyone down or do the 'protection money' stuff like in the old days."

Then Larry warned, "But the Perez and Gorvetti men are holy terrors. Don't ever get wrapped up with any of *those* people. I'll check to find out how the Levine Family is doing for income on their movies and get back to you on it. Just play it cool for now would be my advice."

Gorvetti's men were gathered from those with backgrounds like his own. They were from abusive parents, broken homes, or large families and had very little, if any, religious or spiritual training. These men were only too ready to find a family of "brothers" on whom they could trust and rely. With Jerry Gorvetti being the eldest and most experienced of the gang, they learned from him.

This leader had been taught by his older brothers how to steal, take, cajole, or bribe what they wanted or needed, be it food, clothing, cars, or cash. He learned how to silently break into homes, cars, and stores. There were rules to go by, such as wearing gloves, dark clothing, soft-soled shoes, or sneakers. They would always carry a clean rag to wipe away any fingerprints, stuff into a boisterous mouth, or help silence a loud gun. Gorvetti laid the rules down to his men; no child abuse, no rape, and no back-talk. They either followed his orders or get a bullet in their head, and they knew he meant what he said.

When this lot learned that the Perez gang was making a tremendous amount of money from the porno racket, it was time for them to muscle into it themselves. As Perez moved south to Glendale, San Pedro, Hermosa Beach, and Acapulco, the Gorvetti people moved north to Oakland, Sacramento, and Fresno. As they went, Gorvetti's men overtook pool halls, massage parlors, and smaller casinos. While their investments grew, so did their families.

Unlike the Levine Family, these two 'gangs' were ruthless, merciless, and sometimes careless, which caused grief to their leaders and perhaps death to a member. However, that was a sure way to keep everyone in line. It became necessary for Perez and Gorvetti to ensure the men close to them were also extraordinarily faithful to them. They needed to watch out for any soldiers who hoped to make rank to sergeant or lieutenant, thus causing suspicion in the armies. Having to sleep in a bullet-proof vest didn't make for a restful night. As the saying goes, "It's lonely at the top."

Gorvetti found strength in numbers as he built his stronghold with faithful men who enjoyed a more lucrative lifestyle without the strenuous labor. During his investigations, Gorvetti learned about the porno movie industry. For him, that looked to be lucrative.

The not-too-intelligent men that Perez took in were enthusiastic in using their physical powers, while Juan Perez did the planning, scheming, and decision making. It didn't take long before his name was well-known, or at least notorious. Of this, he became proud.

It was a long way from being bullied in high school for his ethnicity, lack of stature, or looks. The girls who befriended him were not particularly attractive, but they were kind to him. Even kinder, when he helped them raise their grades, for which, they raised their skirts in appreciation, which in turn, he appreciated.

Having realized his ability to better improve his female relationships by using his God-given intelligence, Perez soon realized that also worked to get a masculine following. For their higher high school grades, they were eager to protect their tutor outside of the classroom. It was not long before he became feared by many of whom he had previously feared.

These young men were now well into their mid-twenties, hungry for adventure, fast cars, fortune, and the females which all that attracted. Perez had not grown any bigger or more handsome, but his wisdom grew by experience and adventure, which led to his new fortune. This man found that it was better to receive than to give. He rather enjoyed men begging for mercy just as he had once done.

Good transportation came by breaking a window. Fast money was made in an alley with a knife. With that same knife, Perez had all the sex he wanted. When he bought a good gun for far less than wholesale, Perez found how easy it was to get all the liquor he wanted, and as a bonus, money from the till.

In swearing an oath of allegiance, these seven "brothers" knew they had each other's backs, even unto death. They were able to call in "cousins", who were faithful men outside of the immediate family, on whom they could rely if they were needed for assistance.

It didn't take but a few viewings of pornography movies than for Perez to want to try that out too. He learned the movie theater trade, teaching his men to perform individual functions until his own movie house was orderly and running smoothly.

Some of his men might scout the local towns for other theaters that may be for sale. Or they could be prompted to sell with a bit of "persuasion" from some of the Perez Family via cold hard cash or cold hard brass knuckles, whichever worked best. Not a very popular method, but it seemed to work many times. And the money was considerable for one and all.

Chapter Five

ROY EXPLAINS PORNO

When Carla was nearly finished refinishing their home, Roy moved in to be with her more and save time driving between places.

It was gradual, but she noticed his personality changing during the third and fourth months of their living together. Not only was he not as romantic, he was also becoming a little curt at times in his answers or questions. He sometimes spoke to her as though she were an employee. However, Carla tried to brush this off due to his growing business, one that was flourishing because of the eloquent theaters she had designed. Now she was preparing the home for their life together.

Carla took a work break one day to begin making wedding plans and arrangements. Roy came home from the office to see her pondering over a guest list. She had few people to invite since her family was small and that she had been away at college, also for her months overseas. Roy suggested having a small family service to avoid choosing whom he should or should not invite. And then there would be all the fuss of ordering flowers and decorations plus the preparation of a reception.

"You've been through enough just working on the theaters, and now you're becoming worn-out from redecorating our house. Planning a big wedding will exhaust you, wouldn't you agree?"

He spoke in such a firm manner that Carla thought his mind was already set on having a small wedding. But why? It certainly wasn't as though they couldn't afford a large one. Was he hiding something from her? Or perhaps it was because most all the guests would be his people. Although, she *was* overworked. Carla was confused, and this was not the time to get into another argument.

"I guess you're right. I've been trying to get the house finished."

She paused for a moment. "I wanted to know what kind of ring to get you. Do you want a diamond in it or maybe your birthstone? A ruby or sapphire would look good. A lot of people are getting away from diamonds. I know one couple who..."

"Ring for what?" Roy interrupted.

"Your wedding ring, of course."

"I'm not wearing any wedding ring," he coldly said.

"Why not?"

"I'm just not, that's all."

"My question was 'why not?'."

"Because I'm not. I don't wear rings except for some special social occasion."

Carla looked up at him. The clenched muscles at the back of his jaw, his furrowed brow, and tightened lips silenced her tongue.

A ghostly cooling came over her. She knew why Roy didn't want to wear a wedding band; he didn't plan to be faithful to her. She stood up to face Roy. His jaw was set tight with gritted teeth. Because of his deception, he tried not to look into her eyes.

"Well, that saves us both some added expense. I won't wear one either. End of conversation."

She turned to walk away when he grabbed her arm. "You *will* wear a wedding ring. I'll be damned if you're going to be running all over the country as my wife without one!"

She turned to him, this time with her teeth gritted as she spoke low and firm. "How about if I don't wear your name then? I'll just keep my name as Martin so you don't think of me as an object or a pet that you own. Maybe I just won't marry you then. That way, I won't have to wear any symbols of marital attachment, just like you won't."

Roy picked up his keys and money from the entry table.

"Where are you going?"

"To get something to eat." He grumbled.

"I have dinner on the stove," she argued.

"But it's not on the table." He firmly shut the door behind himself.

With a deep sigh, Carla went into the kitchen to make a drink of Scotch and some water to settle her nerves. She sat for a while on the large, thickly padded, and extremely comfortable sofa. Moving her hand over the luxurious fabric, she smiled to herself.

Mrs. Jacobs-to-be, or not-to-be, looked around the room. She said aloud, "You did an excellent job here, Carla. Why, thank you very much, Carla."

After a while, she considered getting another drink when Roy drove into the driveway. He didn't speak when he walked in to set his money and keys on the hall table once more.

She grinned at him, "What's the matter, you get lost? You need a map to get out of the neighborhood?"

Finally, Carla had turned their spacious house into a fantastic home. Her husband-to-be, whenever they get around to it, became more involved in showing erotic movies at one of his Salem theaters, and then two as the first one drew in many more customers. Who wouldn't want to see "forsaken films" in such a lovely setting? The luxury added to the seating, plus money to the box office as the films became more pornographic.

Wives who complained that these films were "leading their husbands astray" were kindly invited to view a movie for free. Many women who were huffy as the men brought them to the theater left smiling when they took their husband's arms on the way out. Often, women who would come in groups of two and three for the matinee were seen again with a husband at a night-time show. Not to forget the ladies who bought a single ticket and would leave with a man.

It was not very long before those movies turned into triple X-rated ones, which drew an even greater audience. So much so that the condom machine needed to be re-stocked often for men to use while watching the show-all carnal films.

Roy reveled in the surge of box office receipts until one night a man cried out, "Oh, my God, that's my *daughter!*" The man approached the owner with wrath for having his darling daughter exposed to the world in such an outrageously despicable manner. Roy defended himself for only showing the film, it was his daughter's choice to make that movie.

"Our daughter wasn't that kind of girl. She was a *good* girl. We gave her everything that money could buy and anything that she ever wanted!"

Roy admonished the father. "Well, perhaps it wasn't everything that she needed... like love, attention, and affection. These girls get all of that and more while making one of these movies. And maybe she does it because she just likes doing it," he added smugly.

One night, a few customers demanded their money back for having already paid to see the same movie under a different title. Their demands were met with the deepest of apologies and a free pass to the next movie.

There was no time to be wasted for Roy to buy a movie projector to preview all the movies in his own home before any public showings.

One living room wall was perfect to use as a screen; the blank wall opposite the fireplace and across from the room-length windowed wall. With the drapes closed, nothing could be seen from outside the house. The A-shaped glass of the cathedral ceiling, above the curtained windows, would only show the flickering of the films, although, no more than a television that was on. Roy strolled the street in front of his home to reassure himself that he would be above suspect.

When Roy pulled the coffee table toward the fireplace, Carla asked why he moved it.

"So I can set the projector on it."

"Don't you dare, you'll scratch it!"

After grabbing a kitchen towel, she raced to cover her prized piece of furniture. While she held the cloth steady, Roy set the machine down, along with two rolls of film. He loaded the third roll on the projector and then sat on a dining room chair while running the film. He set a second chair to his right and invited his wife to join him.

Carla stood with her hands on both hips. "I'm not going sit there and watch all that *garbage* with you!"

"Honey, I'll only watch each reel part-way through, just enough to know that they're the correct ones. Please?"

Even with Carla's protests, he enticed her to watch the movies with him. Roy asked for her suggestions on any improvement.

"You want improvement? I have a *great* idea, burn the whole bunch of them!" However, that was not the answer he wanted.

Begrudgingly, Carla sat through as many as she could tolerate and for as long a time as she could stomach. She suggested that, after walking around the set barefooted, the "stars" could at least wash their feet before making the movies.

"With all the money you make from decent movies, why do you have to show this trash?"

"Because sex sells. It always has and always will. If there are any men around, they'll want to see this. It's the stuff that men think and dream of; stuff they never get at home." Roy worded that wrong.

"Oh, really, now. Like I'm not here for you when you finally get around to ..."

"Knock it off, Carla. I didn't mean you and me. I meant the guys who come and see these kinds of movies. Maybe they can't perform for a woman, maybe their minds are a little warped, and they like the kinky stuff. Who the hell knows, but they *do* come in to see it. These films don't cost that much to rent because they're low budget, but I can charge more to see them because they're porno films, not Disney. It's a matter of demand and supply. And thanks to you, my customers feel better in coming to an elegant theater instead of some trashy joint at the edge of town where the sick perverts hang out." Roy could see that she was listening to him as he shut the projector off.

"It's not like I'm selling them some hooker. Some of these guys can only get their rocks off by masturbating and some prefer that because it's easier." He started to laugh, "And they don't have to take their dick out to dinner first."

"So, the young boys hang out and become male prostitutes for these perverts then?"

"Not just the young ones. Some men don't care how they get their rocks off, just that they get it, and these other guys are willing to give it to them for money. Yes, they prostitute themselves like that. But you have to keep in mind that they're no lower than the person they have sex with." Roy continued to talk while he changed reels.

"I'm sure that you know what a man's thinking when he looks at you. He sees sex because he wants sex, and that's what a beautiful woman like yourself represents to him. It's hard to see a woman like Marilyn Monroe or Sophia Loren for just their acting talents. Those women sell sex, and as I said, sex sells."

"Well, you don't have to sell it by showing all the basics like these movies show. What's wrong with leaving something to the Imagination?"

"Imagination doesn't sell, sex does, that's why. Now how about fixing me a little snack or maybe a sandwich?"

One afternoon, Carla opened the front door to see some unfriendly-looking neighbor ladies. She invited them inside. As they looked around the spectacularly decorated home, one woman remarked that she could see where Mr. Jacobs spent his money. Their attitudes changed greatly when "Mrs. Jacobs" explained that she was an interior decorator. Her talent could be further viewed inside the Regency and Majestic movie theaters that her husband owned. This knowledge garnered respect for her since they had all had been in those grand establishments.

The primary complaint was that their sons could meet great danger in climbing ladders to their home's rooftops to watch the "sordid" movies that Mr. Jacobs was showing in his living room. How dare he do that? With a humble apology, Carla assured the women that she would bring to her husband's immediate attention, and yes, they were right to be upset.

"I just couldn't bear the thought of one of your teenagers getting hurt going up and down those ladders."

When Carla told Roy about the complaint, he went into the living room to gaze out the windows. He studied the house across the street.

"I'll be damned. From the flat roof of their garage, those kids can see through the A-shape space above the drapes." He turned to Carla with a smirk. "I'll have to either move the projector downstairs to my office or send the little bastards a bill for not paying to watch my films!"

Roy went back into the kitchen with a suggestion. "The next time those broads come over here, tell them to have their husbands talk to *me* about what their sons are doing. This has nothing to do with you."

Within a week, Carla could relay his message. Very soon, Roy had the opportunity to meet the husbands. He greeted them with a welcoming handshake.

"Do come in. I hear that there are some problems with your sons that we need to talk about," he smiled.

As the men looked around his home in awe, Roy took the occasion to brag about Carla's great talents when he introduced her and then took them into his lavish office. The men were seated on cushioned swivel chairs or the sumptuously upholstered leather couch in front of Roy's massive desk. Behind this was an oversized, black leather office chair when Roy sat.

"Now, I understand we have a problem with some inquisitive teenage boys," Roy smiled. "Carla said their mothers are worried about them climbing up and down ladders to get to the roof of your house so they can watch the movies I have to screen. Is that it?"

"Well, yeah, that's pretty much it in a nutshell. I mean, you're showing some very revealing movies for them to watch. After all, boys will be boys," one father said.

To demonstrate a more relaxed attitude, Roy sat back in his chair. "Many wives don't look at the situation like we do from our experience of having gone through that exact part of growing up ourselves. They don't know how their son's endorphins are growing inside of them or how their hormones are changing. Suddenly, that thing in their shorts has a whole new life of its own!" The men chuckled with him and began to relax.

Roy got up to open a cupboard door that displayed a fully stocked liquor cabinet, a shelf of varied-sized glasses, and some cocktail napkins.

"My apologies, gentlemen, I'm being a terrible host. I haven't even offered you a drink yet. There's gin, vodka, whiskey, bourbon, scotch, brandy and..." he opened another cabinet that held a small refrigerator, "some imported beer. We have ice and mixer too. I'm a scotch man myself." With a glass in his hand, Roy turned to them. "So, what's your pleasure, men?" All three hesitated briefly. "Carla makes a mean martini if you'd rather..."

"Oh, well, I'll have a bourbon. Uh, do you have any Seven-up?" one answered.

"Sure, no problem," the host jauntily answered. "There's also some Coke, tonic water, ginger ale, club soda and..." Roy looked through the shelf, "and some bottled water, too. Yeah, Carla always thinks of everything."

He served their drinks. "So, your boys climb up on the roof to see my movies, huh? How's the view from up there?" Roy knowingly smiled. Their sheepish grins gave the answer. "I certainly hope you gave them a good lecture on how badly they could get hurt if they fell off that roof, and that goes for you too."

"I need to preview some of these movies to see if the content is proper and not a lot of sleazy trash," Roy explained. "I know that it all has a bad name, but I feel there is a need, and a great desire, for this kind of movie. Your boys need to see this stuff through the eyes of themselves coming into manhood. When boys at that age learn and understand the act of making love and not just having sex, they will have a better respect for themselves and the girls they date. They can let them enjoy having sex instead of feeling that they're being 'used, which is what the boys are doing. After all, boys will be boys, right men?"

As they laughed with him, Roy was aware that he had his neighbors' full attention. They appeared to be gaining more insight and respect for him.

He leaned forward in his chair with a hand gesture. "Come on now, men," Roy grinned, "we all know what's it's like to look at the neighbor girl down the street differently. Suddenly, we see that she now has bumps on her chest that weren't there before, and out of nowhere, we get this boner that we don't know what to do with."

The men could relate to his recollection. They also noticed how well-chosen Roy's words were; he spoke without using expletives or otherwise distasteful language. He then reached into his desk drawer to get several theater passes for the neighbors.

"Your sons can legally go into my theaters with you if they are over sixteen years of age, but if you don't feel comfortable in seeing these films with your boys, then let them sit separately. Each of you can get together with your son later and have a good father-son talk. You can answer any questions that sons need to learn from their father, not trash-talk from elsewhere that will cheapen this 'act of sex' they're learning about. This can promote greater respect and responsibility between a father and his son that a mother could not, and should not, have."

The fathers' eyes were opened to yet another viewpoint on what goodness pornography could hold for them.

"I also invite you gentlemen to take your wives out on a romantic dinner date, and then experience one of these movies together in either of my luxurious theaters. It could improve your own personal sex life immensely. I can't tell you how many men have thanked me for that alone." Roy rested a forearm on his desk and leaned toward the men as he spoke more gently.

"Let yourselves explore new avenues on a journey to a far better marriage. Put your arm around your wife's shoulder and whisper naughty little things in her ear as you watch these movies. Let this be your own little secret. And don't stop with just the one show. Plan to have a special night out together just for the two of you every so often. Get away from the kids, the house, bills. or whatever.

"And don't let her know that the other wives are doing the same thing too. They may just brag about something over coffee that happened or let slip the reason behind the special smile they have that day. Don't kid yourselves men, your wives really do more than complain about their husbands over that morning cup of coffee or the martini in the afternoon."

Standing up with a smile, he thanked them for talking with him and wished them all the best with their sons and their wives, as well. They all offered to shake his hand with thanks for the great advice and free passes as he showed them to the door.

"I see that you're smiling. So, how did things go with the angry neighbors?" Carla asked.

"Just swell. I gave them a whole new viewpoint on how my films can improve their relationship with their sons as well as their own sex life, and they bought it! A few free passes helped too. We have some very good customers now, I'll guarantee you that much."

Chapter Six

ROY'S INDUCTION

R oy was invited to sit in on a meeting with the Family men. When the husbands got together, they became different men. They each drew forth another personality of manliness dignified by the power that money brought and bought. Their unity was of the utmost importance. So, together they stood as one strong Jewish Levine Corporation Family.

Other families in the porno or casino businesses, such as the Italian Gorvetti or the Mexican Perez Families, respected each other's territories and ethnicities. Having had the senior Herbert Levine's status well-established long before the latter two, it was accepted that the Levine Family was, as some would say, "The Cock of the Walk." This was taken in dignity, stride, and caution by the Levine Family.

Don Levine conferred with Hirsh, Philips, and Blum about inviting Roy Jacobs into the Family. When all was discussed, they agreed that this was a good move on their part. Jacobs had several theaters, money, power, and willingness to follow orders. When the offer was given, Roy Jacobs accepted their honorable invitation.

Levine had established his territory in the West Coast cities of Los Angeles, Sacramento, Oakland, San Francisco, and now through Jacobs, moving into Salem and Portland. Going further south would be stepping into the footholds of the Perez and Gorvetti Families. David Levine wanted at all costs to keep peace within all other Families so that everyone may prosper without causing any strife to another one.

When the meeting was called to order, the first subject of the day was to congratulate Roy Jacobs on his decision to take a bride. He was asked how they met.

"Through a mutual friend, Senator Peter Nichols. He invited me to a home-coming party for Carla. I'm graced by God that she's consented to be my wife."

Hirsh told the other members, "This is the woman who beautifully redecorated all of Roy's theaters in Portland and Salem."

Levine nodded for Philips to resume the meeting. When it was adjourned the men were dismissed except for Phillips and Hirsh. Levine waved a hand for Jacobs to sit with them.

"Keep Peter Nichols close to you. Not for his influence as a senator, who may become governor in time, but as a friend who is also a friend to your wife-to-be. Respect him because he brought you Carla to be your wife. My good friend Harry introduced me to Jada, who became *my* wife. She has been my best friend and my soul-mate all these years. Together we made what we have today, just as it can be with you and your new wife-to-be. Always be loyal to your young friends as they will grow old with you, just like Harry and I have grown together. Respect is something that cannot be easily retrieved, if at all."

"Thank you, Mr. Levine. That is excellent advice."

"That was not advice. Now, I understand that some of your stores are doing quite well with the recent films you've been showing."

"Yes, sir, they are."

"We were wondering if you might consider showing our films exclusively in any of them."

"Well, to be truthful, sir, I have been considering that."

"What do you feel about having another one or two be more exclusive?" asked Harry Philips.

"I'm certain that Salem can't tolerate that in the downtown area. And I'm afraid I can't persuade my father to change his two theaters."

"What about outlying towns? Are there not some stores that can be purchase and remolded? Your new wife-to-be would certainly be a great asset to our foundation in that way," suggested Levine.

Roy's facial expression didn't falter, although, his stomach muscles tightened. *To our foundation?*

"Yes, sir, that could work out to be very beneficial."

"Could?"

"I meant to say 'would', sir. I'll look over all of the outlying Corvallis area, as well as the Springfield and Eugene areas. College towns are always quite promising," Roy assured him.

"I can check into whatever Roy finds. I'll look over costs and licenses and get back to you."

"Thank you, Richard." Levine began to move his chair back as the signal for dismissal.

The Don smiled at the newest partner. "We welcome you into our Family, Roy. And in working together, I am confident that you will enrich all of us with your great experience and foresight. I trust that you will find some good stores to remodel, bringing more status and value to the Family. I know you will be very comfortable in getting to know each man and his own family. Their wives will look forward to meeting your fiance'. Also, congratulations on your forthcoming nuptials, Roy. By the way, have you given your new fiance' an engagement ring yet?"

"Not yet, sir."

Levine reached into his desk for a business card. He scribbled "thank you" and his initials on the back before giving it to Jacobs.

"You go to see this jeweler; his father was a good friend to my father. Mr. Kaplin took over his father's business of making fine jewelry and he'll give you a very good price on a lovely ring. His shop will be hard for you to find, so Richard can take you over there, unless you have other plans right now."

"Oh, no, not at all. This is very kind of you. I'd be honored to have your friend do that, thank you." *Do I have any other choice?*

"I will look forward to hearing about some little Jacobs babies in the near future."

"I don't plan on that happening very soon, sir," Roy laughed.

Levine held out his hand to a rather surprised man who readily shook it with pride.

"Now, let me give you a piece of advice. Stay close to your friends and hold your cards and enemies near your breast. Give ego and pride back to Satan, and you will stay strong."

"Thank you, Mr. Levine, that's very kind of you."

"And that beard makes you stand out from the others."

"I'm glad you like it."

"I don't want any of my men to be recognized because they stand out too much, so shave it off."

Carla accepted the ring with immense joy and surprise. Since Roy hadn't mentioned the subject, she hadn't given any thought to an engagement ring, let alone one with a diamond that large. In addition, she was thrilled to learn how well her husband-to-be had been welcomed in the Levine Family, even though she had no idea of what would be in store for her.

As a young newlywed, David's father encouraged him to start a family and have a grandson follow in his footsteps. That proved not to be possible. No matter how he romanced Jada, for many years of trying he could not produce a child. After seeing different doctors, it was concluded that David had a low sperm count. To save her husband's dignity and manhood, Jada claimed that she could not produce fertile enough eggs to conceive.

Therefore, they were proud to be named godparents to the children of Harry and Marni Philips and Richard and Sharon Hirsh. They reveled in holding those babies as their own grandchildren. This gave the Levines the opportunity to be grandparents through them.

Chapter Seven

THE WEDDING NIGHT

Their parents knew about each other, however, now they met for the first time. In an exquisite restaurant, they conversed and got to know one another. Although the Protestant Martins were cool to the idea of their daughter marrying into a Jewish family, they considered Roy's financial status. One of the topics of discussion was to decide on, or rather, politely argue about, which church or synagogue to use for the wedding. Bright and tactful Ms. Martin suggested a compromise; a Unitarian church.

"Carla, they don't even preach about Jesus there!" Mr. Martin protested.

"A very wise choice, my lovely daughter-to-be," Mr. Jacobs said.

Carla located a church in which they were both comfortable. They very much enjoyed the sermons, and the pastor very much enjoyed their financial contribution.

When the wedding day came, the dress was still on the hanger while Carla applied the last touches to her makeup. She examined her image with approval when Roy walked into the dressing room.

"Why do you have to take so long? I've been dressed for over half an hour. I don't want to be late."

"You don't need to do your makeup and hair. Why don't you just go watch some TV?"

"I don't want to get my pants all wrinkled." He looked at the dress. "Is this what you're going to wear?"

"Yes."

"I don't like it."

"I showed you the sketches and you said you like it."

"It looked better on paper. Just hurry up and get dressed, I don't want to be late."

Carla looked at the clock. "There's plenty of time, don't get all flustered. Go pace the floor then, you're going to make me all nervous"

"Well, if you're not ready to go in five minutes, I'm leaving without you!"

As he stomped away, Carla took a deep breath letting the air out slowly. Then she called out from the bedroom door, "Go ahead without me... and explain *that* to your mother!"

The dress looked fabulous and her new shoes went with it superbly. She stood back from the mirror, taking a final approving look. To her surprise, Roy walked into the dressing room holding a mink jacket.

"I thought you'd like to wear this. It's my wedding gift to you." He slipped it on her shoulders. "Are you ready to leave now?"

"Oh, my, this is lovely Roy, thank you. Did Richard make this for you?"

"Yeah, let's get in the car." And they were on their way.

They were able to speak with the pastor ahead of time about the ceremony as the few guests and family came into the building.

"What kind of church is this? There's no cross around at all. You generally see one at the top of the building," Mr. Martin blurted as the Jacobs sat down in a pew.

"This is a magnificent church, son. I see there's no cross around here, that's nice."

"What do you mean by...?"

"That's enough, you two," Eddie quietly admonished as he sat down. The service was brief.

"I pronounce you husband and wife. You may kiss your bride".

Roy looked into Carla's eyes briefly before giving her a short kiss. Now they were officially married.

The Nichols gave them their best wishes. Peter expected to see at least a hundred guests.

"I couldn't afford to buy that many invitations," laughed Roy. However, he saw that Beth didn't even smile.

When all the congratulations and best wishes were over, the prominent question was, "Where is the honeymoon going to be?" The bride waited for an answer, too.

"It's a big secret, but I'll take my new bride out to a fabulous dinner first."

When the new husband draped the new bride with the new mink, his mother became inquisitive.

"That's very nice. Where did you get it? Is this from your father's furrier friend, Mr. Bloomberg?"

"No, Mama, I stole it from an old whore."

She laughed, "Oh, my son has such a great sense of humor, doesn't he?"

"Actually, she was a young one," Roy said. His mother laughed even more.

When the couple arrived at the posh Red Carpet restaurant, they were respectfully greeted and then guided to their table where chilled champagne was served right away. The groom toasted his bride, and the wedding dinner began. Carla didn't have a taste for champagne but bore through the first bottle and then refused more. Roy enjoyed the second bottle while she sipped on a martini. By his third bottle, dinner was done, and the groom was done in. He sent for his car.

Before making his way out of the parking lot, the champagne had taken its course. Roy stopped to empty his bladder before a large window of diners. He was inside the car by the time attendants ran out of the restaurant to yell at him. The mortified bride turned her covered face away in embarrassment. The only words that were spoken on the ride back to the house came from the radio.

"Why are we stopping here?"

"I forget something. Wait here.

Roy went into the house while Carla waited. And waited. And waited. Bewildered, she went to the house, however, the door was locked. She knocked but there was no answer, so she used the key from her purse to get in.

The tuxedo jacket was on the hallway floor, followed by a shirt, shoes, then a sock, and another sock. The pants were on the bedroom floor and the husband was in the bed.

Terribly disappointed, Carla began to undress. After freshening up she slipped into her new negligee and glided into the bed to snuggle up to her groom.

"Yeah, whaddaya want," he mumbled.

She ran her soft hand over his shoulder. "Well, it's our wedding night, honey," she purred.

"So, you got something new for me?"

Carla wondered if she really heard him say what it sounded like. She lay still. The words reverberated in her head, and then they echoed. His words stabbed her heart. She moved away only to hear Roy going into a deeper sleep. She turned to the other side of the king-size bed as far away as she could.

The hurt became deeper, not just in her heart but now burning into her soul... her womanhood. Her femininity was stripped way as though layers of flesh were peeled from her body until there was nothing else to expose but the torment she was now feeling through the stinging of her eyes, and then the flooding of them that tried to wash away that deep, profound hurting so far inside her that it was now a bottomless abyss.

As Carla tried to muffle her sobbing with the pillow, the heat of the relentless tears now gave way to cold chills besetting her body. Drawing the covers tighter around herself, she could no longer weep. She could no longer sob. Her swollen eyes, empty body, and hollow mind finally gave way to sleep.

The next morning, Carla heard a loud noise coming from the living room. It was cartoons on the TV. Burying her head in the pillow didn't help, so she got up. After holding a wet, cold washcloth against her eyes for a few minutes she put on her comfortable terrycloth bathrobe to find her way to the noise with an aching head and eyes less swollen. She heard Roy's loud laughter.

"Please turn that down."

He looked at her quickly and then back to the TV set while he ate out of an ice cream container. "I like to watch cartoons on Sunday mornings. It's the only time all week I get a chance to relax. Come and join me, well, after you go clean up. You look like hell." He didn't turn his head away from the show but kept shoveling the ice cream into his mouth with a soup spoon.

"Will you please turn it down? I don't feel well."

"I don't see why not. You didn't have much to drink last night."

"Well, you sure had your share." She turned the TV set down before going back toward the bedroom.

"Hey, come here and watch it with me. Hey, did ya' hear me?"

Yes, she did, but she didn't listen. Once back into the loveless bed she tried to comfort herself with the pillow, however, the ache in her heart returned.

Her wedding night, is this the beginning of how their marriage will be? The humiliation, the pain in her heart, the bewilderment in her mind all returned. Her head still hurt, not from the lack of sleep but from the nothingness in her soul. Tears again stung her eyes and pain gouged her heart as she began to cry once more. She heard Roy's heavy footsteps coming down the hallway, and then the door opened.

"What are you doing in bed? I thought you were going to get cleaned up and come and sit with me." She didn't answer. "Hey, ain't ya talking to me?" He nudged her and then saw the tears on her cheeks. He sat next to her and stroked her hair.

"You're crying. What's the matter, sweetheart?" His voice was now soft and caring. "Why are you crying? Because I was watching TV? Are you upset because it was too loud?"

Now she began to cry openly and could not control her sobs or the pain in her heart. *Is he that insensitive? Or just that stupid?*

He leaned over to cuddle her, embrace her. "What's bothering you? Did I do something wrong last night? I know I drank too much. I know we got home okay because we're here. Tell me what's wrong, honey?" His voice was now tender.

Doesn't he even know what happened... or didn't happen? Was he that drunk last night? "You said, 'What else could I give you that was new', then you went to sleep... on our wedding night. You turned your back on me... on our wedding night. Of all nights for you to turn me away." The sobbing was lessened now but the hurt, the intense hurt, was still there.

He was silent for a moment. "Oh, wow, I guess I passed out. I don't remember even getting into bed. I'm sorry. Why don't you get up and take a shower? You'll feel better." He left the door open on the way out. Soon she could hear him laughing at the cartoons again.

After a long while, she got up and splashed water on her face. Holding another cold, wet washcloth to her eyes relieved much of the swelling. In her bathrobe once more, she wandered into the kitchen to heat up some coffee while looking for the aspirins to ease her head. After Carla was seated in her comfortable recliner Roy told her to get him a cup of coffee.

"You have two legs, get your own coffee."

"Oh, my, did we get up on the wrong side of the bed today?"

"On my side of the bed where I slept all alone on my wedding night."

"I see that I'm still in hot water." Roy got up for his coffee. "Why don't you get dressed and let me take you somewhere nice for breakfast?"

"Where?"

"I'll surprise you. Just put a dress on, and we can go someplace."

"I had enough surprise last night," she said while holding the cold compress to her forehead.

"I said I was sorry. I promise I'll make it up to you."

After finishing her coffee, Carla showered and then put her makeup on since the swelling of her eyes had gone down by then. Carl got dressed and then fixed her hair while Roy showered, shaved, and dressed in a suit and tie.

He escorted her to the car, opened the door for her, and held her arm as she got in. "Is there someplace special you'd like to go for breakfast?"

"Let's just go to The Crab House," she answered as he shut the door.

"Oh, how so apropos since that seems to be your mood on this fine first day of holy matrimony."

Carla turned her face toward the door window. *More like holy hell.*

Roy drove to the restaurant's valet parking area. When attendants opened the doors, Roy gave them only the ignition key, avoiding the chance of duplicating other keys.

In the restaurant, he told the head waiter he wanted a private window table since this would be their wedding breakfast. They certainly would be shown the best service at all possible, and nothing was overlooked. For the fifty-dollar tip, all the finest was assured Mr. Jacobs. At the table, Roy sat back with the certainty that money *could* talk.

Chapter Eight

THE MANSION REMODEL

Although their home was finished and settled into, it would be a while before the loving couple would be totally settled into their marriage. Even though they had lived together for nearly a year, being married was different. Now there was a verbal and legal commitment to each other. Roy was not used to a set routine of living which furthered the relationship's imbalance.

While sipping on some coffee, he told Carla what her next project would be. "I want you to go down to Las Vegas with me to meet Mrs. Levine, she's quite the socialite. And she said something to Hirsh about having you go over that mansion they bought." Roy saw that he had her attention.

"I told you about it once before. It belonged to the movie director, Harold Metzler."

Carla suddenly perked up. "Oh, now I remember. I know what that looks like, it was done in the typical Hollywood drama style. You know, gaudy, elaborate window dressings, ugly wood or wrought iron staircases, and massive furniture pieces. I'd love to get my hands on that place. But tell me more about the wife."

"Her name is Jada. She's quite beautiful, dresses well, and seems to be very friendly. Loves big parties and the limelight stuff. I think you'd hit it off well with her." Roy smiled, "Sound good?"

"I'd love to re-do her whole home. Maybe I can impress her enough to do that. Those rooms are enormous with really high ceilings." Carla got up from the chair to slowly pace as her mind began to fan the flames of her vast imagination. With exalted enthusiasm, Carla turned to her husband.

"You know how I can find fantastic bargains at old thrift stores or bargain shops and antique shops. I can dicker over the prices to get a real bargain if I find something unique. I can save her some money that other designers would pay full price for. And that would save her husband some money. Oh, just think what that can do with your position with this Don person!"

Her excitement grew, as did Roy's ardor to see her that excited. He wrapped his arms around her. "I just love to see you like this. You come alive and you're so vibrant."

His wife also knew when he was this alive and vibrant, she had to get it while she could. She began to tease him and taunt him until he took her arm, literally pulling her into the bedroom. Neither one could get undressed fast enough. It had been so long since he had become this passionate with her. Then drained of energy, he collapsed on top of her.

"We should do that more often, then you'll build up your stamina. You're getting too fat in your old age," she teased.

"What do you mean, fat? I'm only ten pounds over."

"Sure, ten pounds over the other ten pounds. Go take a shower while I make you a nice low-calorie lunch.

Upon their arrival at the mansion, Carla stood outside, looking around the grounds. She visualized a horseshoe drive that would lead to a covered entrance and then sweep away in a soft curve. A large fountain could stand in the center of the large lawn with an assortment of varying-sized shrubs encasing a flower bed, and so much more.

She was well-received by Mrs. Levine, who promptly said to call her Jada. They took to each other quite well in their personalities.

Carla was impressed by the woman's overall beauty. Jada was a bit less than average height with a trim, engaging figure. Her every move was as though it had a purpose, as did her manner of speech. Each word was spoken like it had been well-chosen ahead of time. Mrs. Levine appeared to have been of a well-bred upbringing in having a pride-in-excellence attitude about herself. The shoulder-length raven hair, sparsely touched with silvery strands, was swept back into a French roll. All-in-all, this woman appeared to Carla as the epitome of elegance.

Jada was elated with the sketches, noting that the designer was extremely creative in her work, more so than most others she had interviewed. She had also seen pictures of the Portland theaters mentioning that the lobby fountain was "simply divine", to Carla' surprise and delight.

And Jada noticed that when Carla pushed or moved items out of she didn't mind getting her hands dusty while handling some of the furnishings. She wasn't egotistical as were most decorators Jada had encountered. Carla offered Jada time to think over her decision and call her if she was...."

"When can you start, my dear?" was her answer. Again, Carla hired her brother to oversee any construction, wiring, and plumbing needs just as he had done with the movie theaters. And Jada offered each a guest house during their stay.

Soon, Carla instructed workers on how she wanted things done, and with courtesy rather than orders. Jada saw things fall into place with immense pleasure as Carla made her dreamed of ideas come to be. When cost-saving ideas were suggested, Jada was impressed even more so, knowing that her husband was concerned with the remodel's overall price rather than the finished appearance.

Roy would stay with his wife for a couple of days when the Family men called for a meeting. He was comfortable in knowing how happy Carla was in her work there and that Eddie could watch over her. This gave Roy time to care for all of his theaters.

After hearing a considerable amount about the new decorator, Stanley Fraiser wondered if she might be just the one to do something spectacular to his manor home. He was tired of the typical flamboyant frou-frou designers of Hollywood who swished with pomp and circumstance as though they were actually artistic.

Stanley had begun working for his father just out of high school. Starting at the bottom, he learned all the different phases of that business.

When Fraiser's father retired he passed all of his real estate and construction business on to him. Having grown up as a close friend to David, Stanley now provided him all the real estate for and the construction of his hotels and casinos at a more than fair price, just as his father had done for David's father. And this same arrangement bettered both their businesses.

Concerning David's porno business, Stanley didn't approve of it, but then again, he didn't know about it entirely. And David was not going to keep him apprised since he was not a Family member.

Stanley wore his position and money well, with the subdued refinement and elegance of a true gentleman. He stood just less than six feet tall with proportionate weight through proper diet and frequent exercise in his home gym. His thick, dark hair was just beginning to turn silver. He was always a clean-shaven, properly dressed man.

As with David, Stanley remained barren of children with his faithful wife of many years, who died too early of cancer. His real estate business kept him busy through the years, although, the loneliness had taken its toll on him. After several years of single life, he made the mistake of marrying the wrong young lady who was not as faithful. Due to her many and obvious indiscretions, she didn't fare well from the divorce. Fraiser failed to fall seriously in love or marry after that.

He was now past fifty years of living and growing richer. Having gone past the multi-millionaire mark, he still made wise investments, if only to support prime charities and fund educational institutions.

Stanley asked David for a private viewing of his home during its transition after all the workers had gone. He could see how grand this home will be when it was finished.

He turned to his longtime friend. "I do hope you pay this woman well and that you show your gratitude to Jada for having her do all this fine work for you. She has been an excellent wife to you, David. She always made your homes seem like a palace for her king to come home to. In all your years of marriage, she has always presented herself as queen to you."

David nodded at his friend with a smile of pride. "I am certain that this home will be a joy to behold when it's finished."

As Stanley again looked at Levine, he added further advice. "And I certainly expect that you'll keep your indiscretions with her very discreet, my old friend."

The following morning Jada was drinking coffee at the kitchen table while looking over some sketches for one of the guest rooms. She was pleasantly surprised when David set a small bouquet of violets on the table.

"I saw a street vendor selling these. I recall how you used to like them when we were young, and I couldn't afford to buy you any pricey flowers."

"Oh, that was so sweet of you." She held them up to sniff their delicate fragrance. "That was so long ago."

He sat next to her. "What are these plans for?" he asked quite sincerely.

She didn't question his reasoning but smiled to see that he may be truly interested. After she explained the plans, he asked to see what was being done to their home. Feeling proud that he showed an interest, Jada took his arm to escort him around and explained everything she and Carla were doing.

Jada coyly suggested a great housewarming party as an excuse to get together with all of their friends to celebrate the completed makeover.

That's a grand idea, my dear. We should do that," he smiled.

Chapter Nine

THE GIRLS GET OUT

When Carla was home Roy's inattentiveness was that he had "a hard day at the office". In her heart that was not a good enough reason or excuse. Her frustrations dissipated when she was away from him in Beverly Hills, entrenched in the mansion remodel.

While she was working, Carla lived in Levine's guest house. When Roy flew down to attend meetings with the Family men he would stay with her. However, his work in Portland and Salem could not go long without his being there to oversee matters. Knowing that his wife kept busy during his absence, Roy felt safe to be on his own, alone or otherwise.

Jada, Sharon, and Marni became good friends with Carla over the months she spent changing the mansion. During this time the wives would get together for lunch and shopping breaks. Marni Philips and Sharon Hirsh were closer to Jada's age than Carla, who was nearly twenty years their junior. However, the four women bonded as sisters in like interests for having husbands in the pornography and theater business.

They all had something personal in common, that of lacking the affection of their husbands who had now become jaded and negligent in their husbandly duties. With the constant viewing or overseeing, directing, and producing these pornographic movies, the men didn't respond to the usual appeal of their own women. The husbands seemed to need something more tantalizing, tempting, and titilating that they no longer saw in their wives. Having sex had now become self-gratification, or a duty to perform, much to the dismay of these four unfortunate beauties.

Each woman was more than just attractive and curvaceous. They each had that certain aura of beauty, grace, and sophistication which came through pride, not vanity, and self-assurance.

Jada Philips was the second-born of a prominent attorney and his wife. Her mother taught her well in the womanly and wifely aspects of growing into adulthood.

Unlike her brother, who spent hours learning about his father's legal profession, Jada paid attention to her mother's cooking, recipes, and housekeeping tips. This was something every young lady needed to know to be a good wife in charge of her own home.

Sharon did rely on her beauty, charming personality, and quick wit to lead the popularity poll. She learned that it was necessary to have girlfriends on her team to ward off unwanted gossip and useless jealousy. Sharon knew that having them on her side was better than having them claw at her back.

Marni was from a better background but with average looks and personality. High school girlfriends taught her to experiment with make-up and hairstyle. She then became far more attractive. Marni was taught honesty, virtue, and absolutely no promiscuity, for which the boys respected her.

And her virginity was not questioned when Marni walked down the aisle in a gown of pure white to wed Jada's brother, Harry Philips.

So, what did these ladies discuss at lunch besides recipes and house-hold tips? Men, of course. Although, Carla still had her concerns about their marriages to pornographers.

Over cocktails in the privacy of Sharon's home, she asked, "How can you approve of what they do in exploiting women like that?" They looked at each other with shrugs.

"We made a vow to them, '...for better or for worse', said Jada. "For one thing, they started out in the casino business, which led to the porno business."

"And for richer or for poorer," Marni laughed. "Maybe I won't make it that far up the social ladder, but it sure beats taking dictation for a living.

Sharon added, "We all struggle with it, but so do our men in a way. They'll never be high on any social ladder either because of this but they sure make great money from it. Let's face it, sex sells. The casinos were good for people who like or need to gamble. Men are addicted to it the same way some get addicted to porn or even alcohol. But that saves them from going out and raping women to satisfy their lust for sex."

"That's what Roy said". And then Carla asked, "But what about the way women are used to make these movies so that our men can make big money from it?"

Jada spoke up. "These are not innocent little girls, my dear. They know exactly what they're getting into. They make good money, the same as their male partners do. Furthermore, they are certainly not forced into making these films, at least not David's. Maybe in China or Korea, but not in our movies. They have legitimate contracts to sign first and can take them to any lawyer beforehand. Most of the time, I will interview the girls, and Harry or Richard will interview the men. We have Dr. Salsberry, our private doctor, check them out physically and see that they don't have any diseases before they're hired. And he periodically checks everyone over to ensure they stay that way. No, my dear, these girls are not exploited."

"But how can you stay married to a man who makes a living from making movies of other women having sex?" Carla bluntly asked. "I mean, does he ever look at you as a lover anymore after seeing all of these younger gals up close and naked all the time? And what about the temptation to cheat with them?"

The question out of the mouth of this babe made all three women think before speaking.

"It does make us work harder at our marriages than most other couples do," Jada said. "But our husbands also know that there are many other men who look at us with our clothes on. What will they do if they see us naked? That's what our husbands never want to find out. Let's face it; we're not the average slob housewife. Yes, they may think that we don't see that they have wandering eyes, but they know that we know what's in their zippers and their bank accounts. So it's best to keep both closed to the public."

Sharon shared her thoughts. "Nakedness doesn't mean taking off your clothes to expose your bodies, it means exposing your life to each other. The bible says you become one flesh with one another; you expose your *souls* to each other. You let the other person see your inner thoughts. Even those that you don't want to share because you're afraid of what they'll think of you if you do. Once you gain that confidence with one another, you develop complete trust in each other."

Carla sat back amazed at her words. "Oh my, how profound."

Then Marni offered her words of wisdom. "Of course, this never works in the real world. These guys still take us for granted and assume that we'll be here when they decide that the grass isn't greener over there. It only had some cute little flower that fades away in the dark. When they see the light of day they always come back with their tails tucked between their legs and hope that we didn't notice the grass stains on their pants."

Often, either Marni, Sharon, and sometimes even Jada would tag along with Carla to the odd stores where she found the perfect item to use. They gave Carla the attention and deserving praise that her husband no longer gave. She began to draw closer to these women. They all seemed to have the same issues concerning their negligent husbands in sharing about the lonely life of being a pornographer's wife.

They gave card parties, went shopping, not telling their husbands what they bought because they weren't interested in what they bought. It may have been a new dress for a card party and a pair of shoes to go with it. Or a new plug-in vibrator that looked just like a penis, or a penis that looked like a vibrator. The latter had more attachments, and it also stimulated body parts much better.

The disillusioned Carla still felt faithful to her beloved Roy. "I think I would feel too guilty to do something like that. Then I'd have to confess to him that I..."

"You silly broad! Does he confess anything to you?" Marni asked.

Jada reached for Carla's hand. "Honey, you know that you just can't get yourself to admit it. Why else does that jerk leave a beautiful, curvaceous, sexy woman like you alone? You need a *man* to take care of you, sweetheart. And at this point, any man. Lighten up, girl. Do you think any of us would go out for some strange stuff if our old man was doing his job? Absolutely not."

"You know that she's right, my dear," Marni agreed. "The only good reason we get by with what we do on the side is that our lovers know that we do appreciate how they treat us and make us feel. They also know to be very discreet because they'll literally get their heads chopped if our husbands ever find out.

"Do you know that seventy percent of women who cheat on their husbands do it because they want what they don't get at home?" Marni continued, "They need someone to make them feel special, wanted, and needed. Not just used for sexual gratification. Does Roy make you feel that way? Hell no."

"Don't get us wrong, dear," Sharon added, "We love our husbands very much. It's just that they aren't there for us like that anymore, even though we're always there for them And they take that for granted. But we don't make this a steady habit, it's just when we can't take the emptiness and loneliness any longer."

"She will come to her senses in due time," said Jada. "Meanwhile, my precious, faithful wife, I have a dear friend who admires your work greatly. As soon as you are finished with my home, he would like to engage you to re-do his. And he has plenty of money so that you don't have to improvise with sales merchandise or thrift store bargains."

"Who would that be?" Sharon questioned.

Jada looked at her with a comely smile. "None other than Mr. Stanley M. Fraiser."

Sharon clasped her hands to her mouth in surprise. "*The* Mr. Fraiser? Of Fraiser fame and fortune, or rather, fortune and fortune?" She turned to Carla. "Oh, my word girl, for that man to ask for you is the biggest compliment any artist could possibly get. My dear, you are *in*!"

"Who is he?" Carla naively asked. The others sat back in surprise that she would ask and then began to explain all at once.

"Oh, that Mr. Fraiser. How did he come to know about me?"

Jada explained that to her, and Carla relaxed, knowing he was a long-time family friend. She agreed to meet him sometime.

Long before the mansion was done, Jada Levine made an appointment for Carla and her to visit the Fraiser estate. Stanley graciously showed the ladies around his more than spacious manor home with mention of his few ideas.

Carla envisioned what she could do for the home, which impressed him tremendously. Even in seeing the guest house and gardens, her mind exploded with ideas, knowing that money wouldn't deter her plans. Of course, she offered to keep the cost down as much as she could, which further awed Stanley.

He marveled at her engaging ideas while watching her every move and listening to her every word.

Stanley was more than awe-struck by her visions, her beauty, and gentleness; he was enamored. His heart was set on having her, if only as his decorator for now.

Jada saw the expression on his face as Carla moved around his home. It was the look of ardor and admiration. She knew it was the look of love. When their eyes met Stanely could see that Jada was reading him. He blushed with embarrassment.

She went to him and patted his shoulder. "In due time, my dear friend. And I'll pray about it too," she whispered. He squeezed her hand to acknowledge her understanding.

On the way home, Jada asked what she thought of Stanley.

"Oh, my, he certainly is a nice person. You'd think that someone with his wealth would be bossy and, well, harsh or rude. I'm kinda surprised that he isn't married, though. I think he'd make the right gal a wonderful husband."

"Oh, it's not that he hasn't tried. He just hasn't met the right woman. They seem to look at his wallet and not his heart."

With exuberance, Carla explained some of her ideas to Roy when she got home. She was surprised that he became so interested but soon realized that it wasn't for her visions. It was for Fraiser's money.

"Oh, wow! Do you know what that means for me? I'll be right up there at the top of the ladder with Philips and Hirsh. I'll bet the Don will see me in a better light for that. Oh, wow, Carla, this is fantastic! When do you start? Will you be staying in one of his guest homes, or will you continue to stay at Jada's place?"

Carla's heart cooled with those words. She lost her enthusiasm for him as she turned away to continue making dinner, for which she now had no appetite.

Her voice was cynical. "Yeah, I didn't quite see it like that. It should put you right up there, alright."

"Carla, I'm happy for you too. That should be a big job and keep you busy for a long time. Just think about how much money we'll make from it."

"We?" She turned to look at Roy.

"Yeah, "we". This is a marital property state, you know," he grinned. "What's mine is mine, and what's yours is mine too." He laughed, although she knew he meant that.

"Well, I guess that's one way of looking at it," she said sourly.

"So, what's another way?"

"Not signing the divorce papers."

"Very funny. So what's for Dinner? Smells good."

"Shrimp curry over rice, steamed broccoli, and tossed salad. Would you mind setting the table, please? I need to keep an eye on the curry."

"Let's use the TV trays. There's a program I want to watch."

"What's wrong in sitting down with each other and talk. We don't often have time to do that."

"Nothing. I kinda like to just relax in the evening."

"Roy, we don't talk to each other very much; like communicate with each other. All we do is scratch the surface of a conversation, we don't discuss things anymore. We can talk about these things over dinner. Like, why do you want my wages put into your bank account? Don't you make enough money for yourself?"

"Because it's easier to keep track of everything if it's all in one bank account."

"Roy, I know very well how to keep track of my money. You only need to be concerned about your own account."

"Honey, it's all community property. Why make it a big deal?"

"It's only that after a judge decides how to split it up."

"Carla, that's only if we get divorced. What in the hell are you talking about?"

"Dinner's ready. Go ahead and dish yourself up whenever you want." Carla wiped her hands on a dishtowel and then picked up her purse and keys before heading to the coat closet.

"Carla, where the hell are you going? You said that dinner's ready to eat."

"Maybe to see a lawyer about a divorce. Put the food in the fridge when you're done. I lost my appetite."

Walking to her car, she asked herself, "Yeah, so what's there to talk about?

Chapter Ten

DALTON

Carla drove for a distance before spotting an older homey-looking tavern with shingled walls. Inside, she stood still while her eyes became adjusted to the dimness. She looked around. There were several couples seated at small wooden tables and a party of six at another. She thought a bar stool would be better than sitting at a table by herself. Carla selected one toward an end of the curved bar where no one would be close to her.

The large mirrors lining the back wall of the bar had wooden shelves holding several kinds of liquor. And customers could view their image while they enjoyed a drink. The bars Carla had seen before were generally rectangular, while this was shaped like an elongated horseshoe where customers could easily view others on either side. *How unusual, but quite pleasant.l*

"Good day, miss, what can I get you?" the attractive bartender asked.

She laid a five-dollar bill on the bar. "Scotch rocks with a splash of soda, please."

He brought her change back with the drink. "I haven't seen you here before. We don't get many classy ladies in here, so I'd remember. Are you new to the area?" he smiled.

She tried to smile, "Thank you, and I've lived in the area for a while. I'm just running away from home for a couple of hours."

"Oh, well, I'm sorry to hear that. If you want, I'll keep anyone from bothering you while you think things out," he kindly offered. Carla looked up at him in mild surprise.

"I'm a bartender. I see and hear but say nothing," he winked. My name is Ben, by the way."

"I'm Carla."

He nodded and then excused himself to go back to his work.

A while later, Ben set another scotch with soda in front of her.

"A gentleman asked to send you a drink. No strings. He *is* a gentleman, at the end of the bar in the leather blazer. He owns a real estate business around these parts but doesn't like to hang out with business people, so he hangs here. He says it's more comfortable."

When Carla became more relaxed, she signaled to Ben. "Give the gentleman a drink on me, please. I don't like to feel I owe a strange man for something." She pushed a twenty-dollar bill toward him. "And get yourself one."

In a few minutes, Ben set a piece of paper down in front of Carla and went about his work. She casually looked at it.

"You should take that ring off. If I can see the sparkle from here, so can some jerks with $ in their eyes. Dalton." He included his business card, which read, 'Benson Real Estate Company, Dalton Benson, Owner.' Beneath that, *In association with the Fraiser Corporation* was in a smaller print.

She looked up at the man at the end of the bar. He tipped his glass to her before taking a sip She did the same in return and then slid her hands to her lap to remove the large diamond wedding ring. After wrapping it with a tissue from her purse, she slipped it into her front pants pocket.

A young man in his mid-twenties set a glass of beer on the countertop next to Carla. She noticed him grin while looking her over but looked straight ahead.

"You play any pool, lady?"

"No, I don't."

"Wanna learn?"

"No, but thank you."

"Just thought I'd ask. Haven't seen you here before."

"I haven't been here before." Taking a pen from her purse, she wrote on the back of her business card, "This guy is trying to pick me up. Care to join me? Carla."

She asked Ben to give it to Dalton who read it and then picked up his drink to walk over to her. The young man was taking his shot at the pool table, so Dalton moved his beer down to sit next to Carla.

She explained that she was considering a job from a wealthy real estate businessman. She held up Dalton's card.

"Do you work with the Stanley Fraiser Corporation, the big real estate mogul?"

"Not exactly. I'm authorized to use the name, but my franchise company reports to him. Fraiser may be a millionaire, but he works with smaller companies to reach the same goals that he's attained. I know his name is tossed around in the news, but he really is a terrific man. So, please don't let the name scare you."

"We always hear about how ruthless these kinds of men are, though," she added."

"Not this man, he's a kind fella'," Dalton chuckled.

"Oh, good, So if I get a chance to remodel his mansion, I won't have to worry about him yelling at me," Carla laughed.

"No, but he lives alone now, so he downsized a few years back. Now, you had a real estate question?"

She was considering her rocky marriage. Did Dalton have any advice as to how she could keep her own money, property, and business separate in case of a marital split?

He thought for a moment to consider that the size of the diamond ring she was wearing. It most likely meant that she's married to a man with money. He made several suggestions for her consideration.

They struck up somewhat of a friendship while they talked about their mutual interest in building, businesses, real estate, and, of course, interior decoration. After all, that's what every business building needs.

When they finished chatting, Dalton reminded Carla of his card. "In case you need any real estate or a home if a divorce does happen," he smiled. She agreed to keep him in mind, again thanking him for the advice and the rescue.

"By the way, Dalton, when I do talk to Stanley, would it be alright with you if I mentioned your name?"

With slight surprise, Dalton was taken aback. Although, he was sure that this was a woman who *would* know Fraiser.

"By all means, Carla. That's fine with me, thank you."

She smiled with a nod to him and Ben before going to her car. *Very nice fellow. Better hang onto his card.*

She didn't want to, however, she was tired, so she drove back home. Thoughts of another argument or at least a lot of questions caused concern. *Maybe he'll be asleep on the couch.*

Chapter Eleven

ROY MESSES WITH CARLA

Roy rummaged through the several movie advertisements on his desk. He picked up one that pictured a familiar-looking man. His bronze, muscular body was alluring. Roy went on to look over other ads and then went back to the one with the handsome young man. As he studied his body, Roy couldn't recall having met him, although he did look decidedly familiar. He phoned Craig, his manager, who was downstairs in the lobby.

In a moment, Craig tapped on the office door before entering. Roy pointed to the ad.

"Sure, Glen's my assistant. I know that you met him before, that's why he looks familiar. It's just that he was fully dressed then," Craig chuckled. "He's dating a gal that we showed a few weeks ago. She's getting booked as "The Blonde Bombshell". She's got really long, light blonde hair and huge tits. I'm sure you'll know who I'm talking about. I'll look for her poster."

Craig opened the large metal file cabinet to go through the scrolls. "Here she is." He unrolled the advertisement. "See? You remember showing this film, don't you? It's called, "The Blonde Bombshell Explodes". She's Glen's girlfriend. He made a couple of pictures with her as an extra. He's trying to break into the bigger films."

"So, how's he making films while he's working for me?" Roy asked.

Craig held up both hands to Roy. "No, he's only gotten a few small scripts to do on his days off. He fills in for me at the Starlight and Gateway theaters. He's sort of as assistant manager, ticket sales, stock-boy, and works in the concession stand if it's busy. No, Roy, he's not screwing you out of any wages if that's what you meant." Craig could see his boss relax as he glanced back at the photo.

"So, do these two ever make films for Levine?" asked Roy.

"No. Glen just picked up some work as an extra on a low-end budget. She hasn't met Levine yet, but she's trying to get his attention. She had a bit of a set-back a little while ago. She got pregnant by an actor. She contacted one of Levine's actresses about getting an abortion from the doctor who gave *her* one. Later, she became depressed and wasn't interested in sex. The doctor hypnotized her and gave her some medication to get her "in the mood" again.

"Glen had trouble not holding back long enough, so the same doctor hypnotized him to have more control. Glen swings both ways, making boy-flicks occasionally. That's to break into porno films by doing what he loves to do and getting paid for it." Craig noticed that Roy became more attentive with this information. "I can call and get him up here in about twelve or fifteen minutes if you want."

"I have some business to take care of right now. You can bring him here in about an hour."

"Alright, I'll make sure the theater's covered by the other worker then," Craig assured him before he went to see Glen.

The handsome young man was more than receptive to hear that he "big boss" wanted to meet with him.

"Wow, I wonder if he might help me break in with any of the bigger filmmakers. Whatdaya think I can do or say to impress Roy?" Glen balked at the way Craig laughed. "What's goin' on?"

"I have a sneaky hunch that Roy will like you a whole lot. Maybe you've got what it takes."

"What are you saying?"

"I don't know. It's just that I saw the look in his eyes when I told him that you do boy films, and he seemed to be very interested in your poster. I probably read him wrong. But I think if you play this right, Roy can get you and your 'Bombshell' lady in with Levine's company. Just be real subtle and go with your instincts on this. Roy's got a lot of contacts and all that."

He warned, "But be damned sure you're not reading him wrong because he can see that you don't ever make *any* movies, too. I'll be back to pick you up in a little while."

The two men arrived to see their employer on time. Roy was seated at his desk while he looked the young man over. "You don't look legal enough for this kind of work."

"I turned twenty-two a couple of months ago."

"You don't even look eighteen. Have a seat and tell me about yourself."

"Well, for one thing, sir, I really like working for you and Craig. You've got some darn fine theaters, Mr. Jacobs."

Glen said with a beguiling smile. "Craig told me that you saw my picture in an ad. I've picked up some small parts on my days off. Since I do look young, I've had trouble getting any parts for movies. But I sure enjoy working around the films that you show."

"I understand that we showed one of your girlfriend's films recently. Doesn't it bother you when she's having sex with other men?"

"No, it really doesn't, and she not concerned with me doing it either. We have a pretty good relationship and understanding. When we're having sex during a film, it's just a job to us. When we're together, we make love. There's no emotion involved on the job. It's just sex, that's all," Glen answered.

"Tell me about this hypnotism and "mood medication" the doctor gave you. Is he dealing drugs or is that some kind of prescription that he gives out?"

"Oh, no, sir. He doesn't deal with any drugs at all. This is pretty much all-natural stuff made from some kind of root and ginkgo leaves. He mixes it with a small amount of something that's been around since World War Two. It has a long name, but they call it 'meth' for short. It gets a gal turned on and feeling very sexy in just a few minutes, and it wears off in about an hour or so. The hypnotism was pretty much the power of suggestion to keep my "stamina" up, so to speak," Glen grinned. It's "hard" to keep up with pressures of the job," he smirked.

"I never talked with any of the actors. Maybe you can tell me what all's involved in making a film," Roy said out more than mere curiosity.

Craig thought this was a good time for Glen to 'go with his instincts'. "Roy, if you don't need me for anything, I better get back to work." Craig stood up to excuse himself. "Why don't you guys go ahead and talk shop meanwhile. I'll catch ya' later."

"Yeah, go ahead. Gotta keep that money coming in," Roy laughed.

More than a week later, he called Craig into his office again to ask about the medication of which Glen spoke. Could he obtain some?

A Cheshire cat grin came over the manager's face, along with a blush. "Sure thing, boss. I got some at home."

Roy's sharp look of interest made Craig confess, "I gave some to my wife. She's been sorta frigid lately, so I had Glen get me some to try out on her."

"And?" Roy's grin widened as Craig laughed.

"Hey, that stuff worked! She was all over me in no time and wore me out. We had a really great romp in the rack. But then she got kinda mad when she figured out that I drugged her. But she got over it. She agreed to do it again because she liked getting her rocks off. You want some to try out?"

"Yeah, I got to thinking about something. Carla's always on me about getting it on with whores and all that crap. I thought if we could set you and Glen up with her, I can take some pictures with my new Polaroid camera. That would shut her up for sure. Plus, just in case she gets any divorce ideas down the line...."

"Oh, yeah, you gotta cover all your bases for sure. So, when do you want the stuff?"

"Why don't you talk with Glen to see if..."

"Oh, hell yes! He'd love to do it. But I'll talk to him anyway and get back to you. Just say the word."

"Carla's going to have to go back to Beverly Hills soon and work on that mansion. So this coming Saturday, I'll make like I'm taking her out, but I'll have to stop here for some reason. Can you set it up for about eight o'clock that night?"

"Sure, no problem."

While Carla prepared the Friday dinner, Roy approached her with his idea. "I made some plans for us tomorrow night. I want you to wear that dark blue dress.

The velvety one that zips up the front with a kind of lacy top that you don't wear a bra with."

"Gotcha, but why?"

"Because that's what I want you to wear, that's why."

"Roy, just once, can you just ask me to do something because it pleases you? Because you'd like me to do something? Because I'm tired of kinda getting orders from you." Carla tossed the kitchen towel down on the counter.

"I'm not one of your whores or a member of your stinkin' mafia, I'm your wife. Is it asking too much for you to just say the word 'please' once in a while? Or do you think that might soften the edge of your sharp tongue too much?"

Roy walked over to Carla using a softer voice, "Honey, I don't mean to talk to you like that. I work with so many stupid people that can't think for themselves, so I have to tell them how to do their jobs. Now, I would appreciate it if you wore that dress because I like it on you. And it would be nice if you wear your garter belt and stockings rather than those silly pantyhose. It turns me on just to think you're wearing them. Is that better now?"

"Yes, it is. Thank you, but what good is it for me to wear ... oh, never mind. *Shut my mouth. I might get lucky.* "So where are we going that you want me to wear the dress that gets you turned on?"

"Oh, that's a surprise," Roy answered.

Oh, boy. None of your surprises are a surprise.

Saturday night, Carla dressed to please her husband in hopes that he might end up pleasing her. However, this looked to be another one of those other 'surprises' when Roy turned the car into the private parking lot behind the Majestic Theater.

Carla looked at him with reservation. "Don't tell me; you're taking me to a *movie* tonight."

He laughed. "No, I need to pick up some money and check a few things with Craig, my manager. I don't want you to stay in the car alone so, can you come in for a little bit?" He walked over to open her car door, "Come into the office with me ... please."

She thought her little speech had gotten through to him, to her surprise. Carla followed Roy as he unlocked the office door.

Glancing at the large desk, she saw that it had many papers and office books on top, as though he had been working there. Her eyes quickly moved to the sofa that he wanted for "naps when he was tired", or at least that was the reason he gave. The two end pillows looked to have very little use. The side table next to the easy chair was a little dusty. All-in-all, the office looked to have been used just as an office, which set Carla at ease.

Roy draped Carla's coat over his desk chair. He then waved a hand toward the sofa. "Please make yourself comfortable. I think you'll find you made an excellent choice. Just wait here until I check the box office receipts and get some cash. I'll just be a minute.

Hurrying down the stairs, Roy caught up with Craig who greeted him with a wide grin.

"I got the stuff all set up in my office already," Craig said as he opened the door to the meager room. Opening a desk drawer, he brought out two half-full pints of liquor.

"I put some in the scotch, so we'll have the brandy. If we put some in the ice water too, then it'll look like you're making her usual drink", he added.

"Good thinking. Get the cups and ice water from the concession stand. What about Glen?" Roy asked.

"Oh, yeah! He thinks this is too good to be true. He gets to show the boss how good an actor he is." Craig motioned for Glen to join them.

Roy returned in a better mood with the two men and a good deal of cash. Craig set down the bottles of liquor along with the cups.

"What's going on?" Carla asked.

"We're celebrating Craig's promotion to head manager. He's been doing a fabulous job running this place. And I think you met Glen before. I'm moving him up to assistant manager. I wanted to buy them a drink for the occasion. Would you care to join in, my dear?"

She returned Glen's smile but didn't did recall meeting him.

"I *defiantly* would have remembered meeting you, Mrs. Jacobs. You are far more beautiful than your husband described. I'm surprised we haven't seen your gorgeous face on the silver screen yet. You'd be a marvelous Cleopatra."

"Thank you, Glen. That's quite a compliment," Carla sat back on the couch. "Are you in films?"

"He takes care of the Starlight and Gateway," Roy quickly answered. "You guys can sit next to my wife and be comfortable. Carla picked that couch out herself, so give it a try. Let me fix us all a drink. Scotch and water for my lovely date. What do you guys want?"

"I'll have that brandy," said Craig. "You'll like it, Glen. I know you don't like scotch."

"I'll have that too." Roy poured the drinks and then raised the glass, "Here's to my new management team."

The men continued to talk shop about changes to the theater while noticing that Carla's mood was changing. She was more relaxed. Much more relaxed.

"I have an idea. Why don't I get some shots of you three with my new camera," said Roy. "You haven't seen this yet, honey. The pictures develop all by themselves. I'll show you. Why don't you men scoot in close to her so I can get the three of you together."

Craig put his arm around her shoulder while Glen held his hand on her knee, slowly sliding it upward as they smiled for the camera. Roy took another picture after telling them to get closer together. The light flashed.

"Why don't I take a picture of you, dear? Everyone says that Roy is ugly, but he's a very handsome Prince Charming to me," she said with a slight slur.

"Darling, you flatter me too much. But, no thanks. Let me freshen your drinks."

Craig moved closer, remarking that Carla did a wonderful job decorating the office. Glen offered his flattery while his hand slid up her knee. She looked down and then pushed it away.

Carla's intuition sent her a warning that she couldn't decipher. A feeling of deja vu came over her. She set the second drink on the coffee table. As she looked up at Roy, a blur run across her vision. She blinked several times to regain her focus. She saw what looked to be a lecherous smirk on her husband's face. However, now she sensed danger.

An instinct of self-preservation came over her. She felt as though a force was invading her being. Not knowing what was happening but assured that something was, and it was not good, Carla tried to reason to herself that she had to get out of that room. She scooted forward on the sofa.

"If you gentlemen will excuse me, I need to powder my nose." She smiled while trying to stand to her feet without faltering. Carla tightened her stomach and buttock muscles as she stood upright. Her body felt heavy as a wave of heat crossed through it while reaching for her handbag.

Roy asked, "What do you need your purse for?"

"My nose powder is in there, silly," she answered sweetly. "Don't you boys go anyplace while I'm gone now."

Closing the door behind her, Carla reached out for the banister to steady her steps down the staircase. Feeling the perspiration tingle on her upper lip and underarms, she glanced around to see that nobody was looking and then walked to the main door. It felt heavier to push open than usual. However, the sharpness of the cool air was refreshing. She breathed in deeply several times to regain her sobriety.

That was more than just scotch. She tried to walk straight to the end of the block. She steadied herself against the light post while waiting for the *walk* signal. Carla noticed that a patrol car was also waiting in the traffic for the light to change.

She made it to the other side of the street and looked around for a taxi to wave down, but it was the black and white cop car that pulled up next to her.

"You need some help, lady?" the officer called out through the open window.

Carla tried to smile at him. "Just looking for a cab, thank you."

"You out here by yourself, without a coat?"

"No, my husband is over there," she pointed to the movie theater.

He turned his head to look. "I don't see anyone. Where over there, exactly?" he asked while getting out of the squad car.

"He's inside talking to someone. He's the owner," Carla was having some difficulty remaining steady as she reached out for the lamp post.

"You don't look any too great, lady. You been drinking?"

"I had a drink with my husband and his friends, but I wanted to go home, and they wanted to stay and talk." Her speech was slurring.

"I need to see your ID. What's your husband's name?"

"Roy Jacobs. And my name is Carla Martin". Reaching into her purse, she stumbled backward a couple of steps before the cop caught her arm.

"I think you had better sit in the car. You look like you've had more than just a drink, maybe two or three?" He opened the car door and held her arm to steady her as she sat down.

He looked at her driver's license, glanced at her, and again at the license. "You say you're married to Jacobs?"

"Yes, he owns that place along with other theaters. I don't like what he does, so I didn't take his name when we got married. I'm Carla Martin."

"And you work for Jacobs."

"No, I am not one of his whores if that's what you're getting at. I am his legal wife. I think he gave me something in the drink. I feel funny...like weird. I just want to go home, please."

Carla leaned her head back to take in a deep breath and then let it out slowly. "Please, I just want to get out of here," she softly begged.

The officer saw her large diamond wedding ring and that she was well dressed, unlike a hooker. He called headquarters with her name and driver's license number. There were no warrants on her and she was indeed married to Roy Jacobs.

"What do you mean that he gave you something, like drugs?"

She nodded, "Yes, they were up to something. Roy was taking our pictures. Please get me out of here before he comes looking for me. I don't trust him. He's a bad man."

Carla turned her head to look thoroughly at the cop. He was handsome and muscular with thick dark hair. She smiled at what she saw and then reached out to touch his arm.

"Will you take me home, please. I'm a damsel in distress. You have to save me from the ugly dragon."

Having heard about how ruthless and cunning Jacobs was, the officer granted her wish. He called the address into headquarters before starting up the car.

During the twenty-five-minute drive, the officer asked more about Jacobs and was surprised at some of Carla's answers. However, they were inconsistent, inasmuch as her mind was unable to stay focused. Words like mansion, mafia, and Levine began to have meaning, leaving him to understand that this lady may have a legitimate reason to get away from her husband.

When they arrived at her house, he helped her out of the squad car. She made amorous advances toward him. With a grin, he pushed her hands away while asking for the house key. Once inside, she became sultry with him. Not used to having such a beautiful woman fawn over him was flattering, although, he also knew that she was with the wife of a wealthy and powerful man.

"Let me check the house over to make sure everything's all right. I think you had better lay down and let whatever he gave you wear off. Is there someone I can call to stay with you for now?"

"You can stay here with me and keep me safe. After all, you're supposed to protect and serve, and I need servicing," Carla cooed. She ran her fingers over his face and neck as the drug took a more significant effect.

He turned to walk down the hallway with a blushing smile. Following him, Carla opened the bedroom door. "You should check for boogeymen in here."

She flipped her hair back and pouted while slowly unzipping her dress. Then she dimmed the lights.

"Oh, now a great big muscular man like you needs a little loving once in a while." She ran her fingers over his shoulders, his biceps, and down to his firm buttocks, smiling warmly.

"You do have a very nice body. *Very* nice," she said in a low, sultry tone. "You have big muscles. I like that in a man. I would like to see you without your clothes, just touch you all over."

Carla let the dress fall away from her shoulders and then to the floor, allowing him to view her voluptuous, curvaceous body as she stood before him in just the bikini panties, garter belt, and dark stockings.

He glanced at her face. "You're a beautiful woman. Why do you do this? You're belittling yourself."

"My husband did this. He drugged me," she sighed. "I got all, I don't know what, all horny. He wanted me to have sex with his employees. He gets his kicks from doing that."

"You're serious, aren't you?" He looked into her eyes that were dilated. "I think your best bet is to lay down and try to sleep this off. I can call your husband to let him know you're safe at home."

"No, let him worry. He'll think I'm wandering around downtown, so let him worry because he's the one who did this. But you can help me into bed, you handsome stud. He won't think to look for me there."

She ran her fingertips moved over his face again. "I want to make love to you. You're so much of a man." She moved one hand to the front of his pants and ran her fingertips over his now-bulging penis that was trying to hide behind the zipper. Her fingers deftly pulled the fastener down.

"I'm married," the cop said, almost as a defense to her touches and his reaction to them.

"So am I. So what? I'll never tell your wife anything. Will you let me see this big thing, please?" she softly begged. "I'd just like to touch it with my hot tongue."

"Oh, shit, lady, don't talk like that." His voice wasn't strong, and his eyes were willing, as was his desire for her.

"How many times do you beg her for sex? And I'm begging to even touch you," Carla purred while she enjoyed what she felt, as much as he loved the way she was feeling him.

He felt the cries in her soft voice, knowing that what she said was true. When did his wife ever talk to him like that? She issued her body out as a favor to him. Carla laid back onto the bed, pulling him down with her.

He felt the heat from her body. This was a woman who cried out for what he could give her. He wrapped his arms around her as they met in a kiss that was fulfilling to them both. As their tongues tasted one another, their lips blended into what felt like the bonding of two souls that needed to comfort one other.

Carla helped him undress and then wrapped her arms around him as he gave her the satisfaction, the need of his body that was now making love to her. They were not having sex. It was not adultery, and it was not dishonest. It was the redemption of two lost souls, of two unfulfilled hearts that belonged to two people who were just now finding one another, as they should have long, long ago. Was it too late for them?

She closed her eyes and mind to all other thoughts, not allowing anything to take away from this once-in-a-lifetime chance at something that felt like happiness. He held the lady close to himself, engulfing her more than womanly body, along with her soul. Their lips again met, and then she whispered, "I'll never forget you."

In a moment, he melted against her body to further embrace her after both finding fulfillment. The officer then gently pulled away with reluctance as he kissed her tenderly. Looking deep into her eyes, he saw the pain in them.

"What kind of unholy bastard are you married to?" he murmured. Seeing that she had become drowsy, he wiped himself with his handkerchief before getting dressed. He gave it to Carla to use.

"I better keep this," she said. "She might figure things out when she does the laundry."

He nodded in agreement. "I have to see you again. Is that possible?" he whispered. Her sleepy smile and gentle touch to his handsome face was the answer. And then they both looked at the phone on the nightstand as it rang.

Chapter Twelve

THE VALE

On the home front, Roy began to be less attentive to Carla as his words got more and more impolite. The "please", "thank you, dear", and "if you don't mind", became "just do it", "I want you to", or "you heard me", much to her dismay. She began to cower to them.

When he watched late television with Carla, Roy would often lie on the couch in his bathrobe while she rested in her recliner. After a while, he'd pull the afghan over himself and fall asleep. He would remain there until two or three in the morning. Carla could barely notice when he got into the far side of the bed to drift into a deeper sleep. This habit annoyed her until she realized how peaceful her night's sleep had been. And his absence meant less quarrels or cross words.

One day, Roy announced that he had to check out the box offices and talk to the managers.

"Richard just called. He says there's an old theater west of Portland he wants me to look at in a couple or so days. It's been closed down for several years, so he thinks we can get it for a good price. It's somewhere in the valley. I thought you might go with me to see your folks."

"I guess I can. My mother needs to remind me of the bad marriage choice I made anyhow. I can watch her scowl at me once more. How far from Portland is this place? I might know where it's located."

"It's right around Trenton."

"I should know where it's at then. What was the name of the theater?

"I can't remember what he said. The Bailey or The Valley, something like that. Richard's sending up a man to go with me who knows real estate."

Carla looked up from her book as her stomach suddenly tightened. *That's the old Vale Theater.*

"That's in my hometown. There's no way you can open a porno theater around there! Everyone is blue-collar, just like my parents. You sure wouldn't want an angry mob tossing eggs and rotten tomatoes at you."

"Yeah, and I got one word for that... lawsuit."

Carla set her book down. "Roy, those people will burn the place to the ground if you put that trash in there!"

"Another lawsuit."

"Dammit Roy, they'll string you up by the neck before you can get a lawyer, then tar and feather you! Just stick to the big cities, why don't you? There's plenty of them."

"There's plenty of old men who don't get any at home, and young ones who don't get any at all. And some horny housewife who needs the old man to see what sex is really all about. So stick that in your pipe."

"Well, it seems to me that I should take you to the movies more often so *you* can learn. Then, when you figure out what to do, you can show me what you learned. If that's at all possible!"

"Oh, the hell with you. I'm going downtown for a few hours. I'll be back later for dinner."

"You might get something to eat while you're out, besides pussy. I may not be here when you get home."

"Where the hell are you going?" he snapped.

"Out, to get something to suck on. Good-bye!"

Carla waited a few minutes until her temper cooled down before calling her parents home.

After explaining the situation, she asked, "Dad, will you go and find the owners, please? And take Eddie with you. I think they still live in the house next to the theater."

"None of them will want a porno theater around here, except maybe the teenage boys," her father laughed. "But if he does that, you'll be able to collect his life insurance."

"What do you mean?"

"Those people will go after him with shotgun, that's what."

"Then I'd better increase his insurance premium again. Oh, I gotta go, Dad. There's someone at the door. Please get down there just as soon as possible because Roy will be there in about two days. I'll call you back later. Love you, g' bye."

The doorbell rang again. "I'm coming!"

A large, casually dressed man was standing in the doorway with a smile for her. Carla clasped her hands to her mouth.

"Oh, good heavens." She continued to look at him.

"May I come in?"

"Oh, yes. Certainly." She stepped back to look at him fully as he walked through the door.

"Surprised?" he laughed.

She tried to gather her emotions. "Yes, I am. I didn't recognize you out of uniform. Please, do come in and sit down. What are you doing here?"

"I wanted to stop in to see you while your husband's gone for a couple of hours."

She looked surprised, but then again, he was a cop. "How did you know that?"

"Oh, a small bug told me. Actually, he told his manager that."

"So, you have the office bugged?"

"Yes, plus the phone lines there, but not here. You don't need to worry about that. We catch enough as it is."

"We?"

"I have a partner who hates porno and pimps a bit more than I do. He's a good buddy, too. So, how have you been, Carla Martin?" he asked warmly.

"Okay, I guess. If Roy stays away long enough, I can get some work done. You have an advantage over me. I don't know what your name is, officer."

"Jim Crawford, Sergeant. How is the interior design work going?"

"Oh, you've done some homework, I see. It's doing very well, thank you, Jim. I just got into a tiff with Roy about a theater he wants to look into in my hometown. I'll go there and buy it myself before I let him turn it into a porno place."

"Where's the hometown?"

"Trenton, just west of Portland a bit. And how's your police work doing?" she grinned.

He blushed and looked down for a second, recalling making love to her. "Just swell, thank you. I must say that you look more beautiful in the daylight, and you're even sober this time. What kind of drug did that, uh, 'jerk' give you anyway?"

"I really have no idea. You should have heard what I had to say to Roy after that. I made sure he slept on the couch too. And to think he had his manager in on the whole thing from the beginning. I never want to see *that* man's face again!"

Carla paused to look at Jim again, "Your face looks great in the daylight too, Jim, if that were at all possible," she murmured.

He looked down again and then at her with a quiet voice. "I can't tell you how difficult it is for me to sit here and not be able to hold you. But I know your neighbors can see where we're at, so I'd best just stay seated."

"You been by my house then?"

"We've staked it out a couple of times. We used an unmarked car parked just up the street or around the corner, and we were out of uniform. I need to get any evidence that I can on him. The city fathers don't want that kind of business around this area. And he hasn't had any women here while you were out, in case you're wondering about that," Jim reassured her.

"That's a wonder, from the way he ignores me."

Jim shook his head. "Carla... well, um, I'd like to help you out in that area any way I can. I hope you know that."

"Oh, thank you. I think this is the part where the girl goes running into her lover's arms, and he carries her off into the sunset."

"Or into the bedroom," he added with a sheepish grin. Jim reached into his pocket for a slip of paper. "This is my partner's phone number. Give him or his wife a call any time you need or want to reach me. They'll get the message to me right away. His wife will call you back just in case Roy answers the phone."

"Yes, that's a good idea. If Roy asks, she can tell him it's for decoration of her home."

"I need to get out of here before I do carry you off, lady. I don't want to raise any eyebrows. I won't come around again without an invitation, but I do have access to a place where we can meet and talk...or whatever," he smiled.

Jim walked to the door and opened it as she followed. He closed it halfway and then stepped back inside, leading Carla into the hallway. Taking her into his arms, Jim kissed her passionately as she returned his emotions. While holding her close she felt his full erection press against her stomach. A thrill went through her body with the instant thought that Roy would be gone for quite a while.

Jim held her in his arms for a moment longer. "I knew we couldn't be seen from here. Please don't wait too long to call me."

"You're going to leave, just like that?" her voice was almost begging him to stay.

Jim heard that plea. He looked at the door and again at her. He shut the door, turned the lock, and then picked Carla up to carry her into the bedroom. He gently laid her on the bed and then removed his shoes and jacket to lie next to her. When their lips once again met, their souls melted into one. Each felt the same bond they knew when first they made love. This time held far more passion and warmth that both secretly longed for since they first parted. The fire was still inside them, but it was the torch of new love.

They lay wrapped around each other after having found complete satisfaction. As their bodies entwined in ecstasy, they were both aware that time was of the essence, Not entirely because of her husband's return, but due to the possibility of any neighbor's probing eyes and wagging tongues. Jim knew that Carla must keep herself above reproach. He had to force himself to part from her.

"I hope you know that it kills me to have to leave you. Just be sure that I'll be waiting for you to call any time you want to see me again. That's if..."

"Oh, yes Jim, I will. After I get back from Trenton, I promise."

After another quick kiss, he got dressed and left. From the window, Carla watched him walk to his unmarked car and then drive away. She sat on the bed with closed eyes, recalling how he felt that first time and so many times thereafter in the privacy of her mind. To see him again, knowing that he was watching out for her, and then to have him once more, gave Carla a renewed sense of security and womanhood. After straightening the bed, she regained her former thoughts.

Carla called Peter to explain the Vale Theater situation asking for his advice on the theater's purchase. She now wanted to buy it with the idea that perhaps her brother could be the manager.

"Is there any way that you can get away to beat him there? Can Jada or someone cover for you with an excuse?" Peter asked.

"I can ask her to call me when Roy gets back tonight. That way, I'll say I have an important client to see so I can get out of here."

When everything was settled, Peter offered to go along to meet the owners. She sketched some ideas for the theater on the way to Trenton.

Upon her arrival, Carla showed them her ideas for the remodel of the long-closed building. She remembered what it looked like when she was growing up in the early nineteen fifties and wanted to make it look the same way. The Hartleys were thrilled with her recollection.

Carla said, "Most of the folks around here will remember the Vale and how it looked when you first opened it. I also remember that when I was a teenager that all of the kids went to the malt shop for sock hops just down the street."

Mrs. Hartley put her hand to her smiling face. "Oh, my, I remember that. Our boys used to go there on Friday or

Saturday nights. They had that rock and roll music blaring so loud that we could hear it down here, but we always knew where the boys were."

"I had an idea. If I can buy the store next to the theater, I could make that into a malt shop done up in the fifties style with a soda fountain, a jukebox, and dance floor, just like when I was a teen."

"Sold. That's ours, but you can have that too. There's just a lot of junk stored in there anymore. Do you two want to see it, Miss Martin?"

"Yes, sir, and just call me Carla. But can I use your phone to call my brother? He can be here in a few minutes. As a licensed builder, Eddie knows about construction, and he'll need to look at the buildings first."

Mr. Hartley walked Carla and Peter through the buildings. They appeared to be in good condition for their age, moreover, having been closed many years seemed to have preserved them. Carla was surprised to see the one-bedroom apartment on the theater's top floor.

Mr. Hartley said, "That's where the handyman lived. He ran the projector and took care of any little things if they went wrong. Sometimes he sold tickets too. We didn't charge him to live here, so he did the work for free." And then he joked, "He could watch the movies for free too."

When Eddie and his parents arrived, the men looked through joists, foundations, and the electrical circuits while the women gloried in the possibilities of colors, wallpapers, and flooring. When all was considered, it was time for coffee and financial matters.

"I am prepared to offer you eighty thousand for both buildings," Carla told the Hartleys.

"That's far too much. We were only going to ask for sixty-thousand. You'll need some extra money to do all of those improvements."

"Make that seventy grand, and we have a deal," said Carla.

Peter was prepared to write up a contract and finalize the deal, but he didn't like the thought of having it in Carla's name. Mr. Hartley suggested putting it in his old Meadowdale corporation name so that it couldn't fall under 'marital property' in case of divorce or other "legal or illegal" problems, namely Roy.

After the papers were signed, the check was accepted. Now Eddie could begin his work while Carla resumed hers.

When Roy returned from his trip to Trenton he was fuming that "a bunch of local farmers" had already bought the theater. That wouldn't stop him from going into other surrounding towns. He had to make the Don pleased with him.

After learning that Jada was still sick, Carla could get away to start the remodel if only Roy would go on another "business" trip.

Chapter Thirteen

A REAL MAN

After having been with a "real" man again, Roy was far less appealing to Carla. Jim was on her mind before going to Trenton. The traffic would be heavy, so she called him to see if he had time to meet and talk for a while. He was thrilled to do that.

"There's a small store at the corner of third and Meeker. I'll meet you in the parking lot and you can follow me to our safe house. It's really private there. I just gotta grab a change of clothes from my locker and then swing by the Colonel's for some chicken. I'll be there in twenty."

Jim's squad car pulled in ahead of Carla so she could follow him. After a ten-minute drive, Jim turned into a safe house secluded from the road.

He took her suitcase in and turned on the lights. The room was already warm. He checked the deadlock to be sure it was turned, and then swept Carla up in his arms with an ardent kiss. Jim held her face in both hands.

"You don't know how much I've been thinking about you. I've missed you so damned much." He kissed her once more.

"Oh, was your phone call a blessing! I have the weekend off, and my wife wanted to spend the whole time with her in-laws' family. It's her sister's birthday, and I didn't want to be in the car for over an hour's drive just to see her. So I lied and said I had to work. Then you called me." Jim kissed her again. "And you don't know how happy that made me." He quickly kissed Carla once more.

"Okay, that's enough foreplay for now. I need a drink. The last two days have been havoc." He turned to reach into the cupboard. "What's your pleasure? There's some scotch, vodka, and bourbon. I didn't know what you liked."

"I prefer scotch. Rocks with a little soda or water, please."

"Coming up. And vodka and short water for me."

"You're sure in a jovial mood. What's up?"

"Not a thing. Just that I'm so thrilled to have the entire weekend off and to spend it with you," Jim answered while making their drinks. Then he turned to Carla, "That's if you want to spend the whole time with me. I didn't even think to ask you."

"Well, certainly, Jim, but I also need to see my family about the new movie theater so we can get that running. I'm scared that Roy will find out what I'm doing before it's all set up."

"Honey, you've been around that disrespectful bastard so long that you haven't felt worthy of being appreciated. He wants to keep you down-trodden and under his thumb so that you'll be grateful for what little he does for you." He handed Carla her drink and then kissed her cheek.

"So, my lovely lady, this is going to be 'Appreciate Carla weekend'. By the way, I picked up some chicken, biscuits, and coleslaw for dinner. I didn't know if you knew how to cook any better than what's-her-name does."

"And that's appreciation?" she laughed. It was Carla's chance to brag. "I'm a terrific cook! You name it, and I can make it. Meat, potatoes and gravy, roasts, casseroles, Italian, Mexican, Chinese, stews, cheesecake, carrot cake, apple pie, pumpkin pie, chocolate chip cookies, peanut butter cookies..."

Jim put his drink down to hold on to Carla's waist with both hands. "You're giving me a hard-on with all of that talk. How about if you teach what's-her-name how to cook, and I'll teach you how to cook in bed." Jim tried to kiss her but she turned her face away.

"Thanks a lot, mister. You *know* I know how to cook in bed. I just need someone to light my fire."

"Yeah, well, will a hot torch do?" He tried to kiss her again, and again she turned away.

"I'd rather finish my drink and make your torch burn for a while. You men need to keep your thingy on ice, anyway."

"Thingy. What's a thingy?"

"You know... a *penis*."

Jim laughed. "Penis? Is that the best you can do? What about a cock, prick, or dick? How about trouser snake, or skin flute, or a ..."

"Okay, okay, I get the picture!" she covered her red face with both hands, but Jim just had to make it an issue with her.

"What about a ramrod, third leg, a tube steak, or a meat thermometer... but you don't ever call a man's pride and joy a "*thingy*", for God's sake!"

She laughed, "Alright! You made your point."

"And you don't have a vibrator that looks like one?"

"Whatever for?

"Oh, sweetheart, am I going to have fun teaching you a few things. Jim looked around the room to see that there were just two straight-back chairs, a dresser, and one armchair. He set his drink on the small nightstand to prop the pillows against the double bed's headboard. He asked Carla to make herself comfortable on the bed while he removed his gun and holster, shoes, and then rolled up his sleeves. He rested against a pillow next to her with a drink in hand.

"Tell me about your new movie place."

She was happy to tell him about the Vale Theater. "We'll have to work fast because I have to go back to work on the mansion when Jada gets better."

However, as she spoke, Jim heard more than her voice. It was the hurt in it. He got up to fix two more drinks and then rested closer to her.

"What did he do now?"

"Oh, he wants to use my customers and connections to make a big name for himself with this Don person. He has no regard for anyone but himself anymore."

"Sweetheart, I don't think he ever did. Your looks struck him for sure, but I think it was also by your business sense, your intelligence, and your strength. Now that he has you hooked, he wants to break that spirit so he can control you completely. This guy is a real piece of work and a sick one at that.

"I know you have men tell you how beautiful you are all the time, but Carla, the beauty that I see is beyond your flesh. It's in your eyes, your smile, your heart," he turned to look at her, "and your mind. You are so much of a woman that I'm nearly devastated that you should choose to be with me. You make me feel whole again."

Jim didn't want to spend the weekend in Roy's shadow any more than Carla wanted to hear about his wife. He laid back against the headboard.

"Now, take me, for instance. Here you have an all-American hero who shoots at bad guys, rescues small dogs from large cats, and I'm more powerful than a speeding locomotive. But I don't jump tall buildings, just sheep once in a while. Innocent young whores turn tricks just hoping I'll frisk them."

"*Innocent* whores?" Carla laughed.

"I can load a six-shooter faster than a speeding bullet. Which doesn't mean a thing because we use twelve-shooters these days." Jim smiled to hear Carla's laughter. "I once had a fat dog that was so ugly I had to divorce her. The only exercise she got was from chasing cars."

Carla was laughing so hard she could barely hold on to her glass, and Jim was thrilled to see her happy at last.

"I was really jealous because she had a better mustache than I did. Actually, I'm so much of a man that I have to put my condoms on with a tire iron."

With that, Carla grabbed her crotch and cried out, "I gotta pee!" Jim got up to set the drinks aside. Scooping her up in his arms, he carried her into the bathroom.

"Not in my bed, you don't. I hate sleeping in a wet bed so much that I don't have nocturnal emissions anymore."

By then, she was laughing so hard she couldn't pull her wet slacks down, so he did. It was almost too late as she sat on the toilet.

"Now, if you only learn how to pee standing up, you wouldn't have all these problems. You can just whip it out and squirt to your heart's content."

"Get out of here, I can't even pee sitting down with your silly jokes!"

"If you need anything I'll be at the laundromat with the blankets." Jim was happy to hear Carla laughing from the bathroom. He took the bathrobe out of his pack and tossed it to her.

"It might be a little big, but at least it's dry." Again, she laughed.

He made two more drinks and sat in the armchair while he waited for her to return.

"That looks real good on you. But I don't think I'll fit into your robe, so don't even ask," he grinned.

"I can take it off if you want," she demurely said while standing near the bed.

"Yeah, and I'll screw the hell out of you if you do." He watched her pull back the covers on the bed.

"What if I don't want you to?"

"You think you can actually resist me?" he grinned.

"Far more than you can resist me."

"Well, if you don't want to have sex with me, I'll just go home and get resisted."

"If you walk out on me, I'll call the cops."

"Then they'll have to arrest me for resisting." He took a sip of his drink. "Oh, alright, if you insist. I guess I'll just have to have sex with you."

"Too late. I'm not in the mood now," Carla laughed.

"Well, that makes one of us then. I'd rather get arrested for rape anyhow."

"Finally, a man after my own heart."

"Well, that too," he laughed. "Hell, now *I'm* out of the mood. How about another stiff drink?"

Carla let the large robe come open. "I'd much rather have a stiff cock."

Jim turned to her. "Now that's an offer I can't resist."

"Well, you can't from there." She let the robe fall to the floor, allowing him to see the fullness of her sensual, alluring naked body before slipping into the bed.

Sober faced, Jim took another sip of his drink. He walked over to the bed and set the glass on the nightstand. He slowly pulled his shirt out of his waistband, unbuttoned it, and then took it off as he watched Carla watching him. She enjoyed what she saw, and he saw that. He unzipped his pants, letting them drop to the floor, and kicked them aside. This exposed his very brief briefs that could hardly hold in his hard-on. He languidly pulled them down over his large, erect penis for her to see his manhood at its best.

He spoke in a low, fervent tone. "This is what you do to me, day and night, with every thought of you."

Carla reached out her hand to touch him. He closed his eyes to revel at the feel of her soft fingers. He shed his socks and then slipped into the bed beside her. He engulfed her large breast with his gentle hand while his savory mouth was on hers. She totally relinquished her body to him. He felt her complete submission, furthering his sense of masculinity. She was entirely at the mercy of his ability to make love to her to his fullest.

He had done this in his earlier years of marriage and since having her the first time. It was only in his innermost yearnings that he craved touching her while touching himself.

Jim made sure his every move was well received. And he knew they were by her gentle moans and purring, her heavier breathing with writhing, and as her fingertips clenched his skin. Jim knew he pleased her when muscles contracted with each arch of her back and the taste of her sweet mouth.

She turned to reciprocate and please him. Her hands felt every inch of his handsome, muscular body, as did her lips and tongue. She felt his flinches and jerks when she hit a sensual spot and savored his round and full buttocks. She loved the deep groan he emitted as her tepid mouth engulfed his penis or while her tongue titillated other parts.

While he was inside her, his muscles tensed. He pushed her away to save himself from ending the complete pleasure of her womanhood too soon. She smiled to know that she could bring this kind of amorous frenzy to a man such as him. This was an erotic love of which she had only dared to dream, merely hoped would happen to her. To have a man in her arms the likes of Jim who could shame Apollo was beyond her outermost prayers.

After both were thoroughly satisfied, they lay together with their arms, legs, minds, and hearts wrapped in the warm emotions of a satisfying and new bond of oneness, which could only be realized as love. There was no outside world, only the soft touches, warm caresses, and tender little kisses with big smiles for them to enjoy. They made light talk about childhood adventures, teenage thrills and shared other small secrets.

As the afternoon grew late, Carla said she needed to be in Trenton. Her family was expecting her and she had to call them. Then an idea came to her

"Do you know anything about construction and building stuff? Maybe I can bring you along as Eddie's helper."

With that, he grinned. "Yep. I can swing a hammer, pour cement, put up drywall, install light fixtures... and lay pipe." Jim looked at her with a devilish grin. "Of course, you already know I'm an expert at that." He bragged, "I even drive a pretty mean power saw."

Carla raised herself on one elbow, smiling widely. "You do?"

"My dad was one of those old-fashioned do-it-yourself guys who taught me a lot about building all kinds of things.

I was his helper starting as a kid." He pulled Carla against him with a gleam in his eyes. "And I can help you out too."

By his kiss, she knew he wanted to bang on something besides plywood, but she gently pulled away.

"I need to call my folks. I'll be there a lot later than they expected."

"I'll drive with the lights and siren on. We'll be there sooner."

"I really should call them."

"You will, in about fifteen minutes... give or take." Then he gave and she took.

After a bit more than the allotted time, the two needed to develop a valid reason why she was bringing a man with her. She'd have to answer several other questions her mother would ask.

Jim had an idea. "We can tell them I'm a cop who's had bad dealings with your husband on other occasions. I'm here to protect you and to watch out for Roy or any of his Mafia pals who might try to stop you from opening this theater. And that's close enough to the truth."

He suggested renting a motel when they got to Trenton. Perhaps she might find a reason to go out for a while.

Carla called her brother to say she was coming with an undercover police officer. And then she asked if he'd make a reservation at the Trenton Travel Inn for him. Their mother rejoiced in knowing that "someone was out to get Roy."

When they arrived, the family was enthusiastic about meeting Jim. They told Carla how much the town was looking forward to having "their" theater running once more.

Eddie welcomed Jim's help in updating any wiring problems and then adding the insulation and drywall. The two men worked well together, so the work went smoothly. And Eddie was enlightened by Jim's great sense of humor.

Even Mother laughed at his little quips, although she noticed the way he often looked at her daughter in less than a professional manner. The thought of even the *possibility* of having this fine, strong young man as a son-in-law warmed her heart immensely. Although, for once, she kept this thought to herself.

Mrs. Martin encouraged Jim to stay for lunch and dinner, and without question, gave Carla the car keys later in the evening.

As the opening day soon approached, Mrs. Martin ran ads in the local and neighboring towns' papers. Eddie hired the projectionist, concession workers, and ticket salesperson. The soda shop was decked out in the early rock 'n roll malt shop style, complete with soda fountains and a small dance floor. The jukebox box was filled with Bill Haley, Jerry Lee Lewis, Fats Domino, and, of course, Elvis Presley records for the teenagers.

Since he had helped with the purchase, Carla asked Peter and Beth to join the celebration by cutting the ribbon for the grand opening. He was pleased with her request and happily agreed. Carla suggested that this would be good for his political image as well.

The well-published grand opening movies would be a double feature, just like in the 1950s. "*High Noon*" and "*Gentlemen Prefer Blondes*" followed the cartoons. There would be a twenty-minute "restroom and concession" break between movies.

All were asked to dress in the '50s fashion. The guys had (if possible) duck-tail hair with pompadours and wore white snug-fitting T-shirts. Or else cotton shirts with short sleeves rolled up several times, and collars were turned up at the back of the neck. Their low-slung jeans were held up by thin leather belts, and without question, the fellows wore blue suede or white buck shoes.

Most ladies showed up in ponytails and poodle skirts. Their Peter Pan blouses were topped off by a cardigan sweater while wearing saddle shoes with crew socks, the fashion for girls during those days.

As the Martin family watched the multitude gather outside the theater, Mrs. Martin nudged her daughter. With a glorious smile of pride, she pointed at the two uniformed police officers helping with crowd control. Carla put her hands to her mouth in surprise.

"Oh, gosh, Mom, it's Jim. And that must be Tom, his partner."

Carla watched until Jim turned to her with the same caring smile. Then, spotting Mrs. Martin, he tipped his hat. She warmly waved in return with a thumbs-up signal.

Before several hundred cheering and welcoming people, the town mayor stepped to the microphone and introduced the new owner, Carla Martin. The Hartley family was acknowledged with resounding applause. And State Senator Peter Nichols and his wife were exceptionally well received.

After a brief speech, Peter used over-sized scissors to cut the ribbon as the crowd yelled with enthusiasm. He announced that the Vale Malt Shop was open for the teens before inviting patrons into the theater. The grand opening of the Vale Theater was a success!

When the excitement settled, the two police sergeants reported that all was fine with no suspicious activity or other interference, so they would leave everything to the local police force and return to Salem.

Jim whispered, "Carla, call me when you get back." It was hard for both to stand so close and dare not touch one another. Although, she saw the twinkle in his tantalizing eyes, and he saw the desire in hers.

Chapter Fourteen

GORVETTI

R oy made an appointment to speak with David and Richard for some advice. He explained that the managers of the Gateway and the Starlight stores in Salem received threatening calls from someone in the Gorvetti Family.

"They're asking what my selling price is. I thought I should run my idea past you for your opinion since this may include the Family. I have a couple of men up my way who would love to take Gorvetti on, but I don't know how big his organization is or exactly where they're located. My guys want their men to strike fast and hard, but I'm concerned about any retaliation."

"Have you ever had any problems like this before?" asked Hirsh.

"No, but the Gorvetti's haven't been interested in these areas before, nor the Perez people for that matter." Roy said, "I'd like to put a stop to this in a way that will catch the attention of both gangs without causing a war of any sort."

"It shouldn't come to that," said Hirsh. "I would suggest that your two "friends" have a nice talk with a couple of

Gorvetti's men. Perhaps they can persuade their leader to back off."

The Don added, "Yes, they can say that the Levine Corporation owns this establishment and that if they don't care to listen to your men, then their "good friend", Mr. Blum and his men, will explain it to them more fully. Perhaps when they go crawling back to Mr. Gorvetti..." a sly, devious grin slid across his face, "metaphorically speaking, that is, he'll understand the error of his ways. Those people certainly know who Mr. Blum is and what his men are capable of."

Jacobs understood that he had the full backing of the Don, however, at what cost? Was it Levine's intention to take over his theaters? This was something that Roy wouldn't question, for now at least.

"That sounds like a great plan, sir. I'll do that and then get back to you with the outcome. I'm sure it will be favorable."

"Yes, Jacobs, I'm sure you'll see that it is," said Levine.

Roy gave the message to his men who did just as Levine suggested. Gorvetti's men got the message.

All was quiet for a while, although, Roy had his men keep vigil over the situation. Feelers were sent out only to hear that the mention of Levine's name seemed to have doused Gorvetti's fire.

Later, Hirsh was pleased to learn Gorvetti's reaction. A silent peace treaty seemed to have been made and the Gorvetti name did not come up in any Salem area discussions. However, he traveled north to a newer territory, Trenton.

There, the young movie ticket salesman was studying for his college acceptance exams. Soon, a dark shadow fell over him. He looked up to see a triple X-sized man wearing a tan poplin overcoat. He wanted to speak to the owner.

"I'm sorry, sir, he owner is actually a corporation, but I can call for the manager." The large man looked perturbed but nodded.

The attendant called Eddie, "Hi, a great big man is asking for the owner, but he'll talk to you."

Mystified, Eddie went down to the ticket booth. Introducing himself, he extended a hand in friendship. The man didn't respond.

"How may I help you, sir?"

"How much do you want for this place? Mr. Gorvetti wants to buy it." That sounded more like an order than an offer.

"I'm sorry, but as far as I know, it isn't for sale."

"That wasn't the question. How much? Mr. Gorvetti wants to buy it."

Bewildered, Eddie tried to smile, wondering how to answer this large, intimidating man. "I'm not at all familiar with that name. I've lived here most of my life. Is Gorvetti from around this area?"

"That's *Mister* Gorvetti," he abruptly answered, "of the Gorvetti Family. He wants to buy this place. What's your price?"

"I'm sorry, sir, but it's owned by the Meadowdale Corporation, and I haven't heard anything about selling because we just re-opened it a few months ago. If you would care to leave a phone number, I can have someone get in touch with Mr. Gorvetti."

"He'll get in touch with you." Eddie watched him get into the back seat of a new Cadillac and then it drove away. He looked at the ticket salesman and shrugged before going back to his office to call his sister.

Carla didn't like the situation at all. She said she'd speak to Roy about it and then tell Eddie what she learned.

However, the Gorvetti name sounded vaguely familiar to her.

Roy knew that name well. "This is a bunch of thugs that call themselves a mafia. They're an Italian gang who tries to muscle in where they can't get in legitimately. They're heavy into drugs and that's one thing the Don won't tolerate. Those guys get high school kids stuck on it, and they deal with street hookers and pimps too. Why do you ask?"

"I thought I heard the name on the news but couldn't put a finger on it."

"Just stay the hell away from any of them. If they come around of your jobs, let me know right away." Roy ran his hand through her hair to look at her with tenderness. "Those bastards are evil men. They would give anything to get their hands on someone as beautiful as you. They would lock you into a room and force you into prostitution. That's the kind of thugs they are, not a real Family like the Levine's."

"Are you telling me each one of these "families" are mafia people?"

"Some are good ones, like our Family. We don't condone that kind of ruthless stuff. We work like gentlemen. If someone doesn't like dealing with us, we part ways civilly. The Gorvetti and the Perez Families do it with a shotgun or a knife. And that's another bunch that I don't ever want you to be around. The Perez are just the same. But we're all protected by the Don." He lightly kissed her cheek.

"So don't worry. Oh, and I'll have to go down to Fresno to see about another theater that I might have you clean up. I'll be gone for a couple of days."

"Alright, I'll be here in case you need to call."

During that time, the police called Eddie at home. After the patrol car passed through the area in the early hours, a large rock was thrown through the glass window of the ticket booth. The alarm didn't sound, since the theater itself had not been disturbed. A police officer was standing guard when Eddie arrived.

Soon after being called, the insurance man arrived to take pictures and make a report. Even before the mess had been cleaned up, the local glass company was there to replace the window a with break-proof style.

After learning what had happened, Carla called Jada who told her just what to do.

"When this 'gentleman' comes back, tell Eddie to let him know that the owner will meet only with Mr. Gorvetti himself, in person and at the theater. And that the owner does not do business with the help. Use those very words. He'll get the message that you're ready to make a deal. As soon as the appointment has been made, call me. I'll send Mr. Blum up to go with you. Give Gorvetti David's card and say that you're speaking for Don Levine. Once his name is mentioned, and they see Blum with you, it will all go away. If not, they know they're dead meat. I know you can do this, Carla, so make me proud and keep Roy the hell away from this. Kissy-kissy."

Eddie gave the message to the big man who set a meeting date.

Carla sat behind the manager's desk, signing payroll checks. While Mr. Blum stood in the shadows at the back of the room, her brother showed two men into the office. Without looking up Carla said that she'd be with them in a moment and to please be seated. They remained standing as they watched her.

"Mr. Gorvetti does *not* like to be kept waiting," the bodyguard lightly reprimanded. She set the pen down, flipped her long hair out of the way, and then leaned back to look up at the gangster. Carla suddenly surprised him with a big smile.

Then Gorvetti grinned widely, "Carla Martin?"

She stood up. "Oh, my word, are you Mister Gorvetti... Mister Jerry Gorvetti?" She stepped away from the desk into his open arms and they embraced as old friends. They parted to look at one another.

"Get you. You're a big bad thug now! You look great. You haven't changed since high school! What's going on, and who's this 'mumff'? Is he the one who threw the rock through my window?" Carla shook her finger at him. "You owe me big time, pal!"

Jerry broke out in loud laughter. "I haven't heard that since we all ran around together." He turned to his bodyguard, "That was a big-time insult back then. It stands for mutha... never mind. Me and Carla went to different schools together. I went steady with her best girlfriend. She was from Trenton, and I was from Brent, the next town over." He looked at the lady again.

"My God, Carla, I didn't think you could get more beautiful than you was, but look at my girl. You look like a movie star!" He took Carla in his arms again, only to notice a mountain step out of the darkness. He suddenly let go of her.

"Oh, my God! Who's this?" he cried out.

"This is my very special friend, Mr. Blum. He watches out for the Family," Carla motioned for them to be seated while Blum stood to one side with his hands folded in front of him.

"Family? You got a lot of kids?"

Blum handed him Levine's card.

Carla said, "We work for him."

Jerry's face turned stark. He looked at Carla and then gave the card to his bodyguard, who was small compared to

Blum. The man appeared even more solemn when he looked at Blum. Moreover, he nodded with a sign of respect and recognition while offering the big man his chair. Blum waved him off with a motion to sit down. They did.

"Do you know who Roy Jacobs is?" Carla asked.

"Sure, who don't from around here? He owns several movie theaters. Man, he did a knockout job in redoing the Majestic and Regency. Must have paid a fortune to get them done, they're real fantastic. Have you been in one of them?"

She gave Jerry one of her cards. "Interior decorator? Did you do that to those places? And this one?"

"Roy Jacobs is my husband," Carla calmly stated.

Jerry sat back in the chair, "Oh, shit." He became irritated as he glared at his bodyguard. "You didn't know about that?"

The man shook his head, knowing now that he was in big trouble.

Carla related the story to Jerry about how this situation came to be, and he became Carla's old pal once more. He shed the tailor-made, camel hair topcoat to sit more comfortably as they talked.

Carla could see how Jerry had tried to better himself. However, in the wrong way since he came from a family who struggled to get what little they had. And it may have been the only way for him to break out of that slum area where his deadbeat parents raised him and his brothers. She knew Jerry used to be a good kid at heart but not well-educated or cared for.

Jerry was concerned about Carla's situation with Roy, asking how he could help. She said to leave her husband and the Levine Family out of their affairs would be best.

Jerry offered to step in with his "service" if she needed help.

"Thank you very much, Jerry, but keep in mind who I work with." With her thumb, she motioned to Mr. Blum.

Jerry smacked his forehead, "Yeah, that was sure stupid of me to ask," he laughed.

Carla asked, "Oh, but if you have any contact with the Perez Family, would you please let me know. Just in case they ever come around and throw more rocks at my windows."

Jerry looked at his bodyguard, who was already taking cash out of his money clip. "Will five hundred cover that, Ma'am?"

Carla took the big man's cash and then sat back to reminiscence with her old pal for a while longer.

Before he left, Jerry offered his phone number. She promised to keep in touch with him. He was pleased to know that Carla was still as much a lady as ever, but his respect for her was even more significant now, especially knowing who was standing behind her, besides the intimidating Mr. Blum.

Chapter Fifteen

GOOD MAN ON THE SET

Since Carla was working on the house again, Richard Hirsh and his wife held the luncheon meeting on the patio while enjoying pleasant weather. Richard wanted to finalize some matters with the film crew about the new set.

"Did you see to that other lighting effect that I mentioned?"

"Yes, Mr. Hirsh," the director answered. "I told the lighting man about it, and he got on it right away. It did make a big improvement, as you suggested."

Hirsh reviewed the list. "Okay, that looks good. Now, who's going to be on the set with this little girl?"

"I thought that blonde one with the great body should be with her on this. They work really well together."

"Oh, no. Isn't that the one who has trouble getting it up?"

"Well, at first. But when he does get going, he does a fine job."

"But damn, we're wasting money and time just to get him going."

Sharon pushed her chair back from table, crossed her legs, and then asked, "What's he like other than that?"

They described the man to be in his early twenties, handsome with a gorgeous well-built, well-kept body. However, an important part seemed to sometimes malfunction during the filming. Sharon asked to be present for the day's shoot.

The man was more than described, much to her delight. When the actors were in place, the director called out to begin filming. The young woman was lying in bed when her partner approached her. He removed his bathrobe to present his muscular body. However, he failed to offer her an erection.

"Cut! How many times do we have to do this before you can come up with the goods to deliver?" yelled the director. The young actor bowed his head in disappointment to him as well as of the himself.

Disgusted by his remark, Sharon stood up to address the director and the filming crew.

"Hold it, you big manly men. How in the world do you expect a guy to show his prowess knowing that a dozen guys are watching him? *And* just waiting for him to get it up so they can get a cheap thrill out of watching him bang the hell out of some little gal? Maybe Jada and I should be running this show. After all, we run your lives behind the camera, don't we?" The men knew full well not to answer that question. Even Levine and her flustered husband were caught short of an answer.

Sharon strolled over to the bed and draped the man's bathrobe over his shoulders. With a warm smile, she pulled the satin sheet over the young lady's body.

"Now, you rest while I speak to your partner for a moment."

Gently taking the man's arm, Sharon led him to one side of the set. Standing close to him, she drew the robe snugly around his shoulders. Her voice was soft, sultry, and womanly. The actor knew she was the wife of the third most powerful man in this Family's business. He listened to her.

With their backs turned away from Richard and the filming crew, Sharon stood close to the actor. Placing an arm on his shoulder, she spoke into his ear. As her magnificent breast pressed against him, her hand slowly moved under the robe to his bicep, his chest, and then to his stomach.

"If you put all these old men together, they wouldn't be half the man you are. Don't let them try to belittle you. I talk with their wives. I know what those men and my husband *can't* do in bed." The actor froze as her fingers moved lower. Sharon's voice tantalized him.

"I'd like you to show me just what I can expect out of having you for myself. I want to see you perform your best with that little girl, and then you can perform with a real woman. I hope that we can get together and practice your techniques." She whispered, "I have not had a man to satisfy my needs in a long, long time."

Her more than warm breath was on his neck and ear as her fingers barely touched his now engorged penis.

"We can practice and practice... and practice, until you think of me every time that camera is on you." Sharon knew not to get the man too aroused, so she slowly withdrew her hand.

"Now, you go give them more than the performance they want. Show these bastards what a *real* man is like in bed." She patted his rear end, "I know you can do it."

Sharon sat next to her husband again to watch the actor stand by the big bed. He was more than ready to give an Oscar-winning performance, cameras or no cameras, leaving the director in awe.

"What the hell did you say to that man?" asked her husband.

Sharon sat back in the chair, crossed her legs, and looked at her fingertips. "Oh, I just gave him a little bit of encouragement. That's all."

The men looked at each other, not saying any more. Although, they accepted that her "encouragement" certainly worked.

Hirsh called Jacobs later that day to let him know that another hot new film was coming his way.

"Yeah, I don't know what all Sharon said to this guy, but he seems to be super enthusiastic about his job now. I should have her give more pep talks," he laughed. "Make sure you show this at our Vancouver store, too. Those farmers up there will really go for this one."

Jacobs agreed to that but didn't like Hirsh's mention of "our" store. It was his theater. However, he wouldn't argue that point at this time.

"How you're doing on that deal for Bend, Oregon?" Harry asked.

"It's coming along fine. I have the owner down to a good price. The Eureka store is catching up to the one in Metford pretty fast. It seems those people enjoy seeing the real stuff on the screen."

Harry laughed, "Yeah, I'll bet that's a lot better than the sheep those farmers are used to. How is that new manager working out?"

"Bradbury? He seems to be doing quite well. Thanks for sending him my way."

"Any time, I'm glad that you can work with him. He's a little ambitious, so don't give him too much slack. Say, I hear you're showing some stuff other than Levine's films."

Now Jacobs knew why he had called. "I got a good deal on a couple of films from a minor company called 'Fred's Fun Films'. They look to be pretty much on the amateur side, but they're quite explicit." Roy realized that he had better come up with a good reason for going behind the Don's back in not showing his films exclusively. "I thought I'd try them out to see what kind of reaction I get before I got with you and Philips about it," he lied. Perhaps that got him off the hook.

"So, how are they doing?"

"Big time. Everyone's leaving the theater with a big smile, and they come back a second or third time. I show them as a leader to Levine's feature films. It's not the quality stuff that he puts out by any means, so I wasn't sure if he'd want to show it in the stores with his name on them. I can get this Fred guy together with you if you want to check them out for yourself. His prices are super reasonable since they're so low budget, but that shows in the movies themselves. They all have sort of a doctor-patient theme to them, but they're very original in their scripts," Roy said.

"Just watch out for the bootleg stuff that's been getting out. There's a small-time outfit that's trying to break into our end of things. That kind of crap can get the cops and even the FBI's eye if it crosses state lines. We don't need attention from anyone like that."

Later, Harry Philips took Jacobs up on the offer to review the home movies and then reported his findings to Levine. After viewing a couple of them, he agreed to their usage.

"Jacobs has a good idea in using those short films for leaders, and I'm glad that Bradbury's doing good up there. Yes, go ahead and show them at a couple of our outlying stores. See how they react to them. They are not going to compete with our quality film, but if it brings more people in, then it may be worth it," Levine told Hirsh and Philips.

"Do you want Mr. Blum to find out the source of those other films?" Hirsh asked.

"I'll leave that up to him. We've seen these little companies come and go. The cops will be looking into them soon enough. They're not any threat to us. They just want to get a foot in the door as best they can, but they never make anything of themselves. The prices of these films are good for now. If they begin to get greedy, then just cut them off," said Levine.

Chapter Sixteen

DEATH IN THE DESERT

Jada told Carla to take some time off to care for her own home. That break was appreciated. One day, Carla reached for the phone on the third ring just as Roy picked it up in the bedroom.

"Yeah, what's going on?"

"We found the shortage." Harry's voice was strictly business.

"The hundred grand?"

"Closer to one-fifty at this count."

"Oh, wow! Who took it?"

"That guy you put in charge of the Metford store."

"Bradbury, my manager? Oh, shit, my ass is cooked."

"I got it covered for you. I told Levine that you and Blum had an eye on him and that if he ran, Blum was on him."

"I owe you big time, pal. You talk to Blum?"

"Yeah. He had been in some hot water with The Don and this was a way to pull himself out. He tailed Bradbury to Vegas where he was holed up in some dive. I guess he was waiting for his contact, but Blum caught up with the guy first and put him to sleep. A couple of men are holding Bradbury in Vegas. We need to get there ASAP or all of our asses are cooked."

"Okay, I'll get packed and meet you. Where and when?"

"I booked you on the three-fifty out of Salem at six-ten. Can you make that?"

"Yes. I'll meet you at the gate when I get down there."

Carla waited to hear Roy hang up the receiver and then scurried into the kitchen to open the refrigerator door. Roy came in and smacked her bottom. She pretended to be startled.

"I don't know what to fix for dinner. How about if I call for some Chinese?"

"I won't have time. I have to catch a plane at six."

She put her arms around his neck. "Oh, Honey, I just got back. I haven't had any time to see you. Now, where are you going to?" She pouted.

"Vegas. I won't be gone long."

"Oh, take me with you, then I can be with you. Oh, please, I won't get in the way."

"Oh, I don't know. Well, yeah, maybe. That way, I can see the Don and you can keep Jada out of his way."

"Yes, and you can make big points with David. You'll get moved up the ladder in no time. He likes the way you think."

"How do you know that?"

Carla ran her finger over his stomach. "Oh, I talk to some people sometimes, and they say nice things about you. I'll go pack our things. What suit do you want to take?"

"I'll come an' help you. Just take your pants off, I'll be right there."

Oh great, I get a quickie before we leave. I'll give him something he'll like. Carla was waiting for him on the bed in just a blouse with her naked legs spread open. She hoped to surprise him.

"What's this?"

"You told me that you never screwed any whores before, so I thought I'd be the first one for you. Gimme some money first, mister." She held her hand out. " You know the rules, pal, No money; no honey." Isn't that what a whore would say?"

With a lecherous grin, Roy tossed a hundred-dollar bill from his money clip on her chest. Then he dropped his pants and briefs to kick them aside. She watched his penis get fully erect in a second. He began to unbutton his shirt.

"No need for formalities, pal, just come here and get it on." She reached for his arm to pull him on top of her. His face became flushed with anxiety as he mounted her.

"You like this, you tramp?"

"Who the hell's the tramp? You're paying *me*. You like spending money to pay for my hot pussy?" She felt her husband become increasingly excited, which gave her an orgasm.

She thought that if this was a key to getting him aroused, he could give her the sex she wanted. "Come on, big boy, can't you pump that thing any harder? I've had schoolboys that can screw better than that", she panted. "I should bring one home for you to watch so you can learn something. With that, Roy let out a short groan, and she knew that he was done. He tried to kiss her, but she turned her head.

"While I'm at it, I'll have the schoolboys teach you how to kiss too."

He buried his face in her neck, "I'll pay you big time to do that."

"Yuk. Go take a shower."

Roy was markedly pleasant to her on the flight to Las Vegas. He was like the bridegroom he should have been to her. Carla thought about how to use and perhaps control her husband. If he liked kinky sex, she could find a way to give it to him even if it did mean with young high schoolboys. But, then again, that wasn't such a half-bad idea.

When she finished the martini, Carla sat back to rest. Roy tenderly held her hand. She turned to look at him. She saw Roy looking like he was again deeply in love with her, the man with whom she had fallen in love. Carla reached her hand over to gently stroke his cheek and then leaned into his face to kiss his lips.

"I love you, you bastard," she whispered. His hand tightened around hers.

"Honey, you don't know how much I love you. I'll give you the world on a string, I promise. Just don't ever stop loving me, please."

"I won't, darling, I won't."

Once they touched down, Roy put on his business personality while speaking to Carla.

"You don't know a damned thing about what's going on, so I'll say that you came along to go shopping with Jada. And don't you dare talk back to me. If you say anything out of line, I'll slap your face so hard in front of these guys that it'll make you bleed. You got me? You don't shame me in front of these men. If you do anything like that in front of the Don, I'll kick your ass stupid. You women are here to please and serve us men and nothing more. Do you understand that?" His words were firm and clear.

Carla knew the role she must now play. "Yes, dear, I understand. I won't embarrass you before your friends, or the Don above all." She reached up to touch his face and then whispered in his ear. "If you promise to take me like that again, I'll wait on you hand and foot forever. I want more of you," she teased.

He grinned, "You'll just have to wait until I have time for you."

The Family attorney, Harry Phillips, met up with them. "I'll have Blum get your luggage." Then he looked at Carla.

"She's good with everything," Roy said as Carla smiled coyly.

"Alright, we have a car waiting to go right out to the desert. Harry got in the Rolls Royce's back seat while Roy helped Carla sit next to him. Then Roy got into the front with Blum.

They drove for several miles. Carla kept looking out the window as though she was an amazed young housewife off on an excursion.

"I had no idea that there was so much desert here. Look at those lovely sand dunes. It looks like a giant sandbox. Darling, wouldn't this have been fun to play in when we were kids?"

"That's enough, Carla."

"Yes, dear." She sat back to get a nail file from her purse.

Blum tuned onto the desert, driving only a short distance. "He's just up ahead, Mr. Philips."

"Drive behind the car but not too close. Roy, this is all yours."

"I got it, Harry."

When the car stopped, Roy looked at the two large men in poplin topcoats next to the black Lincoln. Bradbury stood in front of them in trousers and a casual shirt. Alarmed, he watched Blum and Jacobs get out of the car.

Roy took a briefcase from the trunk of the Lincoln and looked inside. He nodded to Harry, who came to examine the contents before giving it back to Roy. They shook hands before Harry sat in the back of the Lincoln. The other men got in front and slowly drove to the main highway.

Carla watched them from her vantage point in the Rolls. She saw Bradbury make gestures to Roy and Blum, seemingly, in desperation. Then he knelt away from them with his hands on his head.

When Roy walk back to the Rolls with the briefcase, he raised his right hand as though waving good-bye, and then Blum put two bullets into Bradbury's head. When he fell forward, Blum shot him twice more, leaving his body in the sand.

The repulsive sight caused Carla to see yet another side of Blum and her husband, one that was more than abominable. It was more than evil. It was sheer depravity without a soul. Her stomach churned as she fought the tightness in her throat that would come just before vomiting. She opened the door for fresh air, wiped the perspiration from her upper lip, and then took several deep breaths lest she gave way to the nausea.

Blum opened the trunk and set the case inside. After shaking Roy's hand, he opened the back door for him and then got into the driver's seat to start the car.

Roy realized that Carla had a prime view of what had just taken place. He coldly looked at her as he shut the door.

"Did you get a good look at everything?"

"Good look at what, darling? I was trying to fix my nails. I snagged one." She tried to hold her hand from shaking. "What do you think, sweetheart. Does this one match the rest?"

He glanced at her hand and then patted her knee. "They look just fine, dear. Mr. Blum, take us on to our hotel now."

"Yes, sir, Mr. Jacobs."

Carla noticed the smug look on Roy's face, and then looked into the rear-view mirror. The driver glared back at her.

After dinner at the hotel, Roy told Carla to wait there while he met with Philips and Levine.

"I thought I was going to see Jada while we were down here."

"Yeah, I guess so, I forgot. You can keep her busy while I talk to the men."

The ride to the Las Vegas casino was quiet. When they entered the lounge, Jada got up to greet Carla with a warm embrace.

"Now *I* have someone to talk with! These men and all their business talk, I can't keep up with them. Let me show you around. I don't think you've been here before, have you, darling?" Jada asked with a smile.

She was genuinely friendly as she escorted Carla into a smaller lounge for cocktails. After ordering their drinks, Jada's continence changed drastically.

"You look absolutely horrible, my dear. Tell me what's going on. David is in one of his "Mafia Don" moods, so I know something is up."

Carla related what she had witnessed in the desert. It made Jada shudder, but she wasn't new to such happenings. She took Carla's hand in hers. Leaning closer, Jada spoke almost as a mother would.

"Darling, you must do what you can to put that out of your mind. Roy didn't pull that trigger, my husband did. He just used his faithful servant, Mr. Blum, to do his dirty work. Men who steal from men like my husband can *never* get away with that. Having him killed for what he did sends a message to anyone else who thinks they can try to do that. That message is, 'If you mess with me, this will happen to you'.

"Yes, they take the law into their own hands, but the sentence gets served promptly and without a chance of the benefit of a doubt. There is nothing to doubt. If you do the crime, you don't do the time, you just die. That's the whole message." Jada saw that Carla was still troubled. She reached out to gently pat her face and then sat back in her chair.

"Finish your drink, my dear, then put on a smile. You're the wife of a Mafia man now. You have a very high ranking with great protection from the hundreds of soldiers in this army. This Family is now *your* Family, so welcome into it. Whether you like it or not, you are one of us. Sharon and Marni went through the same thing, and they learned to turn a blind eye just like you will have to. It's a good life, other than that. I did, and look where it got me, for better or worse."

"Does it get any worse or better, though?"

Jada patted her hand, "You bet it does," she smiled, and then signaled for two more martinis. "Just like the second drink is always better. So just drink, relax, and forget. Cheers," she tipped her glass to her young lady friend, who now smiled back, or at least tried her best.

Carla got the message. After all, Jada was the wife of the Mafia Don and one to whom she should listen. Moreover, she seemed to be her friend.

When Roy and Carla returned to the hotel, Blum put their bags in the limo drove to the airport. Once there, Roy gave her a paper lunch sack.

"I have to stay and take care of more business. I'll be home tomorrow to check on my stores. Put this in your purse, and don't let go of it. Give that to Larry Cross when he meets you at the airport in Salem, and then he'll take you on home."

Carla looked inside the sack to see cash inside a clear plastic bag. "What's this?"

"Fifty thousand dollars."

Carla waited for Jim to return her call. He could hear the desperation in her voice and agreed to meet her at the safe house.

Jim was on a police call when she got out of her car. He held up a finger to signify that he'd be right with her.

"I'm sorry, but I can't help you right now. I'm on an emergency call so check with Tom. Yeah, run silent, run deep, good buddy. Ten-four, over and out, and all that good stuff." Jim smiled as he got out of his patrol car.

"What was that?"

"One of the guys desperately needed someone to cover for him."

"So you sent him to see an old movie?"

"A movie? Oh, that. No, 'run silent, run deep' is our signal that there's real big trouble ahead; hurry, but proceed with caution. This guy went to a card party and lost a bundle, but his wife thought he was out fooling around and spent it on some broad. So he needed someone for an alibi before she bit his head off and filed for divorce. I just warned him about what I heard.

"I only have a couple of hours for now. So, what's happened with you? You sounded scared to death on the phone." Jim turned the lights on and then escorted her inside.

Carla explained how she had witnessed the assassination and what Jada said. Jim didn't at all like knowing that Carla was now officially a mobster's wife. Yes, she has excellent protection through the Family now, but were those hundreds of mob soldiers going to protect her from her husband? Moreover, Jim was greatly concerned that Roy was a far more deranged man than he anticipated.

A drink calmed Carla. Jim massaged her shoulders and neck until he felt her tension dissipate. He wrapped his arms around her as she rested for a while in his comfort and strength in silence.

Jim now knew that her husband was not only markedly wealthy, but he was using that money to buy himself into the wrong kind of prestige and power. And he was dragging Carla into that depth too.

Chapter Seventeen

LITTLE GIRL LOST

Donald looked through the various magazines on the grocery store's lower shelf. As he knelt, Donald looked up distracted by the pattering of tiny feet running down the aisle toward him. A darling toddler with sparkling blue eyes was laughing gaily. When she got to Donald, she pulled up the full skirt of her dress with both hands.

"See my pee-pee?" She had no panties on. He quickly glanced about the area to see if a parent or anyone was chasing after her. There was no one in sight.

He put a finger up to his lips. "Sh-h-h. Where's your mommy and daddy?"

The child shrugged while looking around. "Daddy's gone. See?" She raised the skirt again as her little face gleamed. "You can touch it."

Again, Donald looked around as he beckoned her to come closer. She did, still exposing her genitals and proudly smiling. He reached out to pull the skirt down.

"Do you know where Mommy and Daddy is?" he quietly asked.

Moving closer to him, she looked around with a shrug. "Daddy's home." Then she put a finger to her lips. "Sh-h-h. Mommy's mad at him," she whispered.

He whispered, "How come?"

"Cause daddy saw my pee-pee, and mommy got mad and spanked him. Don't let mommy see me. She spanks me, too."

"Why does she spank you?"

"I don't know. And she yells at me, too."

"That's not very nice," Donald told her. "Does your daddy spank you too?"

"No. When I'm alone with Daddy, he kisses me all over."

"Oh. What do you do?"

"I lick on his stick."

"Where does he keep his stick?"

She pointed to his crotch. "Down there. Do you have a stick?"

"Yes, but I don't want Mommy to get mad at me and spank me too. Where's your mommy at?"

She shrugged, looking around again. "I don't know. I don't like her. Do you have a nice mommy?"

"My mommy is really nice, and she never yells at anyone. We should go and find your mommy."

The child began to pout. "No, I don't want to see her. She'll spank me again."

"Oh, honey," he cooed, "I won't let your mommy spank you. I think she's mean."

"I don't want to find her."

"Do you want to get away from her?"

She looked around with fear in her eyes. "Yes".

"Well, do you want to meet my mommy?" The child nodded with a look of hope in her eyes. She wrapped her arms around his neck with a tight hug. "Okay."

He whispered in her ear, "I won't let your mommy get you." Donald put his arms around the child and scooped her up. He looked for the nearest exit, away from any customers.

"You just hold on to me and pretend you're sleeping. Can you do that for me?" She closed her eyes while he continued to whisper. "You be very quiet and don't say anything. If we get caught, mommy will spank both of us."

"Sh-h-h, I'm sleeping."

Donald made sure her skirt was down and covering her bottom. He held her head against his neck while pressing her body close to his. A door automatically opened as he casually walked out of the store. When they reached his vehicle he took the keys from his pocket and unlocked the door. Donald gently laid the girl on the clean, carpeted floor behind the passenger seat.

"You lay down just like you're really sleeping. I'm very proud of you."

His eyes darted around the other parked cars. No one paid any attention so he got in the driver's seat. "I'm going to drive away now, so just lay there and pretend to sleep."

Donald looked around the store's entry and parking lot. There was no one rushing out or even looking around. His heart was pounding against his chest wall as sweat broke out. When the light turned green, he drove into the street.

"Don't sit up yet, but are you okay?"

"Be quiet. I'm still sleeping."

Donald smiled after approaching the freeway entrance. *Yes, get out of this area. Way out.* He merged onto the freeway, staying to the right as cars vied for positions in the faster lanes.

After a while, Donald saw road signs ahead. "Food, gas, lodging." He drove into one end of a store parking lot where cars were sparsely parked.

"Are you ready to sit up here with me now?" There was no answer. Seeing that she was fast asleep, Donald covered her with his jacket and then drove back onto the freeway.

What the hell am I going to do now? Jada. Jada would know.

That was the perfect answer, but how would he explain to his employer how he just took a small child out of a grocery store. *No, I kidnapped her. A crime punishable for how many years in prison?*

Keeping the volume low, he twisted the radio knob to catch the news report. There was nothing about a missing child.

Many thoughts ran through his mind about what kind of mother this woman was. *She got mad that her husband was sexually molesting her young daughter? Got mad? There were no police to call? And to let the small child run loose in a grocery store where anyone could have snatched her up in an instant. And with no panties on. What in the hell kind of mother did this child have?*

When they arrived, Donald worried about getting the child into the house. She was still sound asleep, so he dashed inside to look for his pal. Donald briefly explained the situation, asking that Billie kept watch while Donald carried the child into his living quarters.

"Let's go through the dining room," said Billie. Nobody's working in there yet. There's just the decorator lady talking to the painter. I'll go make sure the coast is clear."

When Billie signaled, Donald carried the child through the dining room to his chambers.

While talking to the painter, Carla saw Donald's reflection in the mirror as he moved with the child through the room. Turning to look, he had already gone through the hallway. She shrugged, thinking it was not her business, and resumed her conversation.

Donald settled the sleeping child on his bed.

"She's darling, like a sweet little angel," Billie said. "She just came up to you like that? Wow, I wonder what her dad does to her."

"What could he do? I mean, he couldn't actually fuck her, she's too little for that. What else could a little kid do besides suck cock? I don't know. Well, what do we do now?"

Billie said, "Just hide her in here until she wakes up."

"What if she wets the bed? We got anything for diapers?"

"Sure, a small kitchen towel would do. I'll go get some."

Billie returned with several towels from the linen closet.

Donald put one under the child, another one between her legs, and then placed a light blanket over her.

"Billy, will you stay here in case she wakes up? I gotta go tell Jada. I may get my ass kicked for doing this."

After Donald explained what had happened, he took a breath, hoping he didn't forget something.

"Oh, yes. With her arms around my neck, she asked to see *my* mommy. She didn't want her mommy to spank her anymore. Jada, I just had to get the poor thing away from there. I know I was wrong, but..." He nervously ran a hand through his hair.

"I didn't know what else to do. If I went to the cops, they'd just take her back to the mother. And I was so surprised when she exposed herself to me like that. I thought some other man might molest and hurt her. "

Jada put her hand on his shoulder. "Darling, you just did what you thought was best. Little children are all curious about their bodies at that age. Do you remember wanting to see what a little girl had in her panties?"

"I thought all little boys did that, but not girls."

"Yes, little girls are like that too. They just get curious and want to see what's different from boys. I did when I was little. I wanted to see why my brother could stand up to pee, and I had to sit down."

She pointed a forefinger at Donald. "But many men know about a child's curiosity. They'll play with their genitals, and little girls can tend to like that. That's where sexual molestation begins. They make the little girls promise not to tell Mommy and give them treats, or they threaten them. Some men just don't get enough sex from their wives or have step-children, which isn't incest for them. Some men are just plain sick and perverted, and they prefer little children because they can't fight back and they scare easily. And the molesters can readily kill them if they become a threat to the pervert."

"Oh, that's why so many missing children are found dead."

"Yes, and just think about what goes on inside the church with those men who can't be married. They use the little choir boys for sex, 'in the name of God'', Jada adamantly said. "Think about *that* when you see a priest next time.

"Alright, show me the little girl. we'll watch the news later to see if there's something about a missing child."

Jada excused Billie and warmly looked at the sleeping girl, saying how precious she was. Her thoughts were that of wanting a child, with wished this little one could become hers.

When the girl awoke, Donald asked if she had a good nap.

"I have to go potty," was her answer.

Jada carried the child to the bathroom and held her while she sat on the toilet. "My name is Jada. What's your name?"

"Lilly Marie."

When the girl was finished, Jada said, "Well, Lilly Marie, guess we need to get you some diapers."

"I don't wear them. I'm too big for that."

"What do you wear then?"

"I wear panties like big girls wear," she stated adamantly.

When they joined Donald in the living room, Lilly asked, "Is she your mommy?"

Donald smiled. "Yes, she is. And she can be your mommy too. Would you like that?"

Lilly looked at him. "I think so."

"Well, Lilly Marie, I would *love* to be your mommy. I'll go see if we have some panties that will fit you. Donald will stay here with you, and I'll be right back." Jada excused herself and returned shortly, holding panties with frilly lace from one of the prop dolls.

Lilly's eyes brightened. "For me? Thank you." She put them on and looked at Donald.

"See? I don't need diapers anymore."

"Excuse me, Madam, but should Mr. Levine be informed of anything?" Donald asked.

"Not yet. And David has business to tend to. He won't be home 'till after nine tonight."

They took Lilly into the central part of the house to show her around. Her eyes darted about, awed by what she saw.

"Is this your house?"

Jada smiled. "Yes, it is, and you can stay here for a while."

The girl's smile became brighter.

Jada called Nona in to meet Lilly with a brief description of what had taken place. Nona held the position as head housekeeper for nearly eighteen years and experienced dealing with many odd situations.

She suggested having a cot set up in her room after dinner, so the child could be in bed by the time Mr. Levine got home. Nona even found a stuffed, fuzzy kitten that one godchild had left behind.

"Well, Lilly, we have lots of fun things around here for you to see. Would you like to see the fishie pool?" Jada got a positive answer. And to the little girl, its sight was more than impressive.

"Those are pretty. What do the fishies do?"

"They swim and eat if they're hungry."

"I don't know how to swim."

"I can teach you sometime. Are you hungry?"

"I don't think so."

They played games until it was time to eat. After dinner, they watched cartoons, bathed Lilly in the great enormous bathtub, and time to get ready for bed. But what about jammies?

Donald offered one of his T-shirts, and Lilly thought it was a nightgown when she put it on. That was perfect. Jada showed the girl her bed, assuring her that Nona would be there if she needed anything. Then she tucked Lilly into bed with the kitten and a kiss. She was soon fast asleep.

While watching the news, Jada wondered what to tell David. However, oddly enough, there was nothing reported about a missing child. It was unusual that a kidnapping wasn't mentioned, especially with a child that young. There certainly wouldn't be a twenty-four-hour waiting period. Jada called Donald and Nona to see her. Nothing was reported on any of the news channels.

"It's not like a ten-year-old ran away because he's mad at the parents," Nona said.

"Yes," Jada agreed, "but what if the parents didn't report the child as missing? If the mother was mean to Lilly and the father was sexually abusing her, wouldn't they worry if the police found out? I imagine the father would either want to find the girl right away, so nobody would know what he did to her or not look for her at all."

"I didn't see anything of the mother in the store. You'd think she'd be calling out her name or tell the manager or a worker that Lilly ran off. It would only take a moment for someone to kidnap her," added Donald. The two women looked at him.

Donald put his hands up in defense. "No, no, I *rescued* her!". "Really!"

"We know, but try telling that to the police," Jada answered. "It would mean many years in prison for you. And I could get jailed for harboring you. I should have turned her over to the police as a missing child in the first place. But, like you said, they'd just give her back to the parents. Any way you look at it, we're all in trouble. Let's let it go until the early morning news.

"Nona, I'll have Donald take you shopping, so you both can pick out some clothes for the child. Maybe some pant and top sets, socks, and shoes. Oh, and underwear and pajamas. Pick out some beautiful dresses too. I want her to look fantastic when David meets her. But tomorrow, he'll be leaving early in the morning and won't be home again until late."

The next day Lilly was thrilled to have a breakfast of pancakes with syrup and some cocoa, something she never had before. She was thrilled to see the new clothes, especially the pants and tops.

"Daddy never let me wear pants," she exclaimed. And Jada knew why.

After that, Jada and Donald enjoyed playing games with her. One was hide-and-seek. After finding Donald behind the couch, it was Lilly's turn to hide.

Carla had just finished hanging the dining room wallpaper and stepped back to see the overall appearance. A giggling toddler ran into the room, abruptly interrupting her thoughts.

Carla reached out for her. "Whoa there, who are you?"

"I'm Lilly. I'm playing hide-and-seek from Uncle Donald and Mommy Jada." Her eyes darted around the room until she spotted the dining room table and chairs. Tarps that fell to the floor covered them entirely. Lilly put a finger to her lips.

"Sh-h-h. Don't tell on me. I have to hide." Then she crawled under the tarps.

"Okay, I won't say that I saw you."

Carla assumed this was the child Donald carried into the house. Soon voices called Lilly's name. Donald came into the room and looked around.

"Did you see a little girl around here?"

"Oh, you must be Lilly's Uncle Donald. What would she be doing in here?" Carla nodded to the table with a forefinger to her pursed lips. When Jada walked into the room, Donald held up his hand with a finger to his lips as he pointed to the dining table. Jada nodded and stood still.

"Well, if she isn't here, I better keep on looking. Thanks," and then he left the room. When Lilly crawled out from under the table, Jada scooped her up in her arms.

"I gotcha!" She swung her around as the girl screamed out in delight. Then Jada stopped to look at the wallpaper.

"Oh my, that's absolutely delicious, Carla."

"What's lishous?" ask Lilly.

"You are!" Jada put her mouth to the little girl's neck. "Yum, yum, yum, yum. I'm going to eat you all up."

Lilly wiggled and squirmed as she giggled and cackled.

Donald came back into the dining room. "There you are! I got you now. Come with me." Jada set the child down, and she ran "Uncle Donald". "Let's go back to the playroom. You shouldn't be down here where people are working," he gently scolded.

Standing back to look around the dining room, Jada brushed the stray hair back with a joyous smile and a brightened face. "I love that wallpaper, it's quite elegant. This place is going to be so spectacular when you get done! I can't wait until it's all finished." She left Carla to her work.

There were no reports on any news programs in the morning or afternoon, so Jada waited to watch the eleven o'clock evening news while her husband worked his in office. The couple wasn't pictured when reporters read their statement that the child had disappeared from their front yard that morning. The most recent photograph of "Lilah" was a year old, and newscasters asked viewers to contact the police with any information they might have.

After the broadcast, Donald, Billie, Nona, and now Mr. Blum met with Jada for another conference. Jada was concerned about bringing David into the picture.

"I know Mr. Levine hates child pornography, and he abhors men who abuse little girls like that," said Jada. "No doubt the story will be on tomorrow's news, so I'll make sure that David watches it with me. I'll take full blame and responsibility for everything if need be. Once he sees that precious little angel, knowing what her parents did, I think he'll take to her and come up with some ideas on what to do."

Blum suggested, "He knows the police chief well if we need his help. Would you like me to find out more about the parents?"

"Yes, please do. I need to know as much about them as possible. Meanwhile, we need to keep our little darling undercover a while longer. We can't take Lilly out of the house until all this is settled. You're dismissed, except for Donald. Good night and thank you for your help."

"Donald, I'm sure if he knows what the daddy did to her, he will take to her more readily."

"I have an idea, Madam. You have such a kind way with your godchildren. What if you had a special talk with Lilly tomorrow and get her to tell you everything her daddy did? I can have a recorder next to you so you can play it back to Mr. Levine. And you wear a wire too. Mr. Blum can set that up to record you separately, so if the police become involved, you can prove the recording wasn't tampered with."

"Why, Donald, that's brilliant! I'll think of what all to ask her, and you boys can set it all up after David leaves tomorrow. So, you go bed and sleep well".

Jada massaged her husband's back, which helped him sleep since he had to leave early in the morning to tend to one of his casinos.

The next day Blum reported his findings on the child's parents. The woman was twenty-two and unwed when she gave birth to Lilly. She was a waitress at a truck stop where she met and married a part-time truck driver when the child was ten months old. The step-father tried to fill his off days by doing handyman jobs.

This gave Jada enough information to understand what kind of home life the child had. It was now most essential for Lilly to receive David with the confidence that he will be nothing like her step-father. Jada hoped that if he fully understood what that man had done, David would receive Lilly into his heart as well.

Lilly ate scrambled eggs, bacon, and toast with jelly for breakfast, a terrific change from corn flakes. They watched some cartoons, and when Jada thought the timing was right, she sat down in the comfortable over-stuffed rocking chair with soft music playing. With Lilly on her lap, she signaled Blum to record their conversation.

"Mommy Jada would like to know more about your other mommy and daddy. Donald said that daddy played with your pee-pee. What did it feel like to you?"

Lilly hesitated, "It felt nice."

"When I was a little girl like you, I wanted to see how a man went pee-pee. Did he show you how he did it?" Lilly nodded.

"He took his stick out of his zipper and made water come out of it."

"What else did his stick do?"

"It got real big and real hard when I kissed it. Daddy asked me to lick it. I liked that."

"Did it taste good?"

She nodded. "It tasted like candy."

"Did it do anything else?"

The girl giggled. "It spit at me. Daddy would pump it, and it spit at me. I can see how far it went on the rug. It went more than his friend did."

"Did they both pump their sticks?"

"Yeah. Daddy's friend gave me presents."

"What kind of presents?"

"Chocolate candy or a toy."

"Do you know what his friend's name was?"

She shook her head. "I don't 'member 'cause Daddy said it was a big secret from Mommy. She would yell and spank me if I told her. His stick got bigger than Daddy's, and it tasted good too."

Jada made up a story about herself. "When I was little, I liked it when a man touched me down there. I liked to show him my pee-pee. Do you like that too?"

Lilly nodded again. "Sometimes. Sometimes Daddy licked me there," she pointed to her crotch, "I liked that."

"Does his friend lick you too?"

"Uh-huh, but Daddy isn't there all a time. He wanted to see me to go pee when I stood up, and my legs got all wet. He put me on the bed and licked me dry and put his stick by my mouth."

"Did you like that?" Jada asked.

"No! It was too big, and it hurt my mouth."

"What did he do then?"

"He stuck it by my legs and laid on me, but I couldn't breathe!"

"Oh, my!" Jada softly exclaimed. "Did you get mad?"

"No, I started to cry. The man said he was sorry and kissed me all over. He pumped his stick and made it spit on me."

"Oh, you poor darling. Did you tell daddy what he did?"

She nodded. "He didn't come back no more."

"Did any other men come to see you?"

Lilly held up a finger. "This many."

"Just one more. What did he do?"

"He had me kiss his stick, but it tasted awful." Lilly bowed her head. "Mommy came and yelled at all of us. She hit Daddy real hard, and the man too. An' she yelled and spanked me," Lilly sobbed.

Jada cuddled her closer while stroking her hair. "That was very mean for her to do that. Did she spank you a lot?" Lilly nodded but said nothing.

"Do you mean 'yes' or 'no'?"

"I don't like her. She spanks me all a time, and yells at me, and pulls my hair." Lilly Marie became sullen. "I don't wanna' talk anymore. I *hate* that mommy."

Jada held her close as she fought back her tears for the child. "We won't talk about it anymore."

She rocked her while humming along to the radio's soft music and stroking her head. Jada spoke softly to the child.

"My darling little angel, you won't have to go back there ever again. And your old mommy will never yell at you, or hit you, or spank you again. Mommy Jada promises that she won't ever do that."

After a while, Nona came into the living room with some games. "Excuse me, Ma'am. Donald took the liberty to get some children's games. Would Lilly like to see them?"

"Shall we see what they are?" Jada jovially asked.

With one game, if Lilly put the right pieces into the correct spaces, to her surprise, it turned out to be a kitten. Another game had cards with large numbers. A hand was drawn on the other side to show how many fingers represented the number. Lilly was going to learn how to count! Soon it was time for lunch and then a nap in Mommy's great enormous bed.

After Lilly awoke from her nap, Jada asked Nona to get the child changed into one of the new dresses. "I want her to look like an angel stepping off a cloud when David first sees her."

When her husband was home for the evening, he relaxed with his first drink. Jada turned the TV news on and sat next to him on the couch.

"Let's see if there's anything new about that missing child. Apparently, the grandparents claimed the parents weren't fit to take care of her. And they'd protest her going back with them."

"I don't understand why they don't give the parents' names," David said. "Oh, well, the police have all the information. It's probably so everyone doesn't bother them while they're distressed."

"What if they don't want the child to be found?"

"Now, just who wouldn't want to find a missing child?" He noticed that Jada was quiet. "You mean if they had something to do with her going missing?"

"Yes. Darling, I have something for you to listen to, and I don't want you to get upset until you hear everything."

"Everything about what?"

"Just a moment, and you'll understand a lot of important things that are going on," she gently answered.

Jada brought the tape recorder in so he could hear the entire conversation. Leaning forward, he listened intently in bewilderment that soon turned to anger. He then understood what she meant by "important". When the tape stopped, the realization set in.

Almost in disbelief, he calmly said, "You have that child."

Jada nodded. "Just sit there, darling, and you'll see why."

She called Nona to bring the girl to see her. When Lilly saw David, she pulled back to stand behind Nona.

Jada stood up. "Oh, look at my pretty little angel," she bent down with open arms. "Come here to Mommy Jada, darling." The child ran to her. "David, this is Lilly Marie."

David smiled at her as he stood up, not feeling anything but empathy, pity, and warmth for the child.

"Hello, Lilly Marie. I'm David. I live here too. Do you like being here?" he cooed. She nodded with a finger to her mouth and then hugged Jada's neck.

"Well, you certainly are a beautiful little girl. I like your dress. That's very pretty too."

"Mommy Jada got it for me. See, it has lace on it."

"Oh, yes. I like that. Did Mommy Jada get you other clothes?"

She nodded. "She got me jeans and sneakers!"

"Her daddy wouldn't let her wear any jeans or pants, just dresses." David certainly understood the reason.

"Would you like to sit down and tell me about yourself?"

She looked at Jada, who smiled at her.

"David is my husband. You'll really like him, and he won't spank you either or touch you like the other daddy did. He's a real nice man and loves children."

Lilly thought about it and looked at David again. He sat down first to show submission. Then Lilly sat next to Jada.

The child could see that David *was* a nice, gentle man. He smiled, paying close attention to all that she told him. He was good at reading facial expressions and body language. In a short time, she was telling him about the games Uncle Donald got her.

"How did you meet Uncle Donald?"

"I found him in the store, and he took me here."

"Were you all alone in the store?

Lilly shrugged. "I think so."

"Where was your other mommy and daddy?" David gently inquired.

The girl shrugged, shaking her head as she looked down. "Daddy stayed home 'cause mommy spanked him."

"Well, Lilly Marie, you won't get any spankings here. I promise you that." He knew it was time to change the subject. "Did you see the fishie pond?"

"I saw them. Do you like to play cards?"

"Yes, I do."

David made sure the evening together was pleasant, even if it meant him losing at 'finger cards'. After a while, it Lilly's bedtime. Jada tucked her and the kitten in bed for the night.

When David and Jada were alone, he momentarily held her close before sitting on the couch with her.

"I just don't know exactly how to react to what you did, my dear. I know you think you did the right thing, but this puts me in a very awkward position. How can I explain to the police, or anyone else, how the child came to be in my possession?" His face showed great concern.

"I'm sorry, but we can't possibly take her in under those circumstances. For one thing, the police could arrest Donald for kidnapping." David put a hand to his head while he thought.

"I'll have Mr. Blum look into the grandparents. If the parents are that negligent of the child, perhaps we can get her to the police chief somehow, and he can take it from there. I certainly can't let a child go back home if she's been sexually violated by that man and beaten by her mother. I just couldn't possibly do that. However, by hearing the recording, the police chief would understand. I should confer with my men and see what Mr. Blum can find out first."

He held Jada's hand. "I understand what your intentions were, my dear. I'm quite aware of how much you've wanted a child of our own, but I just can't have the Family involved with a kidnapping like this. And how can we explain where she came from to people outside of the Family? You understand my position, don't you?"

Saddened, Jada tried to restrain her emotions. "Yes, my love. I understand that you will do what's best for the child." Patience, respect, and letting David be in charge is something else that she learned to do long ago. "I was wrong to get my hopes up." He patted her hand and then put an arm around her.

"I'll meet with the men tomorrow to get their thoughts on this as well."

"Alright, dear."

"Is there anything else, my love?"

"Oh, yes, there is, now that you asked. I think you need to talk to your new little star. It seems that Cindy has been overstepping her boundaries around some of your men, including the hairdresser. He complained to me while he was doing my hair. She wouldn't want to have her pretty face marred by some angry wife's fingernails."

David knew this was something he should address. "I will look into that."

The next day David called his partner aside to ask about Cindy's recent activities off the set. Richard acknowledged the girl had approached him in a more than suggestive manner, and the word had gotten back to his wife.

David shook his head. "The last thing I want to happen is to let any wife loose on one of our girls, let alone my star. I don't have anyone that good to replace her. Check with the hairdresser, see what happened there."

The stylist told Richard that the young star showed a close interest in him.

"I thought she was just feeling horny and told her that my girlfriend would get pretty upset if I stepped out of line. I think she took the hint. She's getting her makeup done now for the shooting today. Did you want to see her?"

"No, I certainly do not. Not without my wife present. Just send her over to the set as soon as she's finished then."

The makeup artist was having difficulty with Cindy sitting still long enough to get the eye shadow perfected. Her fingers reached toward to his crotch. She was extruding pheromones.

"Now, honey, you simply must stay still so I can get you looking beautiful for that camera."

She grinned, "Oh, how can I sit still with you standing so close to me?"

"Well, darling, you want me to get you all beautiful. So, just put your hands on your lap and let me finish with this pretty face," he gently scolded.

She sighed while touching his zipper.

The makeup artist stood up straight. His finger gently touched under Cindy's chin, tilting her face up to look at him.

"Now darling, I don't think you want to look in there," he murmured with a comely smile, "because you will find that I have the same kind of plumbing that you do. Now just put your hands back on your lap and let me do what I get paid to do. Or I'll just have to break your little fingers right off." Message understood.

Cindy strolled onto the set where everyone was waiting for her. She slowly walked past Richard with an enticing smile that suddenly faded as she watched Sharon and Jada step forward to sit next to their husbands. The star moved onto the set to begin the filming.

Cindy was lying on top of her partner during the shoot. She turned to look at the film crew and then sat up.

"I can't do my best work while women are watching. They put me off my game."

"You are an actress, and I'm paying you to *act*, not play games. Now, I want to see some damned good acting out of you," Levine sternly told her.

She glanced at Richard Hirsh but saw only his wife with a sharp glare and her arms folded across her chest. Jada sat next to her husband with a knowing smile on her lips. Suddenly, Cindy remembered Jada was her actual boss. She turned back to her partner.

"Where were we?"

"You were laying on me, and I'm going to turn you over." When he did, with his back to the camera, his cheek was next to hers. He whispered, "You better do a damn fine job of acting because if I lose my job over this, I'll have your ass. And that won't be very pleasant either." With that, Cindy performed her best acting role ever.

After the filming, the Family was called together with only the immediate members present, Don Levine, Philips, Hirsh, Blum, and Jacobs.

Before the meeting began, Phillips said, "Oh, by the way, Roy, our director was happy that you sent that Bombshell and her boyfriend to us. They work very well together. But since Glen looks so young, he wants to use him in some films with older women, say around forty-five or fifty. That could be like a young kid learning the ropes and all."

Roy smiled. "Sounds great, Harry. I'm glad that they're working out for you."

That subject led to a discussion about child pornography and abuse. Then Levine mentioned what had been in the news recently. The men had heard of the child's disappearance. They agreed that something was awry.

"This is more than just a suspicious concern. We have something invested in the problem that needs our attention." Levine warned the men to pay close attention to what was said on the tape as he turned on the recorder. They listened with disgust on their faces. When it ended, Philips spoke first.

"May I assume that this is the child who has been in the news?"

David nodded.

"And is she now under your protection?"

Levine gave another nod.

"Excuse me, sir. I have further information on these parents. I have their names, phone number, home and work addresses, and descriptions." Blum explained, "The grandparents are clean, with good jobs, and a fine home. They will fight for full custody of the child."

"Do you have a full description of the child?" asked Hirsh.

"I have something much better," David pressed a call button. "Will you bring Lilly in here to meet her other uncles, please?"

Jada walked in, holding the child's hand. "David wants you to meet some of his very good friends," she assured the child.

David reached out for her.

"Come here, my pretty little angel. Come and sit on my lap."

She readily went to David before looking around at the strange men.

As David held the child on his lap, Philips leaned forward in his chair with elbows on his knees and hands clasped. "Well, hello, little lady. I'm Uncle Harry. It's very good to meet you."

"Are you like Uncle Donald?"

"Yes, honey, I am."

"Do you know Auntie Nona?"

"Yes, I know her very well. She has lived here a very long time, and she helps Jada."

"How old are you, Lilly Marie?" Roy asked. She held up three fingers.

"We have some special cards. Tell us about them," said David.

Lilly looked at him, "You know about them. You're learning how to count. I can count to sebum. Wanna see?" Before David could answer, she began counting on her fingers. "One, two, tree, poor, pibe..." Jada leaned over to whisper 'six'.

"I know. Sticks and that's sebum!" she exclaimed. When David looked at Harry, he began to clap his hands lightly as the others joined in.

Then Lilly spotted Blum and turned closer to David. He quietly asked if there was something wrong.

She whispered not too quietly, "That big man is awful dark. Is sompin' wrong with him."

As the men stifled their laughter, David quietly explained the reason. She sat back in surprise and then looked at Blum again.

"You mean he was bornt that way?" she asked. When she heard the men laugh, she admonished them.

"That's not nice. He can't help it. Maybe the stork bringed the wrong baby to his mommy."

David said, "His mommy and daddy are black too."

With widened eyes, she asked, "*Really*?"

Blum said, "Lilly, where I come from, there are a lot of black people."

With surprise, she advised, "Well, maybe you should go back and live *there*."

The men tried their best not to laugh.

"I've been told that a lot of times, Lilly," Blum said with a wide grin. Even David couldn't help but laugh.

Lilly thought she made them feel happy and laughed too. Then she got down from David's lap and curtsied to them.

She took Jada's hand. "Let's go."

"Don't you want to say goodbye?"

Lilly turned, "G'bye." Then she waved farewell to them, and they waved in return. After she left, the men were still for a moment.

"What a precious child. Her father molested her?" Richard solemnly asked.

"It was her step-father," Blum said.

"Yes, and he needs to be dealt with," Levine answered. "Jacobs, what would you suggest we should do with a man who indulges himself sexually with a young child?"

He wasn't at all prepared for that question. Taking a deep breath to have a couple of seconds of thought, he came up with an answer.

"It's apparent that this is a man who does not recognize God." Roy couldn't possibly think of any scripture for reference other than the one that he thoroughly misquoted.

"The Bible says that we should do to others like they to you. I would say that this isn't even a man, but an unholy creature who is less than a snake in the grass. If that were my daughter...," he looked at Levine. Raising both fists, Roy demonstrated, "I would tear his chest open, rip out his still-beating heart, and shove that down his throat. And then his privates!"

"You may have the pleasure of dealing with this child's parents," said Levine. "And Mr. Blum may assist you if you would like." Surprised, Jacobs hesitated, although, nodded in agreement.

"If there are no more issues to discuss, I suggest that our meeting is adjourned."

That evening Roy was waiting at the guest house to take Carla to dinner. He was pleased to see her so cheerful, thinking it was because of him. To his disappointment, she bypassed his greeting to change her clothes. When he asked how her day went, Carla answered with happiness.

"Oh, Roy, you should have seen the look on Jada's face when she swung that little girl around and played with her. It was as though Lilly was her own little child. Jada's face was just glowing with love for her. Lilly seemed to fill a great void in her heart. And she's the prettiest child I have ever seen. She's just so full of life and so darling, kinda like little Shirley Temple."

"Oh? Whose kid was it? I know the Levine's don't have any," Roy asked in false inquisitiveness.

"She's Donald's niece. I don't know how long she'll be there, but I'm sure Jada will be thrilled to have her around as long as possible."

"Did that give you ideas about having one?"

Carla seemed surprised by that question. However, Roy's facial expression was one of disapproval.

"Oh, heavens no, not for quite a while, I have a career to manage. I can't take out time for a baby when I'm just getting going on it. Why? Are you considering starting a family?"

Roy smiled with relief. "Oh, hell no. We've got a good thing going just as it is. Kids can come along later, if at all."

"Good, I was afraid that you're getting weird ideas all of a sudden. We can always rent one later on."

"Rent one?" laughed Roy.

"You know, take in a foster child or adopt one. You don't want me to lose my girly figure now, do you?"

Roy looked her over. "I like you just like this." He quickly kissed her. "Let's go eat. I'm starved".

Chapter Eighteen

TAKING CARE OF THE PARENTS

Roy got the information regarding Lilly's parents. To impress Levine, he felt he must have a spectacular, although, quiet ending to this couple. An idea came to him of magnificent proportion. Roy jotted down some notes and then called Blum in to discuss them.

"What did you find out about the grandparents of this little girl?"

"They seem to be real earnest about getting her because they knew the mother was slapping her around, and they detest the husband. The grandfather is a dentist, and she's a substitute school teacher for primary grades. I've reported that to Mr. Levine."

Roy was pleased. "That means they have a good income, and the grandmother is used to being around young children. I'm considering that we could pick up the parents and deal with them in the manner they deserve, perhaps in some out-of-the-way place. How does that sound to you, Mr. Blum?"

He grinned. "I like the way you think, sir. I know of a particular motel that we can use.

"Good, but we can't use any of the Family cars or license plates."

"I have access to such a vehicle, sir."

"I expect that Mr. Levine may just have a friend or two on the local police force?"

"Would the Chief of Police do, sir?"

"Terrific. Since the parents' names or pictures were not shown on the news, perhaps the police can help deal with this matter if we need them."

"I'm sure they would, sir."

"That's good." Roy held out his hand to Blum. Even with a sheepish grin, he didn't take it. "Come on, we'll be working together. It's okay."

Then Blum shook his hand with a generous smile, seeing that was Jacob's way of showing *him* respect. And Jacobs knew it was best to keep on the good side of a man like him.

Blum reported that all was in order. They have until the eleven o'clock news to convince the parents. Roy asked Philips to draw up some needed "legal looking" adoption papers in about two hours. He called to reserve the motel room from a payphone.

Blum had contacted the parents to meet Roy at the store's candy counter where "Lilah" went missing. He described him as he would look in disguise; with graying dark hair, mustache, horn-rimmed glasses, and wearing a tan poplin raincoat.

Roy was picking through several candy bars when a man walked up to the display.

"Sure a lot to choose from."

Roy looked at him with a kind smile. "Sure is. I'm trying to decide what a child likes best. I know they all like candy, that's for sure."

"Oh, you bet. But, they really like chocolate more than anything."

"I guess you're right."

"How old is the little girl?"

Little girl? Roy caught that. "Oh, about three."

"What does she look like?"

"Like a little angel. But then you already know that. Would you like to see her?"

"Well, sure. Where is...."

Roy spun the man around to frisk him for a gun or a wire. He was clean.

"Are you a cop?"

"No, but I can get one if that's what you want."

"No, but..."

"But nothing. You want to see the girl or not?"

"Will it cost me?"

"I don't want your money, but I have a proposition for you and your wife. Where is she?" Roy opened his raincoat to show a harnessed pistol. "Is she armed?"

The man was shocked. "No, we don't have *any* guns."

"Your dead if you're lying, mister."

The stepfather turned stark as he swallowed. "I'm not lying, mister, I swear."

"Then, where is she?"

The man raised his hand to point. "Over there. Honey, come over here. Right now!"

She obliged him. "What's going on? Do you know where our daughter is?"

"Yes, and I also know what both of you did to her." Roy snapped, "If you want to see her, you'll come with me right now!"

He led them out to the limousine where Blum opened the door. This surprised them, although, they didn't hesitate to get in. However, Lilly wasn't inside. Jacobs assured them that the girl was well and in reliable care. They could see for themselves when they got to the destination.

While Blum drove, Roy asked about their treatment of the child.

"Did she give you permission to sexually molest her?"

"I never..."

"You did too! How many times did I tell you not to do that?" the woman demanded.

"How many?" asked Jacobs.

"What?"

"You heard me. How many times did you tell him that?"

"Several times. He never listened..."

"How many times did you report him to the police?"

"Well, if I did, then..."

"You never reported him. How often did you spank 'Lilah'?"

"Just when she was bad, which was most of the time."

"What do you mean by 'bad'?"

"Well, she wouldn't mind me when I told her to do something. And she always..."

"What things did you tell her to do?"

"Well, to pick up her toys and clean her room, maybe wash the dishes."

"How old is she?"

"She's three, but you have to start when they're young and teach them responsibility."

Jacobs looked at the husband. "How often did you have sex with the child?"

"I never had sex with her!"

Jacobs continued to look at him with a harsh and knowing glare. He moved the front of his coat as a reminder of the gun.

"I only, uh, taught her about... you know, the birds and the bees."

"By licking her privates and having her suck on your dick?"

As the woman began hitting her husband, he held up his arms in defense. "See? See how bad her temper is? She's always slapping the girl around too!"

Jacobs said, "I wonder why you let her do that. Now sit there and be quiet, or you won't even get where we're going — alive."

They obeyed until they drove into the estate. In wonderment, both marveled at the mansion and its well-manicured grounds. To them, it was a fairy tale.

"Lilly is staying here?" the woman asked as she stared in awe.

"Lilly?"

She caught her mistake. "Oh, uh, her name is Lilah, but we call her Lilly sometimes, as a nickname."

"Follow me inside," Roy ordered.

Inside was even more spectacular. Their eyes moved around each area of the great room and its posh furnishings, and then to the grand staircase and balcony.

Roy acknowledged the papers when Harry set them on the coffee table.

Then, with both hands in his pockets, Mr. Levine stepped into the doorway to view the couple. Jacobs introduced him as the owner of the house.

The father stepped forward with his hand extended, but Levine didn't take it, so he stepped back again, more nervous than before.

"This is a fantastic house that you have, sir. Um, is my daughter here? Can we see her?"

Levine gave Jacobs a quick nod after glancing at the papers, and then he left the room.

"He's a quiet one," the man said.

"Sit down, we'll talk about Lilah." Jacobs waved at the couch while he sat in a chair across from them.

"As you can see, this is a wonderful place for your daughter to live... without you. You haven't convinced me you'll take any better care of her now than before. I'll make you an offer that you had better not turn down." He pointed to the coffee table. "I'm prepared to give you fifty thousand dollars in cash for your signatures on those adoption papers."

They looked at each other with brightened eyes. Roy knew their answer when the man tried to make a better deal.

"That means we'll be giving our daughter up for good, and that would break my wife's..."

"There is no negotiating. My offer stands for..." Roy looked at his wristwatch, "thirty more seconds."

The wife said, "Well, just a minute, sir."

"Twenty-five seconds."

"When do we get to see our daughter? How do we know she's even here?"

"After you sign the papers." Reaching to the side of the chair Jacobs brough out the dress Lilly was wearing when Donald found her. He tossed it at them. "Fifteen seconds."

Roy stood up when Jada walked into the room with the tape recorder. After setting it on an end table, she turned it on. Before the tape was finished, she shut it off, glaring at the parents.

"Sign those papers, or you won't even see nightfall, let alone daylight!" Then she looked at Jacobs.

"Yes, Ma'am, I'll take care of everything," he assured before she left the room.

Roy turned to the parents, "Your time is up and the pen is on the table." He opened his coat to expose the Beretta 92 as Blum stepped forward. His mammoth hands could easily choke both at the same time. The wife picked up the pen reading none of the contract before signing it. Her husband did the same.

Roy took the papers into Philips, and then he and Blum escorted the couple to another car.

"No limo?" asked the husband inadvertently.

"We'll be going to another part of town where your daughter's waiting for you. A limousine would look suspicious," Jacobs said.

Blum ushered the woman into the front seat. He motioned for her husband to get in the back with Roy. There was no conversation during the drive to the motel until the wife asked about the money.

"It's in a suitcase. I put it in the trunk for safekeeping. You'll get it when we get there," answered Blum."

"There" was several more miles ahead and off the main road with only a gas station, diner, and small grocery store near the motel. Jacobs paid cash for a three-day stay, giving the clerk an extra twenty-dollar tip for holding the room. He asked not to be disturbed because he was a writer and "needed the peace and quiet".

Blum ushered the couple in with the suitcase, but no daughter was awaiting them. He told the couple to sit on the side of the bed and be quiet. He went into the bathroom, returning with a roll of heavy duct tape.

The woman excitedly yelled at him. "What are you going to do?" She turned to her husband, "Honey, make him stop!"

Blum smiled at them. "Stop me?" He slapped her face and then put tape on both their mouths. Jacobs took his coat off, although, he kept on his gun and holster.

With a devious grin, he turned to his partner, "Don't you think they look a little too warm, Mr. Blum?"

"I agree, sir. Way too warm." He ripped their clothes off, throwing them in a pile for Jacobs to gather into the empty suitcase. When they were naked, he taped each one's hands and feet together and then pushed them on the bed.

"So you to enjoy slapping a helpless little child around? Do you like getting slapped around?" Jacobs asked. They both shook their heads frantically as their eyes spit fear. "Mr. Blum, why don't you let them know what little Lilly Marie felt like when they slapped her around and pulled her hair?"

Blum's demonstration pleased Jacobs, although, the recipients were not all that delighted. When blood gushed from their noses, Blum fetched a towel from the bathroom and then slapped their faces with it to "clean them up."

"Now you got that nasty red stuff all over Mr. Blum. Shame on you. What do you think we should do about that?"

As the couple leaned against each other, Roy said, "Perhaps we should have her sit in this comfortable chair where she can rest so the loving father can lie down on the bed. My, my, he looks so tired."

Blum picked the woman up by her shoulders, threw her into the easy chair, and then tossed "the loving father" down on the bed.

"So, you like to have little Lilly kiss and lick your 'stick' after you rub jelly on it? Mr. Blum, would you like to do that?"

"Not without any jelly on it. Perhaps he would, though."

That brought a bit more than mere fear to the frightened father's face. The great man could just yank the object out of his body, but Blum thought of something a little kinder. Taking a switchblade knife from his pocket, the 'stick' was on the man's lap in just one swipe.

Naturally, the wife didn't sit calmly by to watch her husband writhe in excruciating while blood and urine spewed out of his spasmodic pelvis.

"It's too bad that he's making such a mess for you, Mr. Blum. You can't even finish your surgery now. I can get you another towel."

"I wouldn't want you to go to a lot of bother, sir."

Jacobs gave him a towel, "No trouble at all, Mr. Blum." Blum grinned at the horrified man who was trying to scream from the torturous agony.

From bowing to others all his life because of his great size and dark skin he was denied the satisfaction of doing to others who had done unto him. Something was now released inside himself; he could finally lash out and lash back, and that release felt good. Too good. Blum smiled to himself for that sence of inner freedom and satisfaction.

"Oh, you be still now so I can take some nice pictures to show your daughter after I'm all finished with you."

"It would be very kind of you to do that," added Roy. And then he noticed the woman had lost control of her bladder.

"My, my, have you no manners, lady? Mr. Blum, I think this woman is going to need a nice warm bath when you get done with all of your surgery. And hurry with the scalpel so he can enjoy the results before he passes out from all the ecstatic pleasure you're bestowing upon him. My, my, he won't be able to thank you without his tongue. That's just rude of him, don't you think?"

"Yes, it is, sir." With another whisk of the "scalpel", Blum tossed a set of testicles on the man's stomach. "Just as I thought, they aren't very big, but at least you have some, right where they belong," Blum laughed, and then he slapped his face.

"That's very rude of you not to thank me. Cat got your tongue?"

Blum ripped the tape off the man's mouth and stabbed his tongue, slicing it down the middle. He slapped the tape on his mouth again before the man slumped in convulsions. Blum watched with a grin.

"Some folks just don't appreciate good fun," laughed Jacobs. Then he stepped aside as Blum carried the woman into the bathroom where he dropped her into the tub. She writhed in agony and fear. Her face contorted as she tried to scream.

Blum patted her head. "Oh, don't worry, you ain't got no balls either." While the warm water ran, she squirmed and twisted. "No, you ain't going to drown. You just lay there nice and peaceful so we can wash you up."

As she tried to defend herself, the woman had such a horrendous look of terror in her eyes that Blum couldn't resist hearing her last words.

"If I take the tape off your mouth, do you promise not to scream? I hate it when ladies scream at me." She shook her head fervently.

"Alright then, make it quick and make it good." He pulled the tape from her face.

"Mister, I am *sorry*. I didn't mean to hurt my daughter. I was trying to raise her like the Bible said to. That you have to beat the evil spirit out of the child. I'm truly sorry. I'll never do that again," she gasped. "I promise that I won't, please, *please*!"

Blum smiled, "Now, are you really sorry that you did that? Or are you just sorry that we found out about what you did? If you're really sorry, then stick your tongue out so I can see if it's lying."

In fear of what he'd do, she turned her head aside, screaming, "No! *No*!"

Blum laughed and then slapped the tape on her mouth again.

She threw her head backward in anguished torment. In what she now knew were her last moments of life, her thoughts turned to God, asking that He forgive her sins, and to cast this fiend into the pits of hell and fire for all eternity.

When the tub filled with enough water, Blum held out his knife to her taped wrists. Then he saw the water beneath the woman turn a chestnut color.

"Oh, good gravy, don't you have no manners at all, lady? How disgusting of you! Just hush now. You'll be asleep in no time." The razor-edged blade gashed the inside of her wrists.

Jacobs stepped into the bathroom, looking at his watch. "Jada wanted us back before dark, so we could let her know everything was done on time. I'll go get the camera for you."

"Certainly, sir." Blum slid the knife across her throat.

After taking several pictures of the couple, Blum checked the husband's pulse to find that he still had one. He slashed his throat, ensuring the carotid artery was severed.

Jacobs checked the rooms and wipe anything that either may have touched.

The camera light flashed as Blum took pleasure in capturing his work on film. He left a dim light on and ensured the door was firmly locked when they left.

Upon their return, Jacobs changed his clothes and removed the disguise before reporting to Phillips, who would later inform Levine they had taken care of everything.

"Yes, the couple was 'fast asleep', and we left a lamp on. I told the clerk that I was a writer and needed my privacy. He was pleased with the twenty-dollar tip," Jacobs smugly assured Phillips. "I'll bring you the pictures as soon as Blum gets them developed,"

"Thanks, but you've done enough for the day, Roy. Just have Mr. Blum bring them to me. That will be all."

That sounded more of an order. However, Jacobs agreed before bidding him a good night. Walking away, he knew

Blum would give Levine the full, gory report and get the praise, not him. *Damn it!*

Philips and Levine were in the office when Blum reported. They looked over the full-size glossies, speaking ambiguously as in their meetings.

"Whose idea was all this?" Levine asked.

"We both thought of it, sir."

"These are wonderful pictures. Did you take them?"

"Yes, sir, I did. I'm glad that you like them, sir." Blum knew Levine had just praised his work.

Then Philips spoke up. "Did you and Jacobs work together on all this?"

"Yes, sir. We collaborated all through the project. My partner was very easy to work with, sir. And he had several artistic ideas of his own."

Mr. Levine smiled, "Extremely inventive poses on your subjects. This shows originality. I wonder if it was you who directed the models to pose in such unique ways."

Blum beamed with pride at hearing the Don recognize his "personal touch" and the depths of his capabilities.

"Yes, I was that artist, sir."

"I appreciate that. Was anybody around to inspect your artwork?"

"No, Mr. Levine. We don't expect to have a formal showing until the day after tomorrow. That might be delayed in case of rain."

Phillips spoke up. "If you don't mind a suggestion, don't you have some very influential friends that might be interested in a private viewing before the general public is invited to the open show?" His reference was to the Chief of Police.

"Yes, I do. Thank you for that idea. They could appreciate the true value of Mr. Blum's artwork." Levine again looked at Blum with recognition and then motioned to Philips.

"Well, Mr. Blum, Don Levine and I certainly want to thank you for all of your time and effort on this project, and for these pictures. Do you have copies of them?"

"Yes, sir," Blum pointed to the envelope of negatives on the table.

"Good. I'll put all these away in my files." Philips meant his fireplace. "I took the liberty of preparing a receipt to sign that will release these pictures to us."

Blum beamed while signing his name, and then he accepted the envelope containing three thousand dollars.

The following day, David let Lilly stay overnight so Jada could have a little more time with her. This also gave the situation a "cooling off" period.

Harry Philips contacted the police chief, to inform him the child had been found. He could release Lilly to her grandparents, along with the adoption papers and a cashier's check for three thousand dollars, plus another one for two thousand dollars as a contribution to the police guild. The chief accepted the offer without question.

After Jada said goodbye to her, Lilly rode to the police station with "Uncles" Harry and Donald, along with her new clothes and the kitten.

From another room, they watched the girl run to her grandparents. Seeing them again, she leaped into their arms with tremendous joy. The chief presented them with the adoption papers and cashier's check, which surprised and thrilled them immensely.

With a firm handshake and a big grin, he also accepted the two thousand dollars cash "on behalf of the police guild".

Moreover, he mentioned that officers reported the discovery of two mutilated bodies.

"These could be the child's parents. We won't know for sure until they do the autopsy. I just thought you might want to know that." He laughed, "As the old saying goes, 'Evil is as evil does', right?"

Philips returned to give Levine the report, who was pleased and relieved with the news. Although, Lilly's absence left a void in Jada's heart.

After dinner, Carla was cleaning the kitchen when Roy came in for another cup of coffee. She had noticed a change had been coming over her him, thinking it was not for the better. She suspected what may have influenced him.

"While you were gone, I read a lot of that book you left by your chair. Now I can see why your personality has been changing of late."

Roy turned to look at her. "What are you talking about?" he snapped.

"That! That's what I mean, your attitude, your composure. It looks like you're taking on the personality of one of those characters in that book," she smirked.

"Carla, what book are you talking about?"

"That mafia book. The one with a guy named Don who runs a gang of Italian killers."

Roy's expression relaxed. "Oh, *that* book. They're Sicilian and not a 'gang'. They're part of a mafia family. The Don is the head of that Family, just like David is the Don of our Family."

"Oh, so now we're all related. I guess that makes Jada our mother then. What do we call her, the Donna?" Carla laughed as she snapped the dishtowel at him.

"Very funny, Carla."

"I suppose that Larry the lawyer is the consigliere."

"No, Larry's my lawyer. Levine's lawyer is Harry Philips."

"Roy, my love, you're talking like it's really happening now. That's a book of fiction that happened in the past. It was written in the past tense, like the used to be."

Roy was now getting perturbed. "Carla, that kind of stuff is happening today."

"But it's still a made-up story. Do you think that your 'mafia' pals are those characters? Like if David is a Don, then who would you be?

"Dammit, Carla, you don't make fun of him like that! He *is* the Don," Roy blasted.

"You didn't answer my question, Roy. If Levine is the boss, and Harry is the attorney, then that makes Richard the son. Blum would certainly be Luca Brasi. So that only leaves you to be..." Carla burst out laughing at her thought. "That means you must be *Fredo*!"

Her laughter suddenly stopped when Roy's face erupted into fury. He raised his hand to strike her but stopped in midair and then lowered it. "The next time you say something like that to me, I won't be so lenient," he warned in a steady but threatening voice.

Carla stood staunch with both hands on her hips, teeth clenched, jaws tight, and fire spitting from her eyes. "Roy, the first time you hit me will be the last thing you will ever do with that hand."

Roy's countenance relaxed into a mischievous grin. He glanced at the wooden knife block, "I suppose you're going chop my hand off."

"I may have been the only girl in my family, but I was tough. I always played football, baseball, and cowboys and Indians with all the neighborhood boys," she snapped back. "No, Roy, I won't just chop your hand off. I'll tear your dammed arm off and shove it down your throat. And you can bet your teeny little weenie on that, big boy!"

While trying to look undaunted, Roy walked away muttering, "Gawdam fuckin' bitch."

His only warning was a sharp hiss as the steel carving knife embedded its razor-sharp blade into the wall next to his head. Roy's eyes rolled sideways to see the eight-inch blade still quivering only inches away from his face. His body froze.

"I said that I played cowboys and Indians, didn't I? Guess which part I played?" Carla jeered, "Yep, I was Pocahontas!"

She laughed aloud to see her big, brave husband run into the bedroom. In a moment, she heard a flush of the toilet, and then the shower water began.

Carla sighed, "Oh dear, the damned stupid bastard just messed his pants."

Chapter Nineteen

CINDY

Carla was nearly finished with the fabulous mansion remodel. Now it was time for Jada, Nona, and Donald to make a guest list for the elaborate housewarming party. There were a considerable amount of people to consider. They also needed to decide on which caterer and florist to use. Their plans were interrupted by the doorbell, which Nona answered.

She returned with a bewildered look. "Madam, there's a little girl who came in a taxi. She's asking to see Mr. Levine, saying that he is her daddy. She's starting to cry. What do you suggest I do?"

Nona was uncomfortable in handling this situation since she knew too well how the Levine's were unable to conceive a child in all their years of marriage. This couldn't possibly be his child.

It took only a second for Jada to consider this. "Her daddy, huh?"

"Yes, ma'am."

"Why don't you let me take care of this, dear."

Jada saw a girl who looked to be ten or twelve years old. She had shiny brown hair parted in the middle with long braids to either side. Her cute, round face was turned downward with a pouting lower lip. She wiped what looked like tears with the back of her hand. She was wearing a tan poplin raincoat, wrapped over in front and tied with a long self-belt. Jada saw the girl wore sandals without socks. She gently reached out to touch her chin, raising her head upward.

"Let me look at you, honey," she spoke in a soft, motherly voice. "You are a beautiful girl."

"Thank you," the girl murmured as she looked downward again.

"My, how could any mother let her little girl go out into this big city all alone? Do you even have a mother?"

"Yes, but she doesn't care for me. I wanted to see my daddy and maybe he would like me."

"You actually think Mr. Levine is your daddy?" Jada gently stroked the child's face and jaw to feel which muscles tightened as she spoke, something Jada learned from her husband long ago. In this, she knew well not to lie to him.

"That's what my mother told me several times. She said that she has proof of that." Again, Jada wisely thought this was not a ten-year-old child because ten-year-old children have mommies, mamas, or moms, not mothers.

"How did you get here, honey? Did you drive?"

"No, my mother gave me all the money she had and sent me here in a cab." She didn't say she didn't know how to drive or wasn't old enough to drive.

Jada put a gentle hand on her shoulder. "Why don't you come in the house with me, and we can talk about all of this where it's more comfortable. I want to see that you are taken care of, my darling child."

Inside, Nona was waiting for Jada's orders. "We'll go into my office where there's more privacy. I'll have a martini rocks and bring the child a glass of Coke, please."

Jada showed the girl to her office that looked more like a small living room with a spacious desk. She waved her hand in a gracious gesture.

"Sit wherever you wish, dear. Except here, this is my favorite chair." That was a wing-back, armed chair covered in soft upholstery velvet.

She watched the girl look around at the equally luxurious furniture. The small couch and matching armchair were covered in a luxurious print fabric. The coffee and end tables were carved walnut matching Jada's desk, and the carpet had a rich, thick pile. The girl whirled around with a wide smile and wild eyes.

Choosing the armchair, she asked, "You have your clients come in here for business?"

"I like to have my guests be comfortable."

Cindy glanced at the furnishings again, "I'm sure they *will* be."

After Nona served the drinks, Jada asked, "What is your name, my dear?"

"It's Cynthia, but most people call me Cindy. That's what I like."

"Well, Cindy, did you think that a man like David Levine would see you?"

"I just thought that if he saw me, he might know who my mother was because everyone says that I look just like her."

"I see. Well, honey, a man as important and rich as my husband would know better than to have a child alone in a room with him. He would have his assistant, or myself, with both of you. After all, if he is your father, then I am your step-mother. Do you understand what I am saying?" Cindy bowed her head and then looked at Jada with her charming eyes.

"Yes, Ma'am."

"And if he thought that you might look old enough to be in one of his films, he would have me interview you. Do you understand all of that too, Cindy?"

She smiled coyly, "Yes."

"Then stand up and take your coat off," Jada ordered.

Cindy was surprised. "What?"

"You heard me," Jada bluntly said. The girl knew her bluff was called.

"How did you know..."

"Just do it!"

Standing to her feet, the girl loosened the belt and then opened the front of her coat, letting it drop to the floor. Just as Jada assumed, Cindy wasn't wearing clothes. She viewed the girl's naked body with no emotion, just business.

"Now, turn around slowly. Okay, let me see your profile." Cindy obliged, letting Jada get the entire perspective of her ample D-cup breasts, tiny waist, and curvaceous hips. And then she flexed a well-contoured leg. At Jada's order, she showed a full front view again.

"Put your coat back on and sit down. I will only ask you questions once, and I want truthful answers from you. If not, I will call to have you arrested."

"For what?"

"Never mind. I'll think of a good charge before the cops get here."

Cindy leaned back into the chair. With a 'naughty girl' grin she parted her legs. "And I'll guarantee you that I won't even see the inside of the courthouse, let alone a jail cell."

Jada was not impressed. "How old are you?"

Cindy sat up to look like a proper lady. "Depends on who needs to know. For you, I'm sixteen and have ID to prove it. For most men, I'm eighteen and have an ID to show for it. I can be ten, eleven, twelve, or up to twenty-five with the right make-up for moviemakers. For cops, I can be any ol' age they want to fuck. And I do a damned good job of that. Just ask any of the cops on the LA or Beverly Hills beat. So, go ahead and call your cop friends. I'll bet they know me intimately," she answered with confidence.

Jada relaxed with a slight smile. "So, you know your way around the bed, so to speak. You have much to offer, or give if that's the case. Or do you sell it?"

"Sure, I'll sell it to anyone who wants to part with their hard-earned money. Some guys I just reward for a job well done, like cops or our service boys. I know a whole lot of unhappy husbands with spending money."

"That's why you want to get in our movies, then. So you can get paid to get satisfied.?"

"Sure, why not?" Cindy leaned forward in the chair. "I love having sex. I am not a slut or a whore or a tramp, I like to fuck, just like guys do." Cindy stopped to take a sip of her drink.

"I don't understand why girls have to be tagged as whores and tramps just because we like to do what men do. But they're the ones who want a piece of ass or get some strange stuff now and then, 'cause they can't get anything from their old ladies. You wanted an honest answer, so you got one, lady. If you think that I'm a whore or a slut, then fuck you." She sat back in the chair with a defiant attitude.

"But, before you kick me out on the street, I would appreciate some rum in my coke and to fuck some of your hired help first."

"Good lord, girl. I'm rather surprised, pleased, and impressed with you all at once. *But*, I prefer you curb your language. We do not use vulgarities in the Levine household. And certainly, you can have some rum. Would you like a fresh cock, I mean, Coke?"

Jada called Nona for another martini and a rum and Coke.

Sitting forward in her chair, Jada smiled, "And yes, sweetheart, I will certainly see that you can have all the men you can handle before you leave. I am sure they will be quite thankful for that."

"I want to say this is now an official interview for a job. And in possibly many movies. I think you know my husband *can* make a top movie star out of someone like you. And if your sex drive is that strong, you can make a fortune with it, and make that little pussy of yours very happy. However, I give the okay to even see how you'll look on film."

Jada asked if Cindy was on birth control.

"Oh, that," she laughed. "Quite a while ago, I told my mother that I was having bad cramps each month, and the school nurse said I should see a doctor. So, I told the doctor what the real problem was. I said that I just loved to fuck, I mean, have sex. Sometimes I couldn't get enough, but I was afraid of getting pregnant. I said that if he could give me an IUD, I would have to come by several times to have him check it out and make sure it's working right."

"So, did he?"

"Oh, lady, he put one in right then and asked me to come back after his nurse left that day so that he could check it."

"And?" asked a very interested Mrs. Levine.

"Oh, hell, he was real happy to see me. He even put a warm flannel sheet on the table for me," Cindy laughed. "He was polite to me, but he was really quick. I didn't like how he did it, so I only went back twice to make sure the IUD was working right."

"Good for you, dear. Women are here because men need taken care of. Otherwise, sex would not be such an important commodity. Men think they can use us, but we are the real users and never forget that. I got this mansion, all the beautiful clothes, jewelry, and furs by making sure my husband is happy, even if he thinks he's getting some "strange stuff" now and then. But keep that to yourself, young lady, and we'll get along just fine. If you ever cross me, all you'll get is dead."

"Oh, don't worry! I certainly know how to play the game, Mrs. Levine, and you have my word on that."

Jada asked Donald to come to her office.

"I want you to meet Cindy. She may be our newest starlet. Stand up and let Donald see what you look like." She did, and Cindy liked the way he smiled at what he saw.

"That's enough for now, close your coat. Donald, my pet, I'd like to have you get a couple of young men together and show Cindy some of your best ways to welcome her. I'll call when I'm ready. That should give you enough time to get everything nice and cozy. Start with a good, hot bath and someone to wash her back.

"I think she can keep all of my boys smiling for a long while. They work better when they're in a good mood, don't they, Donald?"

"Oh, yes, Madam, they certainly do at that! Excuse me, ladies, I'll go prepare everything to suit our guest beyond her expectations."

"Since you are under a doctor's care, may I assume he is keeping you free of all diseases? We keep a special doctor on staff. All of our people who engage in sex get checked every month and even more often for some. We see that they stay clean. If anyone contracts even lice from you, I will see that your sweet little pussy is cleaned out with a gasoline douche and a match."

Cindy's smile dropped. "Oh no. I mean, yes! I've been checked several times, and no, I *don't* have anything. All of the doctors made sure that I didn't get an infection from the IUD, even. Oh, yes, Ma'am. I am clean. *Very* clean, I promise you. I will swear to that on the Bible."

Jada's voice softened, "Alright, just relax now, dear."

Cindy welcomed the relief the liquor brought to her body that had suddenly tensed. In a few moments, Jada saw that she was once again at ease while discussing her taste in clothing.

"Oh, my, what am I thinking? You have nothing to wear, do you?" Jada called Nona in to determine the girl's clothing and shoe size. And then she called Donald to get Cindy.

After they left, Jada kicked her shoes off. With both feet up on the desk, she thought about what to tell David. She knew he could make Cindy into the big star he needed for his movies. However, that would wait until she got the full report from Donald.

As she sipped on her martini, a slight, mischievous smile crept over her lips. Dear sweet Donald. He was her main man, her bottom man, her very trustworthy friend. What would she do without that young man? He knew many of her secrets, and he knew too well what was in store if he ever betrayed her, or if she even thought he had.

Although, he wouldn't do that, would he?

Chapter Twenty

VISIT TO THE DOCTOR

Jada looked at Carla with concern. "I didn't want to say anything to you before, my dearest, but I've noticed that you have been looking a bit, well... quite tired of late. I know this job has been a strain on you. Have you seen a doctor lately?"

Carla responded to her concern. "Oh, no. I just need to take some time for myself. Just give me a little while to recuperate after I'm all done."

"Why don't you see our doctor for a check-up? Have you had a pelvic exam and all that girly stuff in the past year?"

"Oh, the last time I saw a doctor was before I went to Europe and got all my shots for the trip."

"My dear, do let me get you in to see our Family physician, Dr. Salsberry, for a full going-over. I want to make sure you have all of your parts in working order. He's a nice doctor and very gentle. He takes care of all our actors, too. You'll love him, and I'll feel better if you get a good once-over, okay?" Carla knew she should accept her offer, so she made the appointment.

Talking to the doctor was comfortable for Carla. He was in his early fifties, with three children and a lovely wife pictured on his desk. He spoke kindly to her with a great understanding of the situation. Dr. Salsberry sensed she didn't feel at ease, so he tried to reassure Carla of the necessity to include a pelvic examination to ensure overall good health.

"My nurse will be present at all times," he said. However, Carla was still uneasy. "Have you ever tried hypnosis to relax you?"

She shook her head. Dr. Salsberry explained the procedure, noting Carla's interest.

"I will be very gentle in slightly stretching out the muscles of your vagina, then take a tiny culture which you will hardly feel. Then I will give you a rectal exam to see that you don't have any growths or hemorrhoids. You will relax those muscles and not feel any discomfort. And my nurse will be there at all times during the examination."

The doctor held her hand in both of his. "When you awake, you may feel as though you just had sexual relations, but you certainly won't feel violated. Now, do you understand all of this, Carla?"

"You hear all kinds of stories on TV shows about being hypnotized and all that," she nervously replied.

He patted her shoulder. "Oh, yes, but those television shows are only for entertainment. I've had many years of experience doing hypnotism, and I haven't lost a patient from it yet," he laughed. "I'll have you remove all your clothing and then put on this gown with the opening in the back. I'll be back in a few minutes. Nurse Connors will be in after I have hypnotized you, so you can thoroughly relax during the process."

After Carla was in the gown, the doctor dimmed the overhead light. While sitting at the end of the exam table, she observed the small red light on the upper left-hand corner of one wall. The light grew a little larger and then receded repeatedly while Dr. Salsberry's soft voice invited her to relax and concentrate on the light.

As he murmured, her eyes closed until she was fully asleep. The doctor told Carla that she would feel passionate and want to make love to him and his friend.

"You will yearn to touch us, to have sex that will make you fulfilled. We are the only men you will think of. You will want to please us."

He told her she would remain that way until he said the word "rhinoceros". Then she will fully awaken and not remember anything except that she felt fully refreshed. He helped Carla lie down on the table before letting Nurse Connors in.

"Hi, got a brand-new patient I see, and an exquisite one at that."

"Yes, Fred. This is her first time, so we have to go easy."

Nurse Fred ran his hand over Carla's hips and thighs smoothly. She moaned with a soft smile. He helped her sit up and then offered her a glass of the orange juice concoction to give her more "vitamin C". Within a few minutes, she became amorous, to their delight. Carla writhed and move with their touches.

"That feel good?" Fred whispered. Her smile widened. He ran his hands over her shoulders, her thighs, lower legs, and her feet. His warm hands caressed her arches as he noted her expressions of enjoyment. The not-so-good doctor smoothly ran his hands lightly over the inside of her thighs.

"Carla, Fred and I are going to make you feel wonderful, like you should have felt for many years. We'll make you feel like a woman again. Would you like that, Carla? Would you like to feel what a real man is like?"

"Oh, yes, it's been so long."

Salisbury stripped down since Fred had already undressed. He then nursed her full breasts while his soft hand slipped over her belly.

She moaned softly, "Oh, doctor, that feels so good. I should feel guilty."

"No, you should not feel guilty. Do you want to feel Fred? He has a very nice body."

She responded to that suggestion. However, not enough to his liking, so Fred offered her more to drink. Carla was now at the mercy of the drugged juice. The two men took turns having sex with her, long enough to approach orgasm, and then stopped to delay their enjoyment. Carla obliged them orally when they asked. They reciprocated when she asked. That brought her to a clitoral orgasm.

Salsberry picked up his camera. "Will you let me take some pictures of you? I want to look at them when you're not here, then I can think of you." She smiled when the bulbs flashed.

Fred mounted her again but could not hold back that time. The doctor took his turn as he tried to control himself. With eyes shut tight, Carla gave way to the ecstasy of a vaginal orgasm. With that, Salsberry submitted to an intense orgasm himself.

Carla raised her head. "Does that mean we're all done?

"You want more?" The two men weren't prepared for this.

"Can I have some more orange juice? My mouth is dry."

Salsberry gave her some cold water. He became concerned that the effect wouldn't wear off fast enough and that she might want more sex. He gave her an injection of antihistamine to counterbalance his "sex drug".

Both men applied cool cloths to her head, neck, and even her crotch to revert Carla's mood. They watched her relax while Dr. Salsberry got dressed and prepared to take her out of the trance. Once she seemed back to normal, he breathed easier.

Having gotten her douched, washed, and sitting up in the gown again, he placed the sheet over her lap while Fred went into another room to get dressed.

"Carla, when you wake up, you will forget all this. You'll only remember that you were very relaxed, and the pelvic exam was not at all disturbing. Rhinoceros."

Carla looked at the doctor. "Well, that wasn't as bad as I thought it would be. I'm even feeling better now. Will there be anything else to do?"

"No, you may get dressed."

At the reception desk, Dr. Salsberry gave Carla some prescription creme. "Use this if you feel any discomfort."

After Carla was gone, Fred looked at the films. "This has got to be the best one yet. Her beauty makes the other gals look like old housewives. I can't wait to see the films developed!" exclaimed Fred. "Let's check the cameras, and maybe we can put in a third one for the next time. We can make a fortune off these as home movies, don't ya' think? I can't wait to get the snapshots developed. We can sell them to high school boys who need to know what a nice pussy looks like. At least they'll be great for kids to look at while they jack off."

However, upon showing the exclusive 'home movie' to a group of men, a well-traveled customer was among them. He mentioned that the star of stage, screen, and examining table looked a lot like the wife of a wealthy theater owner who was pictured in newspapers recently. Is there a possibility that she might be...? And *her* in a home porno movie? Lawsuit! Lawsuit! Or possibly blackmail, or worse? Well, scratch that idea.

They devised a better plan. The following "movie star" will heretofore use an anonymous name and wear a wig and mask. Also, there will be a more comfortable table for the lady with more cameras and better lighting, plus an abundant selection of 'doctors', just in case.

Chapter Twenty-one

MARNI'S NEXT

Jada stopped by to see Carla's remodel work. "Hello, dear. My, everything's coming along absolutely wonderfully. "Some of my friends are asking when you'll they can hire you. However, I said that my dear friend, Mr. Fraiser, was next in line. By the way, how do you feel since you saw the doctor?"

"Jada, I feel so much better. Thanks for referring me to him. You were right. That wasn't as bad as I thought it would be. I hardly felt a thing. And he was so gentle."

"I thought you'd feel better about that. You simply must take care of that lovely body. Falling ill from exhaustion would put you right over the edge. Now I just need to convince Marni of that too. Maybe you can talk to her. She's been avoiding a full exam for way too long. I don't want to learn that she has something wrong with the way she's been feeling. Marn at her wit's end with Harry of late. You'd think those men would know when it's time to back off and lie low. But n-o-o-o, they just have to have their pussy and eat it too."

"I'll call Marni and talk to her," Carla said. "Sharon thought this might be good for her too because the marital stress has been grating on her nerves. Perhaps a good check-up could help her."

After Carla explained how comfortable her visit was with Dr. Salsberry, Marni agreed to see him. Carla made her an appointment with the suggestion that light hypnotism could lessen the tension for her.

Carla escorted her friend to the office. After an initial talk with the doctor, Marni told her not to wait. "I think that I'll be alright with this doctor. He's nice, just like you said. I'll call a cab when I'm done here. I may go shopping later, anyway."

When she was seated in the examining room, Dr. Salsberry asked about her health, recent issues, and current problems.

"You've been through a great deal of stress of late. How long has it been since your last full exam; blood pressure, heart, lungs, breast and pelvic exam, a general going-over of everything?"

"I can't recall, to be truthful. It was usually just one part at a time."

Since her day was free, Marni agreed to a complete examination. The doctor instructed to undress and put the gown on with the opening in the back. As Marni sat at the end of the exam table, she noticed the small lighted red dot on the upper corner of the wall. It repeatedly became larger and then smaller.

The doctor re-entered the room, dimming the overhead lights even more.

"Yes, isn't that fascinating? It helps you relax, doesn't it?" His voice was smooth, nearly as fascinating as the red dot. He continued to talk to Marni until she was fully asleep, but could still hear his voice.

"Today, your name will be Anna. You are going to a masquerade ball where you will meet a very handsome prince who is in love with you. He wants to make love to you, and you will let him. He will fill your body with ecstasy and pleasure like you've never felt before. And you will yearn for my body and make love to me as well. You will wear a disguise and become a lovely princess that no man can resist. Do you understand all that I have said to you, Princess Anna?"

"Yes."

"My name is Don Juan, and now Prince Fred will place the lovely mask on your face."

Fred lightly kissed her bare neck and then tied on the mask. She blinked her long lashes, adjusting her eyes to the holes.

"Now, he will put a wig on your head. You will look just like Marie Antoinette." Before doing that, Fred kissed her neck again and then her shoulder. She smiled with delight.

"When you wake up, you can go to the ball, Princess Anna. Remember all that I have told you, and you will feel amorous when your prince beholds you as his princess. And you will yearn for me. But you will forget all of this when I say the word, 'hippopotamus'. You will wake up, and you will have forgotten that any of this ever happened. Do you understand this?"

"Yes, doctor."

"Then, welcome to the ball, Princess Anna."

She looked to see Prince Fred standing before her in a red satin cape and holding a large hand mirror in front of his masked face.

He turned it toward her with a smile. "Behold, the fairest Princess Anna."

She looked into the mirror with approval. "Oh, how beautiful I am, and so is my Prince Charming."

He kissed her fingertips. "I shall fetch a cool drink for you, and then I will taste your warm lips." Fred poured an orange-flavored liquid into a silver cup and helped Princess Anna to sip it.

"I drink to your eyes and the joy they bring to me." However, his cup was empty.

In helping her lie back, Fred placed a satin pillow under her head. Then he slid the gown away and touched her flesh lightly, as though a butterfly was fluttering on her bare skin. Anna moaned softly. Her smile showed pleasurable feelings as goosebumps rose on her skin. A sense of passion and arousal beset her.

As with Carla, the men took turns mounting her until they could no longer hold back. Then it was time to wash and dress her.

Soon, Marni was on the table and in the gown again. Salsberry returned with the exact instructions as with Carla. He said "Hippopotamus" to bring her out of the trance.

Marni opened her eyes and smiled. "All done? So, will I pass for another year?"

"Yes, all of your tests were good. Before you go, I'll give you some vaginal cream to use if you feel a little sore. Other than that, just call me anytime you feel the need. You may get dressed now."

Salsberry was sitting behind the reception desk when she was ready to leave. "I took the liberty of calling you a taxi, Mrs. Phillips. He's waiting out front for you. Enjoy the rest of your day."

A few days later, Jada and Sharon were seated at a restaurant when Marni and Carla joined them for lunch. It was only moments before the server brought their drinks. They were happy to get together again, and Jada remarked how content they looked since their doctor's visits.

"I'm all set for another year," Marni said. "And Harry was happy that I saw the doctor. He even remarked that I was more chipper."

They shared the ease and comfort of the examination and how much the hypnotism helped with the relaxation.

Jada became concerned. "The what?"

Marni explained, "Oh, it wasn't any big thing. He just talked to me to get me to relax. I think it was that little red light that..."

"Wasn't that charming?" Carla interrupted.

"What little red light?" asked Sharon.

Looking at both women, Jada rested her forearms on the table. "Do tell us more about this little red light."

They explained the little red light, which now alarmed the other two. Both said that when the exam was over, they just felt relaxed.

Sharon and Jada looked at each other. "They were hypnotized. My lord, Jada, you wouldn't think something strange went on? I mean, he's the doctor who works for David."

"Sharon, if it is, we'll have to find out. What if they're the ones causing all that trouble with David's company? I mean, Dr. Salsberry has access to all the actors. He could hire some girls who aren't working steadily. For some, it wouldn't matter who they worked for as long as they get paid. Oh, my gosh."

Jada turned to the other two ladies with a gentler tone. "I wonder if we should check him out?"

"Oh no, I don't think he's *anything* like that. He's too kind of a man," said Carla.

"Well, if he *is* all that good, I'd sure like to see him," Sharon said. "I haven't had a check-up in a long while, maybe too long."

Jada asked Carla to get Sharon an appointment with him. After lunch, Carla made the appointment, and then Sharon and Jada talked to Blum. He was sure that he and his men could get into the clinic after hours and look for any hidden cameras or recording devices.

Blum found those cameras. It seemed those were the men who sold "Fred's Fun Films" films to Jacobs and Levine. And most likely to other dealers. Blum installed his cameras and an electronic device to record and listen to all conversations. Jada, Donald, and Blum would listen to what took place during Sharon's appointment in the limousine's comfort.

During the examination, Sharon would gather as much "evidence" as necessary. In the instance that she had had enough, the phrase "I've had enough" would indicate, of course, that she had had enough, thus ending the "examination" with the help of Mr. Blum and his men.

When Carla and Sharon met with Dr. Salsberry, Sharon explained she was shy about being touched by men other than her husband. He understood.

Having been forewarned, Sharon knew how not to accept the hypnotism through her husband's past training. It would prove harmful if an outsider could get pertinent information by hypnotizing one of the Mafia's wives. Unfortunately, Mari didn't have that training. However, because of this, she and Carla soon would.

The doctor was indeed gentle. Although, Sharon protested the red light saying it bothered her eyes. She asked that if he would turn it off.

Not to be offset, the good doctor had other training that Sharon could also avert. However, she went along with his instructions as though she had been hypnotized.

Fred introduced "DeLilah" to a gorgeous, sparkling gold mask and a long black wig. He also adorned her with stunning bracelets of gold. Now, nurse Fred would be her "Samson".

When Dr. Salsberry dimmed further, Samson entered wearing a loincloth and carrying a silver challis containing the orange drink. Taking a sip, Sharon tasted what she expected to be the drug to stimulate her sexuality, not that she needed that. Setting down the challis, she ravished Samson's body and dominated the performance, much to his surprise.

The good doctor became a gladiator with a shield and whip. He became disarmed when she turned her charms on him. DeLilah soon seduced him as well. He didn't know how to react to someone of her sexual prowess, except submitting to his manhood.

She stood with both hands on her hips, demanding to know where the real men were—these men who would give her pleasure and fulfillment. To "DeLilah," these were not men but mere schoolboys. She needed to have a *man* fulfill her. The gladiator disappeared into the lobby to address his awaiting army of three.

"Damn, we have a she-beast in there! You better know how to give it to her rough, or she'll eat you up and spit you out. And I don't mean metaphorically. Just toss her on the table and rape the bitch! Shit, I didn't see this coming."

Two of the men barged into the room to lift her onto the padded table. One held her arms over her head as the other one mounted her.

"You like the rough stuff, you whoring bitch? You like getting rammed by a real man?" he panted.

She laughed, "Yeah, just give me one, and I'll tell you what it's like, you wimp!" The next man was about to ravage her lips, but her teeth suddenly looked like fangs, so he politely withdrew.

The only wise one stroked her face as his soft lips tenderly kissed her neck and shoulders.

Then he admonished the other men. "How could you treat such a fine lady like that? She needs to be loved and caressed. Her skin is like silk, and her lips are sweet as morning dew on the roses. You are beasts and should be flogged to treat a gentle woman with such cruelty. Shame on you both."

In a tender voice, he turned to DeLilah, "May I have the pleasure of tasting those tantalizing lips, my precious lady?"

He leaned into her face, his lips touching her cheek, and then her lips ever so gently, so sweetly, until she parted them in response to his. As he caressed her tenderly, she purred into his ear.

"Finally, a real man," Sharon whispered as she relaxed with him. "Send the others away."

"Yes, my love. I will do anything to please you." He turned to the astonished failures. "My angel of love wishes you depart and leave us to enjoy one another in private. Both of you go now."

He turned to DeLilah, who made him question her following few words, "That goes for you too, Blum. Give me twenty."

In the limo, Jada and Donald laughed. "Okay, Mr. Blum. We'll give her twenty minutes of privacy. I think she deserves that much after what she just went through," said Jada. "Although, I'm sure she rather enjoyed it."

Blum turned the device off, and they talked while waiting. When a bit more than the allowed time had passed, they resumed the transmission. Sharon sounded very relaxed and soothed. The gentleman seemed to have pleased her.

"Well, mister lover, I think we had better get dressed now, and you should go. I'll allow you to walk away from this place if you promise never to return." Sharon told the lover.

He kissed her fingertips. "Why is that, my sweet?"

"Because when you've been seen walking out the front door, someone will come in and bust this place. You have been on camera, my dear." She touched the tip of his nose. "But only I will see this film and remember a fantastic experience with you. I can assure you of that."

He wondered, "Oh, my, are you with the police?"

"No, my pet, the *Mafia*. Now go, and fast! I've had enough of this." When he left the room, the other "doctors" came in to see her dressed and tame as a pussycat.

"What did he do to you, DeLilah?"

"Everything you didn't. You boys are all under arrest."

Blum and his men charged into the room, well-armed. "You boys really *are* under arrest," DeLilah repeated as she departed.

Blum's definition was only an arrest because he planned to arrest their drive for sexual activities.

"I know how to teach these doctors a lesson," said Blum. "But I think these other two need to learn that they can't just rape a woman because someone told them to. So, how can we put a stop to that?"

"Why don't Harold and me take those two into the other exam room and examine them?"

"Yeah, sure. Just make it short."

"That's what I mean to do," he laughed.

"Let's get another table in here so we can examine these two wonderful 'doctors' together," said Blum. Two of his men did that.

"Now, ain't that nice and cozy?" Blum heckled.

Harold and Sammy returned with big smiles. "They're socks fit in their mouths real nice. We could hardly hear them scream when we chopped their dicks off," laughed Sammy. "We shoved 'em in their mouth along with the socks."

"Yeah, but they needed something to wash them down, so we poured a huge bottle of bleach and, what's that other stuff?" asked Harold.

"Hydrogen Peroxide."

"Yeah, we poured that stuff down their throats, too. And the socks kept them from throwing up. That's somethin' I didn't want to see. But both of them is 'sleeping' now."

It was time for Blum's men to play doctor. Salsberry and Fred were stripped naked and tied down to the examination tables. Harold taped the socks in their mouths, which proved to be good sound-proofing for them too.

After a good douse of water, the men were thoroughly examined with the bare ends of an electrical cord plugged into a wall outlet. They fervently flexed their muscles when the wires touched their testicles.

"That was so much fun." Blum grinned.

It was interesting for them to learn that touching the point of a knife to the bottom of their feet with just the correct pressure caused sharp bodily reflexes on the "patients" part.

Blum jeered, "What's that you say? I can't hear you with those socks in your mouth."

While looking over the many medical instruments, the men found some scalpels. A little blood-letting always worked in the good old days, so why not now? Besides the scalpels, the play doctors also found a use for the suture needles. Although, not for stitching up the patients' wounds. Orientals used these for the ancient practice of *acupuncture*.

The new team of "doctors" found the white coats and plastic gloves. Now it was time to do more with the scalpels; a doctor needed to always be in good practice. Not knowing how to do a proper vasectomy, Blum suggested removing all the testicles entirely. That should work.

One of Mr. Blum's men remarked, "Oh, dear, the socks are coming loose. We better fix that. We want our patients to be comfortable, after all."

Harold asked how to encourage those men to stop making nasty movies.

"I'm tired of looking at these perverts," Blum told his men. "Let's wrap this up so we can go eat."

After the men washed the two "patients" down with water once more, the electrical wires helped them shake dry.

After that procedure, Blum gave them a chance to ask forgiveness. They both seemed to see the errors of their ways while begging for mercy. When he was sure they were repentant of their sins, Blum gave the play doctors a quick lesson on what incredible work the scalpel could do with a carotid artery, since he already had some practice with that. They were fast learners and sliced each throat open with one deft swipe.

"They can just stay in here since they've become so comfortable. We should be nice enough to clean up after ourselves, like everything we touched. It's the *least* we can do," laughed Blum.

He had the men remove all the cameras and other devices that Blum and his men had installed. However, they would leave the actual doctor's cameras and recorders. And they destroyed their gloves since their fingerprints were on the inside.

Before leaving, Blum notified Jada of the outcome. She was pleased to know the doctors and his helpers were at the office, "sleeping soundly". Donald then drove her home.

When going for drinks and a late lunch, the men exited through the back door that Blum firmly locked.

Chapter Twenty-two

CINDY BAD-MOUTHS THE DON

Since Jada told her to use whatever she could find around the mansion for the remodel, Carla ventured into a part of the estate where she hadn't been. In a small storage room, there were old lighting fixtures, furniture, lamps, and framed pictures, to her surprise. While looking through them, she thought she heard voices. In quiet curiosity, Carla moved closer to listen. As the voices became louder, she became more inquisitive, so she moved closer. The sound was like two people in heated passion. She peeped through a partially open door and saw bright lights shining on a couple in bed.

The young woman sharply slapped her partner across his face and then pushed him away.

"What the hell's the matter with you? You can't handle being with a real man?" he snapped.

"A man, yes, but you are less than a dog. How dare you treat me like some slut!"

Thinking this was a woman in danger, Carla's heart beat rapidly. But what could she do? Carla held her breath as she quietly looked and listened.

"You *are* a slut." With that, the man threw the young woman down on the bed to mount her. However, she fought back, using her fingernails to scratch his face and chest. And then she brought her knee up against his groin.

Carla held a hand over her mouth to keep from gasping aloud as the man doubled over in agony. This allowed the petite woman to shove him off the bed. Jumping to her feet, she grabbed the only bit of cover, a short, black lace negligee.

"What the hell kind of men are you giving me? This bastard is no kind of actor. He's a pig! Do you expect me to let some crazy bastard treat me the way he just did? You wanna' show that crap in your theaters to make a fortune? What the hell kinda man are you, anyway?"

From Roy's description, Carla recognized Cindy, the porno star. She suddenly realized that she was observing the making of a pornography movie.

Carla quietly stepped back but didn't want to leave. She looked around in case she could be seen and then continued to watch them.

"Young lady, you *cannot* talk to the Don like that!" Richard Hirsh snapped.

"Don? I thought his name was David," she retorted.

The director rebuked her. "His name *is* David, but he is the *Don* of this Family." She looked at both men in question.

"The Don, the Donald, the David. I don't care what you call that man. He can't just let someone treat me like this. All I know is that the *real* boss of this outfit is Mrs. Levine!" Cindy glared into David's eyes fiery with defiance. "And *she's* who I answer to."

Cindy pointed a sharply manicured finger at Levine while she snapped at Hirsh. "He can't allow one of his actors to treat me like I'm some slut off the streets. I'm selling his pictures, aren't I? And he lets some bastard toss me around on the bed like that. I'm here for the same reason you guys are, to make money for having sex. That's all it comes down to, isn't it? Money!

"You make big-time bucks off all this trash, and you treat us girls like we're dime-a-dozen bitch dogs. Maybe some of these stupid broads want to break into big-time decent movies through you, but not me. I love to fuck, and I know how to do it. And that makes you men *feel* like a man. If you were real men, you'd be out there earning a decent living. But none of us are decent people, so let's not pretend you're better than *I* am. Now, do we get the show back on the road? 'Cause I'm so steaming hot that I'll take on the whole damn bunch of you here and now!"

Hirsh leaned over to David Levine, who was now sitting with his head in his hand. "You're not going to let her talk like that, are you?"

Levine nodded. "She's right. Get that bastard away from her and check to see if he's on drugs. If he is, then get rid of him. Put him to sleep. You know how much I hate that stuff. Right now, Cindy is our golden egg — our star — and we can't afford to lose her. See if we have anyone else who can finish this movie, or else we just lost a lot of money."

Hirsh looked at the director. "Who else do we have for her?" The director shrugged as he looked around.

Having calmed down, Cindy walked back over to the bed. "If I don't get any volunteers, I'll just curl up and take a nap." She inhaled and then slowly turned around to the director with a beguiling grin.

"You want to be first, big boy?" she teased. "You're paying me for my time here, so get the cameras ready and let's just see who thinks they're a real man."

Still in her baby-doll peignoir, Cindy turned her back to the camera to stretch her arms as though she was tired and yawning. Then she bent over to put on a slipper. If that wasn't an invitation for a man to enter the bedroom set, then all those men, as Cindy would have said, didn't have the balls to.

The opportunity just presented the lighting man the chance for which he had been waiting; to impress the Don with his acting. He left his post and walked across the set to the actress, running his hand over her shapely buttocks. The new "partner" removed his shirt, exposing his tanned, well-built, muscular body. Cameras filmed this once-in-a-lifetime opportunity.

Cindy turned to smile in approval. "I haven't seen you before. Do you work around here?" she asked in a lusty voice.

"Yes," he answered. He stood up to drop his pants, showing off a very handsome and erect penis. "I'm the company electrician. I'm here to give you a charge." The man stepped out of the rest of his clothes and slipped the covering from her shoulders.

Levine saw how the well-practiced lover genuinely knew how to approach a woman. Little did he know, or would ever know, that some of that practice was with his own wife. Now this man needed to prove that he could satisfy the appetite of this hungry tigress. And he did, with tenderness, strength, endurance, and timing. Cindy lay back on the bed, saying that she had enough. However, her partner didn't.

"You wanted someone who could take care of you. Now it's your turn to do the same, my little bitch. Let's see what you can do for me," he taunted.

Cindy realized this man would be the right partner for her, so she returned the favor. "Oh, you think I got all that I wanted? Well, roll over, and I'll show you how much of a woman I really am."

He turned onto his back. With that, Cindy mounted him and rolled her hips around slowly and teasingly at first.

Her movements became increasingly faster as he laid his head back, moaning with pleasure while holding her breasts to ease them from bouncing.

Soon Cindy loudly moaned as she had yet another orgasm and then fell away from his body. He held his penis upright for all the world to see as cameras caught the ejaculation. His hand fell limp, as did he. Although, the star of this movie knew better than not to play her part fully. She raised her naked body to lie atop him, kissing his face tenderly.

"Oh, you certainly *did* fix my faulty circuits, Mister. How much do I owe you for your services?"

He raised his head to kiss her gently. "I can just bill you. I may need to come back later to re-charge your batteries."

"Cut! That's a wrap. Print it!" the director called out. "Mister, you were fantastic! Mister?"

Levine saw the two had fallen asleep from their exhaustive lovemaking.

"Cover them up and let them sleep. Just keep a camera around for when they wake up. We may have another episode to film. And give that man a contract and the girl a raise. I need to go thank my wife for being such a good boss."

Afraid that someone might come her way, Carla stealthily returned to her work area. She didn't dare tell anyone what she saw, even Roy, although she wanted to let him know how fascinating her venture was. Carla was concerned how he'd disapprove of her seeing that. And that she had witnessed Levine doing what made him rich, watching people have sex in front of a camera.

While Carla was getting ready to begin work in another room, Jada stopped by to look at the finished great room. She was genuinely delighted with the results.

"Please keep in mind that when we're done, we'll go back and hang the pictures, arrange the furniture, and do other things to complete this room," Carla explained.

Seeking more information about the movie-making operation, Carla asked, "Your husband must make some wonderful movies to provide so well for you. I envy you for that. But I'm a little curious. Have you ever watched the filming of those movies that your husband makes? I mean, it must be fascinating to see the actors at work."

"Oh, I saw that ages ago, but David forbids me to get involved in that end of it anymore. I still screen many actors, but he doesn't like me to watch the actual filming. He feels that I am too much of a lady and doesn't want me to witness it. He says it's 'men's work'," Jada laughed.

"He promised me it doesn't turn him on, but I know it does. He lies to me about it, just like all the other men lie to their wives. They get a cheap thrill out of anything to do with sex unless it's at home. But look what it gets me, so why should I complain?" she laughed.

"And if it weren't for you, I would never have my home looking so grand. I can't wait to get the plans made for a wonderful housewarming party. I think I told you that David gave me his blessings on having one when you're all finished."

"Yes, and I'll bet it'll be spectacular. You must have some fantastic ideas for the party."

"You'll see for yourself, dear. I expect you and Roy to be here. I'll be sending you an invitation. After all, you made it all possible."

"Thank you so very much for giving me the job. I love doing it."

Chapter Twenty-three

THE HOUSEWARMING PARTY

Jada had been collecting reports on how well Cindy was doing in her films. She thought the actress could fit into the upcoming housewarming party. Being seen in person by theater owners could sell more movies in which she starred. Jada asked Donald to bring her into her office to discuss the event.

"You can meet several more of the actors and get to know them. I'll have a lovely gown made for you."

"I'd *love* to be there!"

"Good, and you'll be on your best behavior?"

"Yes, Madam, I'll watch my language to be sure."

"You had better, or else," Jada warned. "And that goes triple for not treating any of the men to a free sample. Donald will fill you in about what to expect, who'll you meet, and what to say. Anything he tells you is as though I said it, so don't forget that. You'll have to sell yourself, and I mean only as an *actress*, to these people so we can make more movies, and then you'll make more money. If you have any ideas for a dress, then make a sketch, and I'll take a look to see what we can come up with too. You both may be excused."

When Jada and Nona later met with the rising star, Cindy had a rough drawing of what she wanted to wear at the party, with Jada's approval, of course. And she did approve of it after a couple of "small" changes.

"Not so many sequins and make that in forest green. Skip the spaghetti straps and make it strapless. That way, she can show anyone who asks if those beauties are real or not." Jada devilishly smirked, "I think she'd like to do that, anyway."

"Nona, I want her brown hair dyed to a medium auburn. She can wear it down with soft curls swept over one shoulder. And she'll wear a diamond pendant with matching earrings and ring. If she loses them, her pussy will be on the chopping block.

"Oh, and be sure to tell Carla to wear something quite stunning, too. I'll need to introduce her as my decorator. I do look forward to this affair. It will be so spectacular!"

Jada and Carla stood at the center of the balcony, looking over the gathering of guests. When they saw her, many clapped their hands while others followed suit. Jada held up her hand for silence.

"Thank you all very much for coming to see my beautiful new home. I must introduce my fabulous designer and decorator, Ms. Carla Martin." They appreciated the loud applause.

Jada continued, "Do enjoy yourselves and help yourselves to the buffet table, but not the silverware." She bowed slightly to the laughter. "Eat, drink, and be merry, for tomorrow we diet!" She waved to their laughter and applause, and then turned to Carla. "Well, we did it, girl, the party is *on!*"

"This is a fantastic turnout, Jada," Carla said. "You sure outdid yourself, especially on the flowers and food.

Everything is just perfect. By the way, how are things going with your young starlet?"

"She is working out just fabulously. I'll have to see that she meets the right people so they can order the films David makes with her. I need to do my share to see that she makes my husband a lot of money for me to spend."

Carla nudged her, "My word, you are despicable, lady." She looked around the vast room. "But gosh, everybody who's anybody must be here. And all the gowns and jewelry are stunning."

"Yes, the women are always busy showing off their glitters to each other while the men talk business. We had better go down and mingle."

Before they reached the main floor, Jada pointed Stanley Fraiser out. "Be sure to speak with him. No doubt he'll want to know when you can start redecorating his home."

"If you see any stray men wandering about, they are some of my husband's soldiers posing as escorts. They are here to see that all this exceptional jewelry stays on the women's necks and hands. They are well-armed and will watch for pick-pockets too. Although, only those who show their invitation cards and sign the guest book will get by Mr. Blum. Of course, there are several people we don't need to check, like Stanley or you and Roy, for instance.

"Now, keep an eye on Sharon over there in the yellow gown. You'll notice that her dress will be showing more cleavage as the evening goes on. She likes to show her enormous beauties off to the young guys. And if I don't miss my guess, she will attract at least one of them pretty soon the way she puts the drinks away." Jada turned to a server.

"Donald, darling, ask one of your men to take Sharon out for some fresh air for a while and see that she doesn't drink too much this early. If she gives you any back-talk, tell her that's my order. Let's try to keep her sober for most of the evening. And then bring Carla and me a martini, please."

"Certainly, Madam." He relayed the message and returned shortly with their drinks.

Carla noticed Marni's husband looking around the room and nudged Jada. "I wonder if he's looking for his wife."

Jada excused herself to stroll over to her brother and lightly kissed his cheek, "Harry, my love, you look divine tonight. Marni must be so proud to be seen with you."

"Thanks, Jada. Speaking of the dear girl, have you seen her recently?"

"Oh, I think she's in the powder room, but have you seen David's newest starlet? She looks fabulous tonight. Cindy is going to be a big-name actress pretty soon. But she's a bit nervous since she doesn't know many people. Why don't I take you over to meet her? You can use that tremendous manly charm of yours to set her at ease and introduce her to other actors. You know how David needs her to be that one bright star right now."

"Sure thing, dear. I'll talk to the poor girl and get her settled. Where is she?"

"Over there in the dark green dress, talking to an escort. Come with me."

"But Jada, she doesn't even look old enough to be here."

"She's barely of age, but you men like fresh young things and don't tell me you don't."

While Jada made the introductions, Carla noticed that Stanley Frasier was looking around the room. She moved through the guests to join him.

They talked about the work she had accomplished throughout the mansion. Soon, Carla blinked her left eye.

Taking tissue from her purse, she blotted it. But it continued troubling her, to Stanley's concern.

"I think I have an eyelash in my eye."

"Let me see if I can get it out, my dear." He took the tissue and asked her to tilt her head back while holding her upper eyelid open. With a gentle touch, Stanley blotted her eye.

"There, I got it." They both looked at the tissue and eyelash. "But you have a little smudge of mascara under your eye. Do you have a mirror with you?"

While looking in her handbag, Roy abruptly made his way to her side. With a push on Stanley's shoulder, he demanded to know what the stranger was doing to his wife.

"He took something out of my eye for me. How dare you push my friend like that!"

Roy noticed the slight redness of her eye red and the mascara blemish. "Oh, I thought he was trying to kiss you."

"Around all these people? Are you *crazy*?"

"No, I'm sure he was just concerned that a stranger was admiring his beautiful wife a little too closely." He turned to Roy with his hand extended. "I'm Stanley Fraiser, a close friend to David Levine." He saw Roy's continence turned from anger to embarrassment.

"Oh, I'm so sorry. Carla told me something about you. Didn't you build David's casinos?" You're the one with all the mon... uh, real estate." However, Fraiser knew what he meant.

Then Carla spotted Senator Nichols and his wife looking her way and motioned them to join her.

"Stanley, I want you to meet my very dear friends, Senator Peter Nichols of Oregon and his lovely wife, Beth."

After praising Carla's work, Beth said, "You'll have to do something with Peter's office. It's so "office" looking, and an outdated one at that."

"I'd love to do that. It wouldn't take long at all, maybe just a couple of days. And then Stanley has next dibs for one of his homes."

"One? How many do you have?" Roy blurted. Carla tried not to show her embarrassment.

"I lease out some of them," said Stanley. But I keep another one where I stay during hot weather."

Roy couldn't help but ask if Stanley had any property to look into; areas where he could build more theaters. Stanley said he didn't know of anything at that moment.

"You might be like me, Stanley. I leave all that stuff at the office, and then I lock the door when I leave for the weekend."

He put his arm around Carla's shoulder. "She's been my best buddy since college. Carla introduced me to my beautiful wife. But I'll have to take the entire blame for introducing her to Roy," he laughed. Fraiser got the message.

Shortly, Peter and Beth excused themselves to mingle with others while Fraiser, Carla, and Roy strolled over to the buffet table where a man introduced himself to Roy. He wanted to talk about movie theaters, for which Stanley was grateful. It was challenging for him to be that close to Roy and not put a fist in his mouth.

When Roy turned away, Stanley told Carla, "I may not be staying long, my dear, but I'm so thrilled with what you've done with Jada's home. I do hope you'll consider working on mine when you recover from all of this. And tell Peter that I'm sorry that he introduced you to Roy too." Stanley kissed her cheek and squeezed her hand before turning away. She smiled and then moved back to join her husband, who was now alone.

"Do you *have* to embarrass me around my friends like that?" Carla quietly snapped at Roy.

"What did I say wrong? Can't I just talk with them?"

"You just can't snap at someone and then hit them up for business like that. Oh, never mind."

Carla left him to rejoin Jada, mildly complaining about Roy's behavior. That gave the hostess a reason to execute a dark plan.

She excused herself for a moment to take Donald aside and talk with him discreetly. "Don't you have a special friend who wanted to see Roy Jacobs?"

"Certainly, and I'm sure that Roy will be delighted to meet with him."

He sent an escort to speak to Roy, who then looked around for Carla. She was conversing with Jada, so Roy followed him to the patio. He opened a secret door to a dimly lit, small, and cozy garden. With a reassuring smile, the escort motioned Roy to step inside.

A very handsome young man warmly moved toward him. He slid his hand over Roy's shoulder onto his waist.

"I understand you would enjoy being pleased," he murmured. "It would thrill me to take care of you."

"Glen, what are you going here?"

"Hello, Roy, I was hired as an escort. I'm here with my girlfriend, called the Blonde Bombshell. It's not like we're strangers, now is it?" he purred. Glen ran his fingers over Roy's body and then to his groin. He felt the porno dealer become erect.

"Will you let me pleasure you again? I have a nice, fluffy blanket on the lawn. Let's lie down where I can take care of you. I'd like that very much."

Roy took off his jacket, "Who sent you here?"

"Oh, a friend said he knew you'd were here, and I wanted to show you a good time. I feel I owe you for referring us to Levine. We're both doing very well with him. So just relax, let me fulfill you, okay?"

Roy grinned, "I can't be gone too long. My wife will start looking for me."

"I don't think we should worry about your wife. I have somebody to distract her so she won't look for you. I thought of everything for your pleasure."

He did take care of everything. Another escort led Carla to a buffet table with tantalizing tidbits. Between nibbles, he made exciting conversation about interior designs. His straightforward, knowledgeable, and agreeable manner was refreshing for her.

Jada looked around the great room filled with guests guests and chatting with one another. She decided it was time to step up the pace and then spoke to the pianist.

"Yes, Ma'am, it's getting a little complacent. I think it's time to have Donald and his men turn the dining room into a dance floor. I'll keep playing until he gets the band set up."

In a second, all lights suddenly went out but came back on again when the emergency generators immediately started up. Above the gasps, Harry Philips called out, "Don't worry folks, everything's okay. David just forgot to pay the electric bill again!" Hearing the laughter, Harry looked around the great room to see that all "escorts" were at attention guarding the most critical guests and their wives or dates.

David, Jada, the Family, Mr. Blum, and his men knew what that meant. Someone had severed the power line. However, since this happened in the past, all soldiers knew their positions and what to do. In only a moment, all was calm again.

Jada looked around for her trusty head man. As ever, Donald had his eye on the lady of the house. Soon, he acknowledged everything was ready to begin the beguine.

When the bugle blasted out with "American Patrol," guests couldn't get to the dining room fast enough to kick up their toes and step a light fantastic. Guests set aside their inhibitions when they heard the very first licks of "In The Mood". It is now time to party!

Those who lacked the energy could dance to the lovely strains of "String of Pearls", or "Sentimental Journey", sung by a close-harmony quartet

Above the bugle blasts several people could barely hear a gunshot. That was quickly followed by Richard Hirsh yelling out, "Dammit, I told you not to shake the champagne before you open it!" Hearing laughter eased him, and he then quickly checked with Blum.

"They cut the line at the power pole. We had silencers on and took down two of their men. The one fired at us, but me and my men all have our vests on. We got everyone, though. The dogs went after the two guys who ran." A sadistic grin moved across his lips, "Early in the morning, I'll have two of my men go out there to clean up the mess and bury what's left."

"Fair enough," said Hirsh.

While she watched the dancers, Sharon took the decorator aside, leading her to a less crowded area. "Carla, darling, I've heard so many compliments on what you've done to this mansion. I know you'll get many calls for work from our friends down here. Your dress is utterly lovely, and *you* look so stunning too. I hope Roy appreciates how you look."

"He just mentioned that he liked my dress."

"Well, darling, many other men looked at you, that's for sure. I don't know if Roy said anything, but Richard wants to do a real high-class, uptown film with you in mink and diamonds. And it would never look like a porn film. He thinks your beauty can make a fortune on the silver screen. But I don't think David will allow a Family member to do that.

Carla turned to see if she was joking. She was not.

"Oh dear, I guess I spoke out of turn."

"No, Sharon, you didn't. I won't have anything to do with his disgusting porno garbage. I've worked too hard to become what I am now. However, until I find another job, I guess I'll have to put up with just being his wife."

"Oh, but Stanley Fraiser wants to hire you to work on one of *his* homes, remember? That'll keep you busy for some time. I'm sorry that I said anything. Let's forget about it and just enjoy the rest of the party. It looks like things are finally slowing down. Maybe I can get Richard to trip a light fantastic. We used to dance well together in our younger years. I'll bet we can *still* make it around the dance floor, or at least try. Now, just where is the old boy?"

Chapter Twenty-four

COPS AND ROBBERS

R oy had just walked into the house when his manager called to say there had been a fire started in the men's room of the Starlight Theater. Luckily, he caught it before it did much damage. Since everything was under control, he didn't need to call the fire department. Roy said he'd come in early to see to the matter.

The following morning, he found damage confined to the wall and floor. This was around the wastebasket where the fire was started. Fortunately, there was minimal smoke damage. Roy brought the matter up at the next Family meeting.

"Do you have an idea who may have started the fire?" Levine asked.

"No, but the ticket salesperson said there were three men he hadn't seen before who came in fairly late. I wonder if it may have been the Perez or Gorvetti men." Roy answered.

David sat back in his office chair. "It was not any of the Gorvetti men. We have an agreement with them. If it was not an accident, then it's probably the Perez people trying to get established in your area. They're more like a ruthless street gang, and I won't make any deals with them. They will not honor their word."

"I've heard that Perez has taken over a store north of Portland," said Hirsh. "Is that one yours?"

"No, my stores are right outside the downtown area."

"You mentioned once before that you have a couple of men up your way who can help you out. I'm sure you can handle this without us stepping in," said Levine.

Upon his return, Roy was informed some men had asked for the theater's selling price`. He was fuming when he got home that night. Since Carla was home, he ranted to her.

"I'll be damned if I let some little punks push me around like that! I'll get my two men up here to take care of those grease-balls!"

"You want to start a war with these guys? Just cool down and let me make a phone call."

Carla got Jerry Gorvetti's phone number from her purse. He was home.

She introduced herself with a sultry voice and a generous smile, which caused Roy to frown. "Hey, paisano, this is your old pal, Carla."

Jerry was delightfully surprised to hear from her again. He donned a full smile to ask why he was so honored by her call.

She explained the situation, saying that she was unhappy that somebody had damaged her fine theater decorating. She asked if Jerry could find out if it was the Perez boys. Jerry said he'd check on it and call her back.

Roy was stymied, asking how *she* could learn anything? Who did she talk to? How would she find out anything? Where did she...

"Don't ask, I won't tell, and it's none of your business. Oh, but get me a scotch and soda, please." The phone rang. Jerry said that it *was* the Perez gang. They wanted to make a deal.

"Can you think of a way to get them to meet me? Maybe I can get you into the good graces of some local boys with white hats." Carla smiled while ignoring Roy's questioning glare.

"What are you saying, my dear? You mean the cops?"

"That's right, good buddy. The one and only."

"You got a foot in the door?"

"Oh, I have more than just that, my old friend," she provocatively answered.

"Oh, wow, my little Carla is all grown up!" Jerry laughed. "I don't suppose the old man knows anything about this."

"And he never will, will he?"

"I didn't hear nuthin' about what you just said. I'm just deaf and dumb. So, what do I get out of the deal, sweetheart?"

"The all-clear. You'll get a 'Get out of jail free' card. Can you let me know in the next couple of days, one way or the other? I want to get those greasers out of the way as much as you do. Okay?"

"You got it, girl."

She hung up the phone to look at Roy with a grin. "So, where's my drink?"

Carla wondered if she could genuinely trust Jerry Gorvetti. It had been a long time since they were friends in high school. On what were his loyalties based? Was his word trustworthy? Who were his real friends, and where did he get them? There was one man in whom she could truly trust. Jim returned her phone call.

He was sorry to hear about the theater, although, excited to know about Perez, a man Jim had his sights on for a long while. Perez stepped up to the big league, the better-quality theaters, having gained all that experience and knowledge. The Starlight was one that he chose to conquer.

Through his police department, Sergeant Crawford found the information about Gorvetti; he stood more to gain for helping with an arrest of the Perez family than to stay on the dangerous side of the law.

When Jim called back, it was with apprehension that he asked, "Carla, do you *really* know who you're up against with Perez?"

She took a deep breath. "Well, he couldn't be any worse than Jerry Gorvetti or David Levine, could he? Or Roy Jacobs? They're all human beings with big flaws. Jerry was a kid who wanted out of the gutters and to make more of his life. He got it the same way as Roy and David did, he took it. Perez is a punk kid who probably has no weight to throw around without his backup thugs. So, what's there for me to be afraid of except fear itself? And I live with that daily with Roy. As long as I have you standing behind me, again I ask, what's there to fear?"

Jim looked down with a smile. "Thanks," he murmured. "First, you'll need to have Gorvetti arrange for Perez to meet you at the theater at a certain time with some cash, and then Tom and I will be there with you."

Carla agreed with that.

Jerry contacted Perez and he agreed to be there at noon on the coming Friday, so Carla called Jim that all was arranged.

After discussing it with his boss, Jim and Tom would pose as Carla's bodyguards, one on either side of her. Gorvetti and Perez could each bring two men along with them.

Jim Crawford made sure the wire she wore was in good working order when Carla sat behind the desk. After all, would any of the Perez men have the nerve to frisk her?

The meeting was set. Just in case there were questions, however, Jim placed a small tape recorder inside Carla's purse sitting next to her.

Every man would check their guns before coming into the office to discuss the merger.

"Are you shittin' me?" was Perez's answer. "How do I know you ain't got no undercover cops in there?"

"You can check everyone's I. D.," said Jerry.

"Yeah, and how do I know if that's real? That's as bad as asking me to trust *you*. We have our guns or no deal."

With a few "After you," "No, after you" exchanges, Perez and Gorvetti agreed to walk up the stairs together.

Perez was notorious for sneaking in some men who stayed out of sight men for these meetings. Crawford had two undercover cops hiding just around the staircase. The two officers each carried non-lethal dart guns to silently render the culprits unconscious.

When the office door was closed, the two Perez men approached the staircase. Darts pierced each one. However, the cops caught them before falling, thus eliminating any noise. After moving them into a squad car, the two cops then silently waited just outside the office door.

"I don't do no business with no broads. Ain't 'cha got no man I can talk to?" Juan Perez tried to sound tough with his two well-armed henchmen standing behind him.

Carla sat behind the desk. Leaning forward, her hands casually clasped together, she said, "The days of women being barefoot and pregnant are well over, Mr. Perez. I'm a businesswoman and have been for many years. It was my interior decoration that made this establishment so lovely."

She then sat back to look thoroughly at this man. "But I'm a little upset that you didn't appreciate my hard work."

He grinned with contempt. "So, you don't like the way I redecorated this place? I coulda' made a real bonfire out of this joint if I wanted to. But I only wanted you to have a little taste of what I can do."

Carla sat upright. "You only set a small fire to scare me?"

"Yeah, and it looks like it worked or you wouldn't be here."

"If you made a huge fire, then you wouldn't want to buy it all burned like that, would you?" she asked calmly.

"No, I woulda' waited until you cleaned it up first, stupid." Perez was caustically grinning.

"It isn't necessary to be rude. If you had only made an appointment with me, we could have avoided that mess and talked like two reasonable people. I'll bet you have a crucifix at the end of that chain around your neck."

"What if I do? What the hell business is it to you?"

Carla pulled the chain out of her blouse to show the cross she was wearing. "I just thought that since we worship the same man, we can honor Him by doing what He asked of us, to be kind to one another." That approach failed.

"Like I said, I don't do no busin..."

"Mr. Perez, I am giving you some credit for being a gentleman here. There's no need for threats, tempers, or guns. We can discuss this issue peacefully. I feel you owe me an apology for causing that damage to my work."

"You ain't getting' no apology outta' me, I want your movie house. I'll give you sixty grand for it."

"We both know that it's worth twice that amount, Mr. Perez."

"You don't impress me none with that 'mister' crap. You wanna keep arguin' about it? That'll just cost you, not me. So make up your mind, *lady*."

Perez looked at his two men and then at Gorvetti. "You think you got a handle on this little chat? I ain't that damn dumb. If you make the wrong move, I got men outside the door, *good buddy*," he sneered. "So, whatcha' think about them apples?"

"You got the cash, good buddy? Put it on the table."

Perez's head man opened the briefcase and dumped some cash on the desk. Crawford counted it.

"Looks like you're about five thousand short, good buddy."

Perez sneered, "It looks like you guys just took too long to answer. You got a title to give me?"

Carla reached into her purse as his two bodyguards made a move for their weapons. She smiled, "Feel free to look inside my handbag, gentlemen. I have no knives or guns in there. I only wanted to give Mr. Perez my card." When she handed it to him, he merely glanced at it. "Is this supposed to impress me, *lady*?" he smirked.

"That's just in case you need a decorator in the future. But perhaps you might be interested in my employer's card. I have redecorated several theaters for him, and he loves the work that I do. However, he was extremely displeased to learn that you don't." Carla handed Levine's card to him.

The man's visage suddenly changed. "How do I know where you got this? Maybe you stole it from somebody. It don't mean nothin' to me."

Again, Carla reached into her purse. "I'll show you a picture of my employer, and it's even autographed."

Perez took the picture of Carla standing between David and Jada Levine. He had written, "To our lovely Goddaughter, with love, David and Jada."

Now Juan Perez's continence changed drastically. "Yeah, well, so whadaya' want to talk about?"

"You want to buy my theater. You'll need to pay me more than the fifty-five thousand that you have there."

Perez put some cash into the briefcase. "I guess you don't like a good offer when it's sittin' right in front of ya." He turned to one of his men. "Let 'em in."

One of his men stepped backward to open the office door. "Boss wants you guys in here." The bodyguard hesitated as he began to draw out his handgun while watching that Gorvetti or his men didn't make a move. He turned his head slightly, "Now!"

However, the two men who stepped through the door with guns drawn were not who he was expecting.

Jim and Tom drew their pistols. "*Police*. You're all under arrest!"

"What the hell for?" shouted Perez.

"Arson, bribery, being discourteous to a lady, you name it!" Crawford snapped. "You all have the right to remain silent. If you give up that right anything you say may be held against you in a court of law. Do all of you understand that? And that includes you and your men, Gorvetti."

Jerry shot a glance of fury at Carla while he was being handcuffed. She smiled with a knowing wink. His composure eased as he tried to reassure his men. "Relax, guys, this will all be taken care of. Just do what the cops say."

They were not sure if he had betrayed them or if it was Carla, but they rebuffed both, as well as the cops.

When all the men were taken away, Jim walked back into the office, closing the door behind him. He took Carla in his arms, warmly kissed her, and then stepped back to look at her with a smile.

"Lady, you are one hell of a broad. Thanks for doing this. I'll see that Gorvetti and his men are set loose as soon as possible. But my boss will want to 'chat' with them first. It's up to him whether they get any time for this or not. But I'll tell him they were very cooperative. I'll also give them a *suggestion* to get out of this business, at least in this state."

He shook his head slightly. "I owe you for this." Jim quickly kissed her again and then joined his men in the arrest.

Carla sat back down with a smile, still feeling Jim's warm lips on hers. Then she put her feet up on the desk to think. After several minutes, she dialed a number.

"Hi, Jada. You'll never guess what I just did. Ya got a minute?"

Chapter Twenty-five

THE BEGINNING OF THE END

"You sound tired and weary. What's going on at home, dear? And don't lie to me. Your voice always tells me the truth. So, what's he been doing now?" Jada's gentle words sounded motherly over the phone.

Carla tried to speak, but words failed her momentarily because she knew she was at an impasse. "I just don't know what to do. It was bad enough for him to go on sudden trips, not telling me where he was going or not call while he was gone, but to come back and not talk to me. I can't take it anymore."

"Oh, not to worry, my dear. I'm certain Roy was merely hiding out while he's shedding his skin."

"Yeah, then he slithers into some broad's bed. It's the deceit, not the actual lying, just not saying anything to me. It's as though he wants me to have reason to start a fight. Carla put her hand to her forehead, rubbing it to bring some relief. Then she slumped back into the comfort of the over-stuffed chair.

"Have you ever thought of making him wonder what you're doing while he's gone?"

"What do you mean?"

"This dutiful, faithful wife stuff has gone on way too long, my dear. I mean, have you ever thought to make him jealous of you? You always worry about what he's doing. Why not just give it back to him like a pie in the face? Make Roy wonder what you're up to while he's gone. That bastard is not man enough to be a man at home," Jada pointed out. "I know this is a shock for you, but why does he avoid having sex with a sexy woman like yourself? Maybe because you don't have the plumbing that he likes."

"Jada, you're *crazy*!"

"Why would he sleep on the couch rather than in your bed? It's to avoid having sex. I know you haven't seen this in him before, but take my word for it, I've met plenty of other men like that."

"I can't believe that! Why in the world did he even marry me then?"

"Oh, I'm sure that he was in love with you in his own way. But he couldn't show it in the normal way a man does. And he needed to have a "handbag" on his arm to show others that he's normal. Now he expects you to whine, bitch, and cry when he comes home, and that gives him another excuse to avoid you. What would he do if you were all cheerful and pleasant?"

"He'd wonder why. Yeah, why am I worrying about what he does? I don't care anymore. I'm tired of fighting for his affection. I'm sure there are men out there who would want to be with me. Oh, I feel a little better now, thank you. I'll just ignore him the way he ignores me then."

"That's *if* you can do that, my dear."

More than a month had passed while the two tried to avoid one another. Roy tended to his movie theaters while Carla threw herself into her work. The tension between them began to dissipate but was still in the air when they were both at home.

Finally, Carla couldn't bear up under this agony any longer. She had no one else to turn to but God, whom she had left out of her life and thoughts for so very long. She got down on her knees by her side of the bed and began to pray. She asked for forgiveness in her neglect of the Lord and that He gave her the strength that she needed to deal with the husband that she vowed to love and cherish.

"I don't know how to love him anymore. I don't even know him anymore. Oh, Lord God, please guide me and give me the strength to hold up under all of this... this tension. Let me be a good wife to him, but *please* let him be a good husband to me in return. I just don't know what to do except to leave it all up to you. Please forgive my weakness, Lord God, but I need your help right now."

Carla heard Roy's footsteps as he came into the bedroom and again became fearful of him.

"What the hell are you doing down there, saying your *prayers*?"

Carla's hand nervously moved across the carpet. "I dropped an earring and was looking for it." She suddenly felt a metal object. Picking it up, Carla saw the gold earring she had lost some time ago. Holding it to her breast she murmured, "Oh, thank you."

"For what?" Roy demanded.

Carla stood to her feet to look at him. She firmly said, "I wasn't talking to you."

With quiet, renewed strength, Carla contended with Roy's gruffness. One day, he saw that his forceful personality no longer impressed her when she showed him indifference. Roy told her to get him a cup of coffee while watching TV from the couch.

"How about if you get it yourself? And you can get me a refill while you're up." Then Carla resumed sketching.

It took a long while, but things finally got back to normal between the two, whatever "normal" was for them. One morning Carla awoke with Roy's warm arm wrapped around her waist. He was amorous. His touches were gentle, and his body was inviting. She turned over to see him smiling warmly at her.

"Morning," he whispered. Carla smiled back.

This began a lovemaking session almost as fulfilling as they ever had. For the first time in many months, Carla was satisfied by her husband. He was also fulfilled. As they lay back together, Roy said he didn't want to go into the office at all that day, but he did. At least not right away.

While he showered, Carla put her on robe and made breakfast with a smile and a song on her lips. Afterward, she offered to trim his hair before he got dressed, which he appreciated.

After making a phone call, his mood seemed to change. However, he asked if Carla would trim and file his fingernails. She happily got her nail files, cuticle nippers, and hand cream together on a TV tray. As she trimmed his nails, she got a chilled sense in the surrounding air. Carla looked into Roy's face that was now glaring at her. She set the file down.

"What's wrong, dear?"

He bitterly said, "I wish I never discovered that position. It takes too much out of me, and you're just not worth the effort."

Carla wondered if she heard correctly. However, to see the piercing look on his face, she knew she had. *Why the sudden change? Was it that phone call?*

Her happiness abruptly drained. Her heart seemingly dropped to her stomach that now churned inside her. She looked into Roy's scowling face again. In only seconds her femininity, her womanhood, her desire were once again torn from her.

Looking straight ahead, Carla rose from the chair. She wanted to toss the tray in his face, although, she didn't dare.

Carla went into the guest bathroom, locked the door, and sat on the edge of the bathtub. And sat. She finally heard the front door firmly shut when Roy left the house. Carla sat there until her body felt chilled, and then went into the bedroom. Another kind of chill went through her while looking at the bed that was comforting and fulfilling only a short while ago.

Taking her pillow, Carla curled up on the couch and lay still, wondering what she had done to deserve that cold, cruel remark from her husband. She couldn't cry. She could only lay and wonder what made him say those horrible words to her, "... and you're just not worth the effort".

After another day had passed, Carla wanted to see Jim. She needed his comforting strength. When she called, Judy heard the stress in Carla's voice. "I'll call Jim and get right back to you."

Carla sat back, wondering how her life got to be such a mess. At least Roy was in Beverly Hills for a Family meeting. So, for two more days she was free of him.

The phone rang. "Jim said to meet him at the safe house at five, but he said he can't very stay long. He must be on a case."

Carla was waiting when Jim arrived at five o'clock, still in uniform. As they went inside, he didn't offer his usual big smile. After having sensed a heavy tension about him, she didn't approach him physically.

"I'll go in the back room and get the bottles."

When Jim returned, Carla had two glasses with ice on the table. He poured the drinks and sat down across from her. He leaned an elbow on the table and then ran a hand through his hair.

"Bad day?" she asked.

He nodded after taking a sip of vodka. "Yeah, it's been hectic." He had yet to look into her eyes. Carla thought something else troubled him.

"What is it, Jim?" He briefly glanced at her and then looked away. "Jim, you need to level with me. I can tell something is bothering you. Did you get fired? Tell me what's wrong."

With that, he sat back in the chair after taking a gulp of his drink. He had mixed feelings of responsibility, disappointment, and shame. *Come on, man. Dammit, ya' gotta tell her.* "Well, um, ... she's pregnant."

Stunned, all Carla could say was, "Oh. How far along?"

"A little over three months. I had no idea because we weren't, um, getting on that well to speak of. The wife knew we were close to a divorce. She didn't want me to stay with her just for that. And abortion was out of the question." Jim looked at Carla now with pain and sorrow in his eyes. She knew the choice he had to make.

"I hope you plan to stay with her. I know you wanted to have a family."

"Carla, I just... I can't..." She reached to take his hand. Instead, she laid hers on his forearm. He looked at her hand.

"Don't worry about me, Jim. We both knew that our situation wouldn't end by riding off into the sunset together." Carla didn't know where the words came from, she just said them. "You're going to be a father now, a daddy.

This baby can help you find what you once had together, and then your marriage will be strong again."

Jim moved his arm to hold her hand. His heart was still troubled. "What about you? I can't just up and walk away from you, Carla. I can't just blot out of my mind all that you've been to me. All the times together and how you made me feel wanted and needed. And I thought that's what you felt too."

"Jim, you *know* you made me feel that way. It's something that I'll cherish forever, and I hope you will too. But in time, it will fade as that baby grows, and as your marriage grows. Jim, you will never go out of my heart. We had a deep bond of friendship and love. It wasn't all physical."

"No, not at all. It was and still is inside of me. Right now, I'm scared to death even to touch you."

She pulled her hand away. "Then don't. You had to make a decision, and I respect you for doing that. You're honoring those vows you made to her. You have a fresh responsibility with that baby. Your seed, your flesh and blood, will come into this world. It's up to you to love, cherish, and raise that child." Carla tried her best to smile. "And brothers or sisters will follow."

"Yeah, I can't have just one child. That's not fair to any kid."

"How does your wife feel about having a baby?"

His attitude perked up slightly. "She's thrilled. Her sister's teaching her how to knit little things, and she's been looking in thrift stores for stuff so we can afford other bills that'll come along. She found an old crib that was in great shape and painted it white. She's even getting the spare bedroom fixed up into a nursery." His countenance changed for the better, although, Carla sensed something still troubled him.

"That's not all," she murmured. "What else is bothering you, Jim?"

He leaned both arms on the table. Jim looked into the glass that he spun around in his hands, and then sat back in his chair to cross a foot over his knee. He cleared his throat and ran a hand through his hair.

"Yeah, well..." Avoiding her eyes, Jim looked above her head, "I uh, that is, Tom and I, got transferred to the Portland PD. Actually, to a smaller precinct just west of Portland. The town's called Brent." Jim looked down at the glass again

Got transferred or asked for a transfer? That's very close to Trenton. "That's great, Jim. I'm sure you'll love it up there. Brent's a delightful town. And with a smaller police department, maybe you won't be working as much overtime. Then you can spend more time with your new family. There's a lot to do and see there, Brent's close to the ocean and mountains. It'll be a terrific new start for all of you."

Feeling less tense, Carla added, "Things are going to be good for you. And for me too, so don't even give that a thought. I have a lot of work to keep me busy, and I'm happy doing it. And I have some good friends to be with."

Carla stood up with a smile. "You better get back to work, mister."

He started toward the door, and then he turned to hug Carla. No kiss, just a quick, warm hug of friendship and comfort.

"We'll keep in touch?"

"You bet! Is it alright if I stay and have another drink? I'll lock up when I go."

"Sure." With a smile, he nodded, and then tipped his hat to her before leaving.

Carla poured a stiff drink and sat at the table again. Unable to hold the tears back any longer, she dropped head against her folded arms and cried, "Oh, dear God, please bless this wonderful man, and his marriage... he deserves it."

Chapter Twenty-six

THE ENDING

After work, Roy sat in his car not wanting to go home. He couldn't stand the friction between himself and Carla, even though he caused most of it. He drove around to find a bar with entertainment. At least he'd have something to occupy himself while he had a drink or two. *Ah, the hell with it.* He drove on home.

Since the house was dark, he assumed Carla asleep in bed. Keeping the volume low, Roy watched the living room TV and sipped on some brandy until he felt sleepy. Using just the bathroom nightlight, Roy undressed and found his way into bed, however, Carla wasn't there.

In his robe and slippers, Roy checked the guest bedroom, the office, and the lower floor. Carla's car wasn't in the garage. Confused by where she had gone, he went back to the living room, sipped on more brandy, and waited. By two A.M., she still hadn't returned. Feeling sleepy once more, Roy went back to bed.

The following morning, he noticed Carla had slept on her side, however, she wasn't home. Where had she been the night before, and with whom? He wasn't sure if he should feel jealous, worried, or angered. After a hot shower, he dressed and then went downtown to eat breakfast before starting his day.

Carla finished with her business and then returned home to see her husband had gone to work. The following day, she left before he came home. This went on for three days until Carla couldn't live this way any longer. On the third night, she waited for Roy to come home, even though it was getting late.

While sitting in the dimly lit living room, Carla tried to evaluate her life. Was a divorce inevitable, or was there a chance for reconciliation?

A phone call answered her question.

"Yes, is Roy there?" she purred.

"He's not home yet. Who's calling?"

"Linda, who else? Who are you?"

"His wife." His wife heard silence and then dead air.

Carla was lying on the couch when Roy returned much later. He snapped on a lamp before speaking. "You feel up to making me something to eat? I didn't have much dinner."

Not attempting to get off the couch, Carla slowly sat up. "What did you have to eat, Linda's pussy?"

As Roy's head spun around, his face turned crimson. He tried to answer, but the usual harsh remarks failed him. "*What*?" he demanded, but his voice had guilt, not terror, in it.

"Your girlfriend called while you were out. I guess she didn't expect me to be home."

Turning away from her, he snapped, "I don't know what you're talking about!"

"The hell you don't." She turned to cover herself with the blanket. "Go to hell and just leave me alone. And turn that damn light off!"

Carla was gone when Roy got up the following morning and asleep on the couch by the time he returned. Unseen daggers flew through the air, and there was silent grinding of clenched teeth. She was going to bide her time until she had complete control of her temper and thoughts before confronting him.

Carla was making breakfast when Roy walked into the kitchen wearing casual slacks and an open bathrobe.

"Carla, I love you." His meek voice was filled with what sounded like remorse.

With her back to him, she asked, "What do you want for breakfast?"

"Carla, I'm sorry," he muttered. "It's all over. It won't happen again. I really love you."

She took some eggs out of the refrigerator. "Yeah, well, what do you want for breakfast?"

"Carla, I really do love you. Please believe me."

"I heard you the first time. What do you want for breakfast?"

With tears in his eyes, he turned her around. "It's all over. It won't ever happen again, *I promise*. I'm very sorry, Carla."

"Sorry that you did it or sorry that you got caught?"

"Carla, I'm very sorry... I *do* love you."

She scowled, "Well, I don't love you anymore. You had to push and push. Just how much do you think I would take? You went way too far, mister. I'm filing for divorce. Now, what do you want for breakfast?"

In his eyes, she saw his heart burst, but it was too late. His deception had gone on too long. She turned and then heard him walk away, whimpering.

She said to herself, "Yeah, it's all over... until next time. And Linda wasn't the first one." She was no longer hungry, although, a nice scotch and coffee sounded good.

On the deck, Carla tried to relax in a lounge chair. While sipping her drink, she heard Roy's car drive away. *Yeah, run off and explain all that to your Don pal.*

It was then that she began to cry. This time it was not out of hurt, or frustration, or anxiety. She didn't know why, but the relief felt good, so she cried.

Peter filed Carla's divorce papers, although, he was concerned that she wasn't ready to withstand the upcoming battle with Roy. He had the money and influence to make the issue go badly against his soon-to-be former wife. Peter suggested moving closer to her parent's home where Eddie could protect her, although he was suspicious of her mother's overbearing influence with Carla.

After Carla gathered what she needed, Eddie moved her into the small apartment above the Vale Theater. She felt safe in the cozy quarters and was comfortable in taking over the theater's management while Eddie cared for the finances. Carla familiarized herself with the employees and their jobs to fill in on their days off.

When Peter heard that Roy found the corporation's ownership, he called for an employee meeting. Since Carla's husband was trying to find her they reassured everyone that Carla was the legal and rightful owner and their only employer. Roy Jacobs had no involvement in the theater or its employees. They did not have to answer to him under any circumstances.

"Is he that bad?" one young man asked.

Peter nodded. "He's that self-centered, egotistical, and that wealthy."

A young lady asked, "Why did you marry him, Carla?"

"He wasn't like that when I married him. He was kind and thoughtful. I thought we were both very much in love with each other. My advice is to have a long engagement so you can have an even longer marriage. But some lessons are only learned first hand," Carla sadly answered.

Two weeks later, Roy came in as a paying customer. He watched part of the show and then found his way to the office. When Carla answered the door she was taken aback to see Roy. He appeared apologetic and humble, asking to come in and just talk with her. Unsure of him, she sat behind her desk, offered him a chair, and waited for him to speak.

"I've missed you. I just can't sleep anymore." Roy expected an answer. He didn't get one.

"I realize I have no right to be here, but I just had to see you again. I'm sorry that I messed up so badly and I know that I was in the wrong. I wasn't being straight with you, and I guess I deserve what I got, so please forgive me. I still love you."

Carla continued to listen while watching his body language. His fingers were steady, not twitching. He was looking straight ahead, not downward. His leg was crossed. These were signs of his self-assuredness, not humility.

Carla sat back in her chair and continued to look at him. "Just exactly what do you want, Roy?" Her voice was steady and firm.

"I just want to talk with you, Carla."

"About?"

He didn't expect this restrained attitude from her. "About us, about how I can make up for what I did wrong."

"Exactly what did you do wrong, Roy?"

"I made you upset with me. I failed you as a husband, as a lover. Although, I provided well for you. I gave you a wonderful home, plenty of work, and a good social life, but I still failed you."

"You have that all wrong, Roy. I gave you a gorgeous home and a better income from the theaters that I redecorated for you. Except for their wives, the social life you gave me was with a Mafia — a well-dressed gang of thugs and killers. All of you men tended to your 'business' and left us alone. And we waited for you to come home and be a husband to us lonely wives".

"Do you think I could not have found other work for myself? Let alone a better husband? Now, I ask you one more time, Roy Jacobs, who wouldn't wear a wedding ring, what do you want?"

Carla looked into the eyes of the man she once knew, trying to see what was behind them. A man's eyes are the window to his soul, but what is there to see if he has no soul? She waited for his answer, seated safely behind her desk.

"Carla, I just want to talk with you, to be with you. Please, just come and have a drink with me so we can talk."

"I'm here now and I'm listening. So, talk."

"It's uncomfortable for me to say the things I want to say in this environment. I just wish you can give me a chance to make up for it." He looked at her with sad eyes. "Please, Carla."

"Make up for what, Roy? You didn't answer my question. Just how did you wrong me? Tell me what you did wrong."

Saying nothing, Roy bowed his head and then stood up. "I'm sorry. I just hoped that... never mind," he murmured and then turned toward the door.

"Well, since you went through all the trouble to find me, then look me up if you think of something to say, besides how sorry you are."

After Roy walk through the door, she relaxed her tight stomach muscles.

Carla waited for a couple of minutes in case he returned. Then she looked out the window to watch him turn the corner. Soon, his car passed. Carla sat down in her comfortable office chair. *The son-of-a-bitch. He'll come back, maybe with an answer then. Maybe not.*

Roy continued to pursue Carla by sending her flowers, calling her, and coming to see her. Reluctantly, she finally agreed to have dinner with him at a restaurant notable for fine dining.

While Carla finished dressing for her date, the doorbell rang. A delivery man carried in an exquisite bouquet and a large box.

The enclosed card read, "I should have given you this long ago. With all my love, Roy." Inside the box was a full-length, Canadian mink coat, and it fit perfectly. She couldn't get to a mirror fast enough to see her full image. It was stunning, and with Richard Hirsh's label in it.

Carla draped the coat over the back of the sofa before finishing any last touches. She wanted to look perfect when Roy picked her up.

The doorbell rang, and she greeted him joyfully.

After helping her into the mink coat, Roy stepped back in admiration. He smiled, "You do that justice."

The restaurant conversation was reasonably light with mentions of David and Jada and, of course, Richard Hirsh. While having after-dinner cordials, Roy presented Carla with a small velvet box.

"I saw this and I just had to get it for you."

She opened the box to find a spectacular three-carat oval ruby surrounded by three rows of smaller, sparkling diamonds.

As she stared at the ring, Roy smiled to see Carla beaming. She fought back the tears to slip it on her right-hand ring finger. It fit perfectly. Carla could see that this man was again the man with whom she had fallen in love many years before; the gentle one, the thoughtful one.

Looking into his eyes, Carla whispered, "Thank you, Roy, it's gorgeous. I love it." Again, she gazed into the dazzling diamonds that flashed tiny rainbows of color at her and smiled.

When they finished their drinks, Roy proudly helped her into the luxurious coat. At her apartment, Carla thanked him for the lovely time and beautiful gifts. Then she gave him a quick kiss.

Inside, Carla took a deep breath and then sat to ponder the night. With a serene smile, she gazed at the ring while stroking the soft mink fur.

So why now and not back when he first… oh, well, better late than never, I guess

Chapter Twenty-seven

THE BETRAYAL

Again, Roy courted Carla. His sense of humor picked up. Although, from what little he had, anything would have been an improvement. And Carla thought he was trying to better himself.

They had dinner at the finest restaurants before attending concerts. Roy escorted her to stunning museum openings, a red carpet Golden Globe Award show, and the Met Gala, where the theme was 'Royal History Passed'. Roy and Carla reprised themselves as King Louie and Queen Antionette, in Versailles' high fashion of the day, which included the queen's plume-trimmed powdered wig.

Roy gave Carla ecstatic evenings to remember. All this lead to an occasional romp in the rack, where Roy had improved. Perhaps, as he told Carla, it was from all the books he had read. Whatever the reason, she didn't complain. He was making her feel complete again. That kitchen grew inviting to her, and the master bedroom tugged at her heartstrings. Yes, she was ready to move back home. It was time to call Jada and tell her the good news.

"Oh, really? Now, are you thinking with your head and not your panties?" her dear friend asked. "I suggest you take it slow for a while longer. See how long this 'courtship' lasts.

If you go back too soon, you will look too eager. How do you know that he won't start right back up again with the way he treated you before?"

"Oh, you should see the way Roy is now. He's just like he was when I first fell for him. My word, he really *has* changed, Jada. I'm so thrilled to have gone to all those unique places. The Met Gala was outrageous! And all those costumes were out of this world, but we fit right in. You should have seen how Roy strutted his stuff. He loved being seen dressed like that!

"Jada, I can't believe how much he's changed. He gave me that gorgeous mink coat that Richard made for me, and you know what fantastic work *he* does. And the ruby and diamond ring is far more than beautiful. You have to see it, Jada. The diamonds alone are fabulous."

"I *have* seen it, my dear."

"What are you talking about? *When* did you see my ring?"

Jada described it down to the eighteen karat white gold. "Some dummy was trying to sell it, but it was just too hot for anyone to wear down here. David was heartbroken that you two split up, so he "suggested" that Roy buy it for you. It was about ten cents on the dollar here, and he knew better than to turn down his Don, so he bought it. My husband told Roy that he'd love to see it on you the next time you come down here."

"Yes, I know exactly what he meant. That Roy had better give it to me if he knew what's good for him," said Carla. "I've gotten to know that much about David." She slowly shook her head, "That son-of-a-bitch lied to me again. At least he gave it to me and the mink coat."

"Well, my darling sweet angel, do you want to know about that fur coat?" She did, so Jada continued. "That bastard had the nerve to bring some whore down this way, and he took her into Richard's salon on the pretense of finding something nice and furry for her.

Richard showed Roy a hot mink coat, you know, one that had been stolen. It was too chancy to be seen in it around here. Richard would have to take it apart and completely remodel it. That was too much work to do, so he showed it to your loving husband. Roy took him aside to say he'd come back to get it later. Richard only had to change the lining and put his label in it. That's the one he gave you.

"And, since Roy didn't get the tramp a fur coat, he took her to an auction and got her a diamond pendant to go with some diamond some earrings that he already gave her," Jada said.

"That rotten scoundrel! I'll bet he stole the earrings right out of my jewelry box because I went to wear a pair and couldn't find them."

"You might see what else you're missing. Like the mink jacket that Roy stole from another whore and gave to you." She heard Carla gasp.

"That was my wedding present! He told his mother that he stole it from an old whore, so we thought he was joking. That son-of-a-bitch!"

"Darling, Roy doesn't want you, he just doesn't want anyone else to have you. He can't stand that you dumped him. His giant ego has been bruised. And, yes, I'm going to tell David about the kind of man he has on his team. The only way I learned about this was from Sharon. Richard was scorching mad that Roy brought that little tramp down here for 'the boys' to see. They knew what she was.

"I will not let my husband get into any trouble by having someone without morals or scruples working that close to him. All it would take is to have a gun put to his head, and Roy would spill his guts to anyone.

"Carla, use that horrible man while you can. Get that house away from him and get whatever else you can get. Get all your ducks in a row before you say anything or sign for divorce because he can make it very nasty for you. But, not while David and I have your back."

When Jada finished her advice, Carla realized what a big mistake she was making once again. Roy had not changed.

"Oh, my lord, Jada, you're right. It was his big ego that was hurt, not his heart. That man is so narcissistic it's a wonder he lets anyone into his life. Why couldn't I see that?" Carla asked.

"Because you're too close to see what's happening. Do you have any projects that you can get away from? I'd like you to come down here for a few days, if not longer. You need to get away from that man for a while."

"I only have a couple of things to wrap up. Eddie can take care of the Vale Theater for me. I don't want Roy to know where I am, though. Got any suggestions?"

"I certainly do, my dear. Stanley would love to see you again. That man will protect you because he cares for you and wants to see that you're happy. He can even take you for a little spin on his yacht. You won't be doing any work down here. I'll call our old friend and let him know that you're coming. And you can always stay in my guest house, Roy won't ever know."

Carla put Roy off to finish her projects before saying she had an emergency call from Mr. Stanley Fraiser. She knew Roy wouldn't check on him.

In her absence, Eddie would manage the Vale Theater. Carla was consulting with her brother when a worker saw the ring she was wearing.

"Carla, that ring is *beautiful*! Is that a new engagement ring?"

Carla looked at it and smiled. "No, actually, it's my new divorce ring."

Jada Levine was sure to talk to her husband.

"Not now, dear. I have several matters of importance on my mind," was the wrong answer.

She knew what some of these matters were since Donald had a particular, and peculiar way of finding out that the IRS was close. It was time to tighten up the ranks, firm up the guards, and close up the books.

"*David,* you must listen to what I have to say."

He stopped what he was doing and sat upright, not turning to look at her. '*David'?* The only time she ever said his name in that tone of voice was when it was of prime importance; like the first time she found out that he had been having an affair with a cute little starlet, which he called "friendly meetings". Naturally, he denied that, and naturally, she began divorce proceedings. But that was resolved, at a price, many years ago.

"This about your Roy Jacobs. "This about your Roy Jacobs. I just talked to Carla and he's at it again. After finally taking her to some exciting places, he's trying to get her to move back home. He lied about that ring and the mink coat. He let her believe Richard made it for her, and he bragged that he saw the ring and bought it for her. I just had to set her straight before she moved back into the house with him. I just couldn't let him do that to her again. He is evil.

"I asked her to come down here for a little while and bring that ruby ring and mink coat with her. I don't want that man to get his hands on her again. You need to cut him loose before he drags you under." Her voice was adamant.

Now David turned to look at her. To his relief, she didn't have her hands on her hips. "I will do that, dear. I wanted to speak to Harry and Richard about him, at any rate. They reported that Roy had disgraced our Family because of his inability to hold his marriage sacred. To behave that way toward a woman such as Carla is a disgrace. Is there something else that you feel I should know?"

Jada's voice softened into that of a caring wife who respected her husband. "It's just that Carla is about to fall completely apart under this strain. I asked her to come down here for a while. Do you think it wise to say something to our dear friend, Stanley? He has been particularly concerned for her."

David leaned back to consider his answer. "I think this would be more of a personal matter that he'd prefer to discuss with you. Since we haven't seen him in a while, perhaps you can invite him for dinner. And you might mention that Carla's coming to visit. Maybe Stanley would like to talk with her about decorating his home. That would certainly interest him. It pleases me that you are so concerned for our dear friends, my good wife."

Jada responded with a gentle smile and a tender kiss. "I appreciate your saying that, my good husband. Thank you for taking the time to talk with me, dear."

"It was my pleasure, darling. Is there anything else?"

"Oh, yes, there is, now that you asked. I think you need to talk to your new little star. It seems that Cindy has been overstepping her boundaries around some of your men, including Richard and the hairdresser. He complained to me while he was doing my hair. She wouldn't want to have her pretty face marred by some angry wife's fingernails."

David knew this was something he should address. "I will look into that."

The next day David called his partner aside to ask about Cindy's recent activities off the set. Richard acknowledged the girl had approached him in a more than suggestive manner, and the word had gotten back to his wife.

David shook his head. "The last thing I want to happen is to let any wife loose on one of our girls, let alone my star. I don't have anyone that good to replace her. Check with the hairdresser, see what happened there."

The stylist told Richard that the young star showed a close interest in him.

"I thought she was just feeling horny and told her that my girlfriend would get pretty upset if I stepped out of line. I think she took the hint. She's getting her makeup done now for the shooting today. Did you want to see her?"

"No, I certainly do not. Not without my wife present. Why don't you check on them, and then send her over to the set as soon as she's finished, then. "

The makeup artist was having difficulty with Cindy sitting still long enough to get the eye shadow perfected. She was extruding pheromones as her fingers reached toward his crotch.

"Now, honey, you simply must stay still so I can get you looking beautiful for that camera."

She grinned, "Oh, how can I sit still with you standing so close to me?"

"Well, darling, I want to get you looking beautiful. So, just put your hands on your lap and let me finish with this pretty face," he gently scolded.

She sighed while touching his zipper.

The artist stood up straight. His finger gently touched under Cindy's chin, tilting her face to look up at him.

"Now darling, I don't think you want to look in there," he said with a comely smile, "because you will find that I have the same plumbing that you do. Now just put your hands back on your lap and let me do what I get paid to do. Or I'll just have to break your little fingers right off." Message understood.

Afterward, Cindy strolled onto the set where everyone was waiting for her. She slowly walked past Richard with an enticing smile that suddenly faded as she watched Sharon and Jada sit next to their husbands. The star moved onto the set to begin the filming.

Cindy was lying on top of her partner during the shoot when she turned to look at the film crew and then sat up.

"I can't do my best work while women are watching. They put me off my game."

Levine sternly told her, "You are an actress, and I'm paying you to *act*, not play games. Now, I want to see some damn good acting out of you!"

She glanced at Richard Hirsh, although, saw only his wife's sharp glare. Jada sat next to her husband with a knowing smile on her lips. Suddenly, Cindy remembered Jada was her actual boss. She turned back to her partner.

"Where were we?"

"You were laying on me, and I'm going to turn you over." When he did, with his back to the camera, his cheek was next to hers. He whispered in her ear. "You better do a damn fine job of acting because if I lose my job over this, I'll have your ass. And that won't be very pleasant either." With that, Cindy performed her best acting role ever.

Jada called about Carla's flight arrival, and to invite her for dinner Saturday night. She would join Sharon, Marni, Jada, and their husbands. Stanley Fraiser would be Carla's escort, so a lovely dinner dress would be in order.

Carla chose a gown to go with the new ring and her diamond earrings. By adding one of Jada's ruby necklaces, Carla was stunning and even more so in Stanley's eyes.

The Levine's elegant dinner was served in the stunning dining room that Carla had designed. The table was set with fine linen, china tableware, sterling flatware and service ware. The platinum-rimmed crystal stemware added sparkle to the setting, while a low centerpiece of flowers and candles added warmth.

Carla saw more of a "regular" family revealed this night when all were light of heart and full of spirit, and not just the liquid kind. She viewed Stanley as a more amiable man. He joked, exchanging fast quips with Harry and Richard while David slapped the table in outrageous laughter. Even Jada laughed with tears down her face. Carla had forgotten what it was like to have fun and be with desirable people who no longer needed to guard their conversation or words. Each person enjoyed a delightful time with one another.

Stanley urged everyone to not overeat. After dinner, they would be his yacht club guests for dancing and gaming. To that, David Levine offered a toast.

When it was time to leave, they took the limousine to Stanley's home where his helicopter was up, running, and ready to dash everyone off to the club.

There, Stanley saw Carla's eyes glance from one wall to another, from one area to another, from one fixture to another while they were being seated.

"I see that you have all the new furniture and chandeliers picked out," Stanley teased.

"Was I that obvious?" she blushed.

They enjoyed more conversation and drinks while the band played. Stanley seemed to amaze Carla more as the evening passed. To her enjoyment, she found him to be an excellent dance partner. Although, Stanley couldn't hold her as close to himself as he wanted. He wouldn't betray his God or himself by interfering with Carla's marriage vows.

When the night's fun slowed down considerably, Stanley asked if everyone would go for a brief walk with him. They moseyed outside to the mooring area where he pointed out his "Yoat".

"Your what?" Carla asked.

"I think it just sounds too pompous to refer to her as a yacht, and she certainly is much more than a boat, so I call her my Yoat,"

He turned to the others. "What about going for an outing tomorrow? I want to get our lovely lady away from everything and take a run down the coast to see if the salmon are biting."

"The salmon?" Harry questioned.

Stanley chuckled, "That's just in case we don't see any marlin."

The date was set. Everyone would converge on his home by mid-morning, or as Marni said, "At the break of noon."

This was an event to go down in Carla's memory book. The graciousness of the host, the comfort of friends, the camaraderie of gal-pals, and the thrill of it all! The excitement and exhilaration for Carla to enjoy and cherish was without scope.

Fishing was included. It was the first time she tried to reel in 'a big one', and all by herself while the others cheered her on.

"Pull up! Now reel, okay, let it go back. Pull it up and reel, that's it, faster, faster!" cried Richard. "Come on, girl, you can do it."

"She's got it! Someone grab the line and get the net!' Stanley yelled.

Sharon jumped around the deck, clapping her hands. "She did it! Look at that beauty! Oh, wow, Carla, that's a *big* one!" It was twelve-pound salmon.

Exhausted, Carla dropped back into the chair and squealed with delight when the others poured champagne over her head. They officially indoctrinated her into the Yoat's fisher-woman hall of glory. And guess what they had for dinner?

In the late evening, while the "crew" relaxed over brandy, Stanley asked Carla to stroll on the deck with him. They enjoyed the setting sun and the orange hues it cast as it fell away into the sea.

While leaning against the rail, he could feel her shiver. Stanley shed his jacket to place around her shoulders. When she looked into his eyes, she saw the depth of his care and concern for her as he drew the collar close around her neck.

"Thank you, Stanley," she murmured. "That's sweet of you."

Save for the splashing of gentle waves against the side of the Yoat, the evening was still. Carla wrestled with the words she wanted to say. Leaning against the rail, she turned to Stanley.

"I haven't said anything before, and I *may* be out of place by asking, but I wonder how you can remain so close to David when he's involved with a pornography mafia that kills people."

Stanley laughed. "I think Roy has filled your head with tall stories, darling. David is *nothing* like that. Our fathers started in business when we were just youngsters, and we grew up together as friends throughout the years. My father built his father's casinos, just like I built the ones for David. Somehow he progressed into the pornography field, which has proven very lucrative. They sell tickets, and he makes money. I don't approve of those kinds of movies, but a *mafia?* No, not at all.

"And I certainly can't see a man like David being involved with anything like murder. So, put those thoughts out of your mind, dear. Roy is an egotistical man who wants to be recognized as being extraordinarily important. He'd most likely tell you all kinds of things that make him feel that way, to you at least."

Carla couldn't possibly mention what she had witnessed in the desert or repeat Jada's words. That would destroy either his opinion

of David or herself, so she accepted his answer and remained silent.

The next day, with Stanley's help, Carla brought the Yoat into port. The excursion ended all too soon, but everyone promised there would be more in the future. However, she first needed to tend to her responsibilities. And Stanley understood and respected her for that because he had to make the same choice for himself years prior. Decisions like that got him where he was. They also taught him how virtuous patience could be.

Carla promised to be back. The visit was exciting for everyone, and the parting was sweet sorrow, but more so for Stanley. This time the distance between them would only be measured by miles.

Chapter Twenty-eight

THE FALL OF ROAMING ROY

Levine, Philips, Hirsh and their bodyguard met to discuss the disgrace recently brought upon them. The Don wanted opinions on what to do about Mr. Jacobs, the man who knew too much. And Roy was well aware that Blum's capabilities could bring any man to his knees, and his silence.

Several subjects might disgrace Roy in return. One being that his wife brought down the two most notorious men in the porno pirate game. She confronted those men face-to-face, and without Roy there to back her up; not that he had the manhood to do it. She had put her faith in the Almighty God whom they all worship, or say they do.

Jacob's infidelity became a Family matter because he had involved them in his indiscretion. These were men who cherished marriage and family above all else. At least *their* affairs were discrete.

The men considered Jacob's situation and their options on dealing with it before Harry notified him Wednesday evening.

"Roy, we have a meeting set for Friday at ten A.M. And I expect to see you there," was all he said.

"Yes, sir," Roy answered, and then Harry abruptly hung up.

They generally gave more notice, so what's up? Must be something pretty important going on.

He caught the flight to Los Angeles, but nobody was there to pick him up as usual, so he rented a car.

At the meeting, everyone was very somber, but not everyone was there, to Roy's unspoken curiosity.

After Levine called the meeting to order he said, "It is my understanding that the Perez and Gorvetti people are now out of the way."

"Yes, they are, sir," Jacob's vaunted

"And how so?"

"I know that Juan Perez was arrested in Salem and is now in prison with several of his men. Apparently, Gorvetti was in on the arrest in some manner, but he was released for being a state witness."

Philips turned toward Levine to murmur, "Shall I tell him what took place?"

The Don leaned back in his large office chair. Looking upward, he took a puff from his cigar and hesitated. And then, with a slight motion of his hand, he said, "Harry, you know how I hate to hear about suicides." Even Blum couldn't keep a straight face.

Jacobs looked around with a sheepish grin. "Did I miss out on something?"

Hirsh said, "You'll figure that out in due time."

Philips told of the FBI and the IRS investigations into the Levine Corporation. They sought information leading to contraband movies that crossed state lines and corporations that filmed minors.

The foremost subjects were then discussed;

1. The people who regularly worked in their films would be the only ones to trust.

2. The Levine Film Production movies are the only films their Family stores would now show; having had trouble with boot-leg film could have cost Levine his license.

3. All extra actors would be on unpaid vacation. Speaking of vacations, maybe Mr. Jacobs would be interested in taking one, perhaps to Europe?

Roy loved that idea. "I never took my wife on vacation. I'll do just that when she returns from the job presently she's on. I'm sure she'd love to see London again." Jacobs expected a better response than their chilled expressions.

"Where is your wife working?" asked Philips.

"I believe she's working on one of the homes of an old real estate tycoon," Jacobs answered with pride, having forgotten the man's friendship with David. "I expect she'll make a good deal of money from *that* job."

"Do you measure your wife's ability by income?" Hirsh asked.

"Well, no, it's just that she's never taken on a client as wealthy as this one. I just thought that he'd be pretty generous with her. She's extremely talented and worth every penny she earns."

"With all the money you have, Jacobs, why is your wife even working?" asked Levine.

"She loves the work. As I said, she's very talented, and people pay her well for what she does. Well, sir, like when she remodeled your home. It makes her happy to do that kind of work."

"And where does all of her money go, Jacobs?"

Roy Jacobs became uneasy. "I have my account, and Carla has hers, although it *is* marital property."

"I would strongly advise that you each keep your accounts separate. Wouldn't that be best for both of you?"

"Yes, Mr. Levine, you're right as usual. Thank you for that suggestion, sir."

"That was not a suggestion, Jacobs. Although, I believe Mr. Philips has some suggestions."

Roy realized this part of the meeting was about him. His stomach muscles tightened and his throat became dry. Levine watched him reach for the glass of water, noting how he tried to appear composed.

"I was not at all happy when Richard told me about your visit to his fur salon recently. You seemed to have been with a, um, "lady" other than your wife. Is there a particular reason you had to be seen with this, well, *lady*, in this area? Are there no furriers in Salem or Portland?" Philips calmly asked. Although, Jacobs knew he was getting his ass chewed out royally. He had to quickly come up with an appropriate answer.

"I was down this way on business and this young lady was interested in a fur wrap. I wanted her to patronize Richard's salon and keep the money in the Family. This ..."

"How dare you to sit there and lie to me, Richard, and Mr. Levine about this little tramp? We know that she's nothing but a *whore*, and you carried on with her the same way you did with your other mistresses, underhandedly! You just had to show us you can have someone other than the woman that you disgraced... your wife! And in doing that, you disgraced the Family and your Don.

Roy knew the power of this Family, and how they could learn about anyone's personal life. He also knew it only took one of the many soldiers in this Family's army to meet him at any time, and for his last time. His answers now had to be truthful.

Philips continued. "The only reason that you have the privilege to even breathe today is that you hold too much prominence in Portland and Salem than to have Mr. Blum take care of you the way he could. We know Carla would be the first one that the cops would blame and we'd never let that happen to her. And, for your concern, your beautiful wife is now in the company of, and working for, Mr. Stanley M. Fraiser. He's been a long-time friend to Mr. Levine. You speak in disrespect of a man who earned where he is today, and on his own. You could have done that yourself, Jacobs, but your arrogance and monumental ego could only be for yourself!"

Philips sat back to take a deep breath and regain his composure.

Setting an arm on the table, Hirsh leaned forward with a reaffirming hand gesture to Roy.

"Look, Jacobs, we suggest you take a nice long vacation in Europe. It's such a big country, and there's a great deal to see. Take this young lady with you, and spend some time there, maybe about three or four months. Seriously consider what you want to do with your young life. Think about getting out of this business altogether and do something else." Hirsh spoke as though he were a father chastising a young and very naughty son.

"Forget about Carla and let her have her own life before you wreck hers entirely. Do you understand where we're coming from? You've had things your way most of your life. Just stay away from Carla and take care of yourself.

"Maybe you can take your parents to Europe with you. I think they would enjoy that kind of trip with their only son. Roy, you had your bit of 'fun' with our Family, now have fun with your family. Okay?" Hirsh sat back, waiting for an answer.

"Yes, I think they would like that very much. Thank you." Jacobs looked at the other men who stared at him in acrimony.

He muttered, "I humbly apologize to all of you, especially to Mr. Levine, for causing the disgrace that I've brought upon the Family. I have done you a great injustice..."

Before he could finish being humble, Philips accepted his apology and then excused him.

"Mr. Blum will see you to the airport, a reservation was made for you."

"Thank you, but I have a rental car to return."

"Don't worry about that. One of Mr. Blum's men will take care of it," Philips said.

Seeing Roy's face lose all color, Hirsh added, "Oh, Mr. Blum won't harm you. We just want to give you a comfortable ride to the airport and make sure you get there safely. I'm sorry that things couldn't have worked out better, but your service was good while we had your allegiance."

With ice on his tongue, Levine said, "You have a nice vacation, Jacobs."

"Thank you, sir." Roy was not at all ensured of his well-being, or his life, as he left the room.

Having known other men in that same situation, Blum asked, "Would you care to use the men's room before we leave, sir?"

Jacobs nodded and then went into the bathroom to relieve his loose bowels. Blum waited, and then walked him to the Rolls-Royce and opened the back door for him.

To Roy's surprise, the car headed for the Levine mansion, leaving him to question why. Blum said it was Mrs. Levine's wish. Once there, he escorted him to the viewing room where Jada was waiting with Donald, who greeted him.

"Hello, Roy. Scotch rocks with soda?" After Donald gave him the drink, Jada motioned for Roy to sit.

"I'm sure you recall the big housewarming party we gave after your lovely wife re-finished my home. So, I want you to see some of the movies we made during the party. I think you'll enjoy this, Roy."

Blum dimmed the lights as Donald started the projector. The film began with Jada and Carla greeting the guests from the balcony and then on to the ladies in their glamorous gowns and sparkling jewelry. It also showed the beautifully decorated buffet' tables. There were several highly renowned people, many of whom Roy recognized. One was Stanley Fraiser speaking with Carla. Roy shivered to see himself push the wealthy man away from her.

Then the movie showed the many guests mingling and chatting. In a short time, Roy saw himself getting "mingled" by Glen in the secret garden. Roy gulped down his drink before the film ended.

"Roy, I hope this is enough for you to know better than to go near Carla again. If I learn that you have caused her any trouble at all, and in the least amount, we will show this film in movie theaters all around Salem, Portland, and Los Angeles. If that's not enough, I will show this to my husband. Then he *will* send Mr. Blum to see you. Now, do we have an agreement?" Jada asked. That really wasn't a question.

Blum escorted Roy to the car where there was no conversation until they arrived at the airport. Before Roy got out of the vehicle, Blum turned to Roy with a stern look.

"I hope you take our suggestion of a vacation in Europe and stay away from Miss Carla. I don't want to have to look you up because you know only too well what I'm capable of. You have a pleasant flight home now."

Roy nodded as he got out of the Rolls and then cursed Carla under his breath with malice on his tongue.

Chapter Twenty-nine

ENOUGH OF THIS

The Vale's concession worker raced to her employer. "Miss Martin, are you feeling alright? Maybe you should sit down." Her grandmother had sudden spells like this, although, Carla wasn't nearly that old.

The young woman grabbed a chair from the counter and pushed it toward Carla. "Here, sit down, Ma'am."

"Thank you, I think I will."

The girl offered a cup of water. "Just sip on it, Miss Martin." *Oh, that sounded bossy.* "I'm sorry, ma'am, I didn't mean to sound like I'm giving you orders..."

Carla held a hand up, "Don't worry, honey. I didn't take that way," she murmured. After a few minutes, Carla stood up but didn't walk further than the lobby where she crumpled to the floor, unconscious and in convulsions.

The attendant dashed to see if Carla was trying to swallow her tongue. She yelled for a worker to call 911, and for someone to bring a coat or something to cover Carla.

"And call Eddie!"

The ambulance sped to the Vale's front door. Paramedics saw the unconscious woman was still convulsing. As they put

Carla into the ambulance Eddie burst through the door with both parents.

"Take her to the Valley Hospital, we'll be right behind you," cried her father. Then he turned to a worker, "Call Senator Nichols and tell 'em what happened — and no one else!"

Eddie asked a worker to take charge of the Vale until he returned.

"Oh, don't worry, sir. We'll see to everything. Please, just take care of Miss Martin for us."

While being checked into the emergency room, Carla was still unconscious with slight tremors. The doctors asked if Carla was epileptic.

"No, she's just having a nervous breakdown. It's because of that bum she's married to," blurted Mr. Martin. "I don't want him anywhere around as long as she's here."

"Yes, sir, but I need to know his name for the records."

Martin glanced at his wife before snapping, "Roy Jacobs!"

"The big theater owner? That Roy Jacobs?"

"Yes, him."

"But you called him a bum, sir."

"He is, just look what he did to our daughter. He's a terrible man. So, what will happen to her now?"

A nurse said doctors were caring for her and then asked the Martins to be seated in the waiting room. Eddie said, "Cara's attorney, Senator Nichols, may soon call. Please tell the doctor it's okay to discuss my sister's condition."

It was nearly an hour before they could see Carla, who was under sedation but calm. She reached for Eddie's hand. He assured her the Vale was under control and that the employees were rooting for her. She tried to smile at her parents. They promised Peter was notified of her situation.

Her father held Carla's hand. "I'll ask the senator to get a restraining order against Roy and keep him away from you." With a wisp of a smile, she closed her eyes.

When Senator Nichols called, Mr. Martin asked about the order.

"I have one in place right now. How is she doing?" Peter fretted.

"She seems to be stable for now, she just fell asleep."

"Thanks, I'll send her some flowers meanwhile. Maybe that will cheer her up. Will you ask the doctor to call me anytime? I'll want to know how she's doing and when we can see her."

Eddie returned to the theater to resume its management. However, within two weeks, Roy stormed into the Vale demanding to see Carla. The employees wouldn't say anything, so he yelled they were all fired and to get out. One young man wasn't afraid to stand up to the angry man.

"The Meadowdale Corporation owns this place, you have no right here. Senator Nichols told all of us that himself," he asserted.

Roy's chest puffed out as he spun around in fury. The sales clerk buzzed the office and then Eddie met Roy on the stairs.

"I thought you were in Europe."

"Well, I found my way back here, didn't I? Where is Carla?"

"She's been ill. I'm standing in for her."

"I want to know where the hell my wife is?" he shouted. Eddie tried to calm him.

His voice boomed, "I will not be quiet! Where's Carla? Where is she?"

"I said that she's not been well, so she's not here." Eddie turned to go back to the office when Roy grabbed him. A worker saw this and called the police to say that someone was attacking the manager.

The police charged into the Vale sooner than expected. The worker pointed to the staircase where Roy had Eddie pushed against the wall with one hand. The other was raised in a clenched fist.

"Stop! Police!" Roy turned to see two officers with guns drawn. He held his hands up to show he wasn't armed.

"Hold it, I'm the owner here. This man knows something about my wife that he's not telling me." He descended the stairs. "I just wanted him to tell..."

"Put your hands on your head and interlock your fingers, mister! We know who the owner is, so don't lie to us. You're under arrest."

Roy moved on down to the landing and yelled, "Just hold it! Do you know who I am?"

"Yes. You're under arrest, for assault and battery and attempted robbery. Turn around and put your hands behind your back You have the right to remain silent..."

"Hold it! I was not going to rob anyone, I was just talking to this guy. He knows where my wife is!" Roy yelled. The cops looked at Eddie.

He calmly said, "Carla, my sister, is part of the corporation who owns this theater. There's a restraining order against this man to not come onto this property or to be anywhere near Carla Martin. Senator Peter Nichols is our attorney if you need to call him."

While Roy resisted, the officers escorted him to the squad car.

The Trenton police booked Roy for breaking the restraining order, however, his attorney couldn't bail him out until the next day. Larry Cross warned him to keep away from Carla since the senator was her friend.

Ignoring the warnings, Roy soon learned in which hospital Carla was staying, and, with flowers in hand, went straight into her private room. To see him sent a hot wave throughout her body, which suddenly became chilled. Carla's eyes darted around the room to no avail. There was nothing and no one to help her get away from him.

Her underarms tingled with tepid perspiration at the thought of being alone with Roy. Although, he tried to assure Carla his only concern was for her well-being. And he'd pay all charges that were accrued during her stay. This with a kindly smile on his lips, but his eyes held animosity.

With no energy to argue or to resist, Carla laid her head on the pillow again, trying not to appear drowsy. She was leery of closing her eyes. If she fell asleep, it would be too easy for him to hold the pillow over her face.

Not knowing how else to ask for help, Carla reached for the water glass on the bedside table. After taking a sip, she coughed and then dropped the glass at Roy's feet as though it was accidental. As he stood to brush the water from his pants, she pressed the call button.

When the nurse came in to help the fear in her patient's eyes was startling. While she leaned over her, Carla whispered, "Husband."

With a nod of acknowledgment, the nurse said she'd return to clean the floor. However, two guards came to handcuff Roy and then called the police. He had broken the restraining order once more.

Having found himself in the Trenton jail again didn't lessen his contempt for Carla. In his mind, the woman he once loved, cherished, and provided for had turned on him, and it was Carla who made him lose his position with the Family. He thought she told Jada about her troubled marriage, and then Jada relayed that information to David.

Roy called his attorney, but he was held over with too high a bail for Larry Cross to acquire in time for the court date.

The judge looked down upon Roy Jacobs to see the man who Roy Jacobs could not see; one filled with bitterness, contempt and defiance. However, he also understood that Roy had connections with a well-known mafia.

"You were a man of great repute in this community and in this state. I am very disappointed that you have reduced yourself to these acts of insurrection. I do not see that you have any business in this town, the Vale Movie Theater, nor the Valley Hospital. You have twice abused your restraining orders to stay away from your estranged wife. I now forbid you to come within the City of Trenton city limits for five years. And I will fine you one million dollars. This money will be set aside for the use of funding local schools. I also want to see that you attend anger management classes in the city of Salem where you live. If you do not comply with these orders, you will see jail time. Case closed."

Newspapers and airwaves were bombarded with headlines, stories, and rumors of the break-up.

"Millionaire Movie Mogul Jailed for Jealousy", "Movie Magnate Messes Up", and "Jacobs Justly Jailed" led news stories. There were speculations of his wife's health failure, suggestions of attempted murder, and mentions of his involvement with a prostitution racket because of the pornography now shown in several of his theaters. It was even suggested that he had driven the poor woman to attempt suicide.

More gossip was now open to the public's scrutiny. Roy's parents were disgraced in the turmoil caused by their son's derogatory publicity. The ferocity shown by Samuel Jacobs's mortification of his son's actions sent out rumors that he intended to sue Roy for defamation of character.

Trenton's newspaper headlines continued to embarrassed public officials of the larger cities, Salem and Portland, where Jacob owned prominent movie theaters.

"Riled Roy Hostile at Hospital; Jacobs just doesn't get the judges' message. Can his money make this one go away?", and "Local Celebrity Checks Into Crowbar Hotel For The Second Time; Jacobs enjoyed our hospitality so much that he returned for another stay, but this time he was told to stay away. His million-dollar fine will fund local schools."

"This is the first time you ever looked bad, but I have to say you sure made yourself noticed," Cross admonished. "Roy, stay out of view and it will all die away. That includes being seen at any of your theaters or favorite restaurants. The public just eats up scandal like this, especially when they see a little tarnish on their knight's armor. And columnists are striving to take pictures and get interviews or statements for their news producers, so heed my warning and just back off!"

Unsettled, Larry stopped. With a hand to his bowed forehead, he took in a deep breath and then looked at Jacobs. "And you better back off of Carla, too. You know damned well that you put her where she's at, so let her get well. Remember that Senator Peter Nichols is standing behind her, so don't get in front of him. You may have the money, but he has the clout. If you want to let off some steam, call me and we can go someplace quiet and get drunk," he scolded.

Chapter Thirty

THE RECOVERY

The Martins were happy to show Carla the newspapers since the gossip had been buzzing around the hospital. She noticed her family's quiet rejoicing, even though she paid little attention to their reports. Her subdued personality frightened them. Doctors expected Carla to respond to the medication and the treatments better than she did.

After a while, Carla became content with her watercolors, drawings, and learning how to knit. Needlework was new to her. The older patients in her ward were happy to teach this "newcomer" their talents of playing cards and board games. In turn, she showed them how to draw, sketch, and paint with watercolors. She had become oblivious to the outside world. This environment was her new sanctuary.

Peter and Beth Nichols were overly concerned when her mother called to say that Carla was "fading away into her own world". Her daughter casually spoke to the family as though they were hospital staff.

Her family begged her to let Peter finish filing for divorce. She looked at him with empty eyes. "If that's what you think I should do, I guess it's alright then. Should I talk to Roy about it first?" Carla asked in all innocence. Peter could now see how far Carla's mental state had fallen.

After listening to her family and friends' urging, Carla said Peter could do what everyone thought was best. He immediately began the final proceedings.

Several days later, a man asked to see Carla Martin.

"Are you a family member?"

"No, I'm a family friend." He gave his card to the receptionist.

She excused herself to speak to Carla's doctor. Looking at the card, he was in disbelief. "I'll see to this."

The doctor introduced himself. "Miss Martin is under my care, and I wasn't informed about your concern with her. I'll have to see some substantial identification, please."

"Certainly, I understand." He showed the doctor his driver's license and Realtor's license.

"Thank you, Mr. Fraiser. I'll take you to see her. She doesn't remember much at all. In fact, she has to be reminded who her parents are sometimes."

Carla was at a card table when the doctor introduced Stanley. "You folks have room for one more player?" he asked.

"Hi, Stanley, I'm Fred. We're short one person anyway." They moved their chairs around to make room for the new player.

Stanley sat in the extra chair. "Thanks a lot. What are you playing?"

"We were going to play Crazy Eights. You know how to play?"

"It's been a long time, but I think I can remember. Will you introduce me to the rest of the gang?

Carla just waved and said, "Hi, Stanley."

Everyone enjoyed playing the game until the nurse said it was time to wash their hands for dinner. Stanley thanked everyone for the game and then spoke to the doctor once more.

"I'd like to take care of all expenses for Carla Martin's stay here. Please send any bills to my office. And you may inform her family that they needn't be concerned about anything." Fraiser gave the doctor another business card. "In case they have questions, and that goes for Roy Jacobs. He knows very well who I am. If he has anything to say about Carla's keep, he can contact me. I don't want him having anything to do with her, and I'm sure her family feels the same way." Stanley held out his hand to the doctor, who received it in gratitude.

"Thank you so much for your care and concern for Carla, Mr. Fraiser. She's been on a very rocky road, but I can see that she has some peace of mind and contentment while being with us. It'll just take time."

Before leaving, Stanley asked, "Please let me know if there's anything that I can do to help her."

As the weeks drew on and doctors came and went, Carla had no interest in anything but her therapy classes, what to choose for each meal, or when it was time to bathe and wash her hair.

Fred and others from the card game asked Carla to join them. She noticed there was an outsider at the table and stared at him.

"Do you remember me?" he asked.

"I think so."

"He played Crazy Eights with us the other week," a woman said. "This is Stanley."

"Oh. Hi, Stanley," Carla said with a slight smile.

As the game progressed, some players had to help Carla select the right cards. She couldn't remember how to play the game.

Stanley's heart was breaking to see her that way. Finally, he glanced at his wrist-watch.

"I'm sorry, I have to go." He excused himself without looking up.

"Goodbye, Stanley," said the other players. Although, he didn't hear Carla's voice.

When he walked toward the door, the doctor saw Stanley blotting his face with a handkerchief, so he didn't speak to him.

Carla's mother was fearful that her daughter may never come out of this dreadful, shallow state of mind. Mrs. Martin became so vexed about Carla's condition that she contacted Jim Crawford through his police department.

Mrs. Martin said that Carla might "snap out of it" if she could recall knowing him. He said he'd be there with Tom and Judy in forty-five minutes.

Upon their arrival, Tom asked to speak with the doctor in charge, saying Mrs. Martin was concerned with her daughter's security and welfare, as were they. For that reason, he and Jim had been observing Roy Jacobs for several months.

With the doctor's approval, they moved around the patients, looking at their knitting and crochet projects, or art and handiwork. Judy admired one lady's drawings.

"Oh, you should look at *that* lady's work. She draws castles and mansions!" She took Judy by the hand to see Carla.

"Show this lady your castles. Please show her what you draw, Honey. Show her that lovely mansion with the enormous bedroom."

"Yeah, but just don't show her that naked man," an older man said.

"You old fuddy-duddy! Just 'cause she won't draw you! Go away," the woman scolded. And then she began turning the pages of Carla's drawing pad to show her sketches.

Jim stood behind Carla and remained quiet while the woman showed Judy the drawings. Some were rooms in Jada's mansion, and another showed the garden's water fountain. On another page were a crystal chandelier and a flowing staircase.

"Carla, these are magnificent," Tom said in wonderment. "They are stunning. You're very professional. Is that what you used to do? I mean, did you design these yourself?"

Carla looked up at him with a slight smile and shrugged. "I don't know. I just like to draw."

"Show the lady your people," a woman said.

"Yeah. Show the lady that good-looking man," said another one. She turned to Judy, "I think she has a boyfriend, but she won't admit it." When she turned the pages, Carla reached out to slap at her hand. "Okay, you do it then."

Judy put a hand on Carla's shoulder. "I'd like to see what he looks like, Carla. Will you show me, please?" Her soothing voice was encouraging.

With an expression of pride, Carla turned the pages to show a man in a police uniform from the waist up. He was looking askance at the artist. With a slight smile, his face glowed with serenity.

"Oh, my. He certainly is handsome," Judy said.

"That one is all mine."

Carla turned to another drawing. The same man was lying naked on a bed, propped up on one elbow while the blanket covered his private section. The rest of his muscular body was exposed as he gazed at the viewers. He showed a more than contented smile.

In quiet admiration, the ladies gathered around Carla to look at the mystery man. She turned the page to show the same nude man standing before a curtain with his head bowed and an arm reaching upward.

Carla tenderly glowed as her eyes moved over the drawing. With a wistful smile, she reached out to touch a finger ever so lightly from his shoulders to his feet.

"Is he standing naked in front of a *window*?" a woman asked.

"No," Jim said, "That's a shower curtain."

Carla whipped her head around to look up. Jim smiled at her and then knelt to look into her face. She studied him for several seconds and then flipped the pages back to the man in uniform. She glanced back at Jim.

"Hi, Carla, do you remember me?" His words were gentle, and the voice sounded familiar. She looked at the drawing and back to Jim again. As tears stung her eyes, she reached out to touch his face.

"Is that you?" Carla whispered.

Jim nodded. He took a handkerchief from his pocket to wipe her tears. When he pulled his hand away, she took the cloth and held it to her chest. "That's mine," her lips pleaded.

"You can keep it, Carla. I'm Jim. Do you remember me now?" he asked again. Carla's eyes darted over his face and into his eyes as tears fell down her cheeks.

"Jim?" she whispered.

"Take your clothes off, mister, so we can see if that's you!" a woman laughed.

Carla jumped up. "No, you can't see him! Nobody can see him! He's mine!" Carla snatched up the sketchbook and ran out of the room. Jim tried to go after her, but the doctor caught him.

"She'll be alright. You made her see what she was drawing was real. She could remember what happened. That's good. I'll go talk to her."

Jim was waiting in the hallway with Tom and Judy, hoping to see Carla again. The doctor suggested he waited a few days to come back, perhaps with a member of her family.

Tom knew how much Jim was hurting for Carla, so they all had a drink and talked before going home

Carla's family stayed near while she recovered. The nurses gave her the proper medications in the proper amounts at the proper time of day. There were walking and exercise routines, game times, bingo, and simple card games. She even learned how to play dominoes, laughing aloud when she made a good move. Slowly, she became more active and respondent.

One morning, Carla lay in her hospital bed with the sense that someone was close to her, but she tried not to look. She then felt a peace come over her. Slowly and cautiously, she opened her eyes. A handsome man was sitting next to her with her hand in his. As her eyelids blinked, she smiled at him.

"Jim...? What are you doing here?" Carla murmured.

His smile was warming, "Watching a sleeping beauty sleep." Jim's voice was soft, filled with compassion and caring as he sat on the edge of the bed. "How do you feel?"

She closed her eyes, squeezed his hand, and then looked at him again with a slight smile. "Much better now, thank you. And you?"

"Just super, now that I can see that you remember me."

"Mom said that you came in to see me, but I didn't know who you were. I'm sorry."

"No need to apologize. You showed us the sketches you drew, and I was thrilled you even remembered me. That made me see you recalled who I was, at least on paper." Jim saw her blush.

"I just couldn't get that man out of my mind, and I didn't know why. He just made me feel very safe, I guess. I hope it didn't upset you, Jim."

"Only how you got here. I was pretty upset for a while. I even thought about putting Roy away somehow. I guess his Mafia buddies even turned their backs on him." With that, Carla had a worried look. He squeezed her hand.

"No, out of their love for you, they won't do anything to him. They were afraid that you'd be blamed, so they made him leave the country. He's roaming around Europe someplace. Levine has men watching Roy right and left. Don't worry, you'll be just fine."

Carla asked, "How's the baby doing?"

"Oh, he's getting pretty big." Jim smiled with pride. "I think he's going to take after his dad because he wants to be a cop."

"And his mother?"

Jim looked down and then back up to Carla with a nod. "She's doing really good too. We, uh... had a real long talk. Not about everything, just enough for her to know that there's someone who she almost lost out to. He squeezed Carla's hand again before he sat in the chair next to her bed.

"Judy got her to understand a cop's life much better. Now I'm not just a paycheck and housemate anymore."

Jim tried to smile while changing the subject. "You were right about living around here. There's a great deal to see. All of us went out to the ocean one weekend. Our two boys thought that was stupendous, and to play in that much sand was heaven right there! You should have seen Tom out jumping the waves when they came in." Jim lowered his head with a mixed-emotional smile.

Carla reached out to take his hand again. "What we had was beautiful and wonderful, Jim. I respect you for making the right decision with her. I'm sure that we can always be special friends in our own little way, and I will cherish that forever."

"Yeah, me too." Jim looked away so she couldn't see the tears on his face.

"Hold me again, Jim," she whispered. He moved over to sit on the side of the bed. They wrapped their arms around each other once more while both wept a few bitter-sweet tears. Then, sitting up again, Jim took out his handkerchief to wipe his face, and then hers.

"I'll let you have this one back," she grinned.

He chuckled at her remark. "Yeah, you don't know how many times that I wished that I took that first one back. I just wanted to hold it and feel you there with me," he smiled.

"I'm here with you now, Jim... and always will be. Someday you can bring that little guy around to see me. I'll bet he'll be wearing a twelve-shooter by then," she laughed.

"Oh, you bet he will."

They talked about his job, Tom and Judy, and possible plans for Carla to resume her work. There were many things to discuss. Nothing got solved, but it was nice just to talk together again.

Chapter Thirty-one

OLD FRIENDS

Day by day, Carla became more active, physically and emotionally. She was more talkative with more energy to do things, such as sketch ways to redecorate various areas of the hospital.

On one visit, Mrs. Martin asked the doctor how long this stay would be. Why can't Carla come home to her family?

Jada, Sharon, and Marni wondered the same thing. Their calls couldn't go through to Carla's room. Mrs. Martin curtly told each of them, "Leave my daughter alone and stop trying to pester her". Even their unopened letters were marked 'return to sender', to their great dismay.

Through Harry Phillips, they learned that the divorce was finalized and Carla had been awarded the house, household belongings, separate bank account, and her car. Harry was sure they could contact their friend in due time. Meanwhile, he kept in touch periodically with Stanley Fraiser and Senator Nichols as to Carla's welfare.

Marni was at odds about staying with Harry. He was the only man she ever loved, and now this love was dying. It was only because of Harry's infidelity that Marni strayed. She yearned for affection and the sexual fulfillment she no longer had with her husband. Even though each had trespassed their marriage vows, there was still a bond between them. Although, Harry was paying more attention to her now, now that he needed her support.

Sharon felt the same with Richard. Although the fur business was in somewhat of a slump, she knew these times came and passed with the economic situations. However, the personal tension between them was nearly unbearable.

As usual, Jada made suggestions for them to consider. "I know this is a troublesome time for all of us. Young Carla was up against a veritable demon who nearly destroyed her, mentally and emotionally. She truly loved Roy and would have stayed with him if he had been decent to her."

"But that situation differs completely from ours. The only man who would marry the ex-wife of a renowned Mafia boss is a man who doesn't value his own life, or another Don. And that would only be to humiliate our Don and me. Do you think I can expect to be treated with love and respect from another man like I have?" Jada sat back to look at Marni and Sharon. "Ha!"

"At least Carla has her work to support herself," Sharon added, "but what would I do for money to even live one, let alone spending cash? Oh, dear me. Is this where the 'for better or for worse' part sets in?"

"What about 'for richer or poorer?'" Marni added. "I just hope it doesn't come to *that*. I can tighten up the old belt, but what about getting cut off entirely?" She shook her head, "I guess we just need to make the best of what we have. At least we still have something and someone."

"I don't want to break in another husband. It took me nearly twenty years to where I can do something with Richard," Sharon laughed. "I guess I'll go home and rub his back like a good little wife should do."

"While you're at it, my dear, try rubbing his front too," advised Jada. "It's time that we all paid more attention to our men. Just because they had some "indiscreet" indiscretions doesn't mean we have to abandon them. They know that we've had our share of fun, too, so why don't we set our tattered feelings aside to show them what kind of stuff *real* wives like us are made of. Don't forget the 'in sickness or in health' part of that oath. If our husbands go under for all the stress they are having now, *they* just might be in the mental ward," said the wise Mrs. Levine. They drank to that.

"Do you have any more tips to share with us then?"

"I sure do. Even if he snaps or yells at you, just stay calm. Ask if there's something they want to talk about, and *smile* when you do that. After you get their attention, tell them just to stay put while you get them a tasty drink. Then sit down with your man and ask them how their day went. And *listen* to what they say, don't just hear them talk. I think it's time for us to go home and put this into practice. Just don't overwhelm them all at once. That won't earn their trust. It will just cause suspicion, and then they won't relax."

Carla was released from the hospital in the care of her parents. However, the strain of their company became stressful for her. Again, her mother was trying to control her life.

Carla talked to Eddie about her situation. She saw the guilt his eyes could no longer hide. He confessed that her friends had not abandoned her. Their mother had protected Carla from going back with that "bunch of thugs and murderers". She *was* trying to control Carla. Of course, as a mother, Mrs. Martin would protect her only daughter in that emotional state. However, to lie to her about friends who truly cared was beyond mere concern.

Jada was stunned to hear Carla's voice after nearly five months. With joyful tears and some laughter, Jada said she had concluded there was no getting past her mother, so they prayed for Carla's well-being.

"My mother convinced me you didn't even send a get-well card. After Eddie told me about what she had done, well, enough of me, how is everything going down there?" There was a hesitation. "Jada?"

"Not so good, sweetheart. David has been in prison for nearly four months now." She heard Carla's startled gasp.

"The FBI tried to get him on income tax evasion, but they couldn't prove anything. Then they got him for contributing to the delinquency of a minor, and the Mann Act," Jada explained. "Then the bastards got to Cindy, his big star. They convinced her she'd go to prison if she didn't testify against David, and just what would happen to a girl like her in a woman's prison with all those women guards."

"But didn't she have proper ID proving that she was legal?"

"That didn't matter. The FBI produced false IDs and pictures of her as a fifteen-year-old girl, and even younger. The judge bought it and gave David five to seven years in prison. At least he was smart enough to know what kind of 'Family' men stood behind their Don. That judge sent David to the Los Angeles Correctional Facility. Whatever they want to call it, it's still a prison.

"Oh, never mind all of that, my dear, can you get away and come down here for a while? Sharon and Marni will be ecstatic to see you again, but no more than I. You can even stay with me. I only have Donald and Nona here anymore. And my brother has Mr. Blum staying here for our protection.

"Little Lilly Mari came to visit on the weekends. She talked to her grandparents so much about me and 'Uncle Donald' that they let her come to see me. And I was extremely blessed to be with her again.

"Oh, that' s wonderful. How did they find you?"

"Her grandfather contacted the police chief, and he called Harry. Well, what do you think, my dearest, can you come down for a while?"

"That would be terrific, Jada. Yes, I can. I've only been staying busy with the Vale. I can't get my mind back into my work yet. I sure want to get together with you and the girls, though. I'll get back to you as soon as I clear things up here. I miss all of you so much."

However, Eddie had other concerns for his sister. "What are you going to do about your home in Salem? You can't just leave it sitting there, and you can't ever go back there to live."

Carla agreed. She remembered the Realtor she had talked with at the tavern. Rummaging through her purse, she found his business card.

"Oh, wow, I'm glad I hung onto this. Let's get a hold of this guy. He's somewhat associated with Stanley Fraiser, so I'm sure we can depend on him for help."

Dalton Benson remembered the beautiful lady. He would be thrilled to sell that house, and then find a new one for her in Trenton. When he asked what she had in mind, she described the many Tudor homes she admired while in England and Germany because they seemed homey and warm.

Carla mentioned nothing about cost, just comfort, so with that, Benson started his search. Although, he went about this transaction with caution. Recalling the drastic publicity concerning her divorce, he contacted Stanley Fraiser.

Fraiser suggested that under the circumstances, Dalton should keep a low profile on the sale and her relocation, and to keep this out of the public eye as much as possible. He added Carla was his dear friend.

"I'd like keeping this between us, Dalton if you don't mind. And I'll see that your commission on this sale is favorable to your firm. Thank you for contacting me on this matter."

"Yes, Mr. Fraiser, thank *you* very much, sir. I'll get right on that and keep in touch with you."

Dalton lost no time in finding the right buyer. In Trenton, he showed Carla and Eddie homes he had located. The third house was exactly what she wanted. Carla could find no wrong, from the heavy carved wood entrance door to the vaulted ceilings, the stuccoed walls, and the solid hardwood floors. Even the colors were compatible with her. And it was reasonably close to the theater, but far enough from her parents.

She insisted Eddie stay in the finished basement "mother-in-law" apartment. This included a separate entrance that would provide complete privacy for him. He agreed to remain there until she became adjusted to life on her own.

Fraiser was pleased with Benson's report. "Just get everything set up so that all she needs to do is walk in the door and be at home, if you would, please," he asked.

Clothes were hung in the closet, the bed was made, dishes were put in the cupboards, crystal and silver service were placed in the china cabinet, and table linens went back into the buffet. Even Carla's favorite brand of Scotch whiskey was in the liquor cabinet. Benson handed her the key, and now this was her very own home.

Carla phoned Jada to tell her the good news and that she'd check back with soon. When she finally became situated and comfortable in leaving Eddie in charge of the house and the Vale Theater, Carla told Jada when she would arrive.

Donald was mildly taken aback to see her walk out of the airplane in slacks, a casual shirt, and loafers instead of her usual glamorous self. Carla wore little make-up, and her hair was pulled back in a simple ponytail. She beamed to see Donald again.

When they arrived at the mansion, Carla looked the garden over. The fountain's running waters were now still, and the lawn wasn't as immaculate as it had been. However, it was still welcoming to her.

In no time, Jada came to embrace her young friend. With both hands on Carla's shoulders, she stood back at arm's length to look at her thoroughly with eyes darting over her entirety.

"My word, girl, you look absolutely... horrible." Then she hugged her again. "Please come sit and talk to me. I just can't wait to hear how much your loving mother has degraded you!" she laughed.

Nona served cocktails while they brought each other up to date. The time together was a blessing for both women.

"Well, my dearest, your "sisters" were totally ecstatic when I told them you were alive and almost well," Jada laughed. "They were so thrilled to know that you were coming down for a while. We can all have lunch together, just like always. Except, we now go to a couple of less popular places so we don't get bothered by flashbulbs. We just wear casual outfits, so you'll fit right in just as you are, my love. Let me give them a quick call to meet us."

When these two ladies walked into the small but charming restaurant, Sharon and Marni couldn't get up fast enough to greet their friend with hugs and ask too many questions simultaneously.

To be with them once more, Carla shed tears of relief and joy. She had all but forgotten the camaraderie and girl-talk they had enjoyed in being together. The three friends embraced her with warmth and sisterhood, and with a better understanding of what she must have had endured.

These four women talked about how much their lives have changed in becoming wiser and more caring through the following days. Each grew to be a stronger person for having undergone their recent experiences.

A saying was that "One learns more from experience than books." And Benjamin Franklin wrote, "Experience is the best teacher, and a fool will learn by none other."

Although, Jada did not perceive any of these women to be fools, they were merely products of situations set before them. It would be a fool who did not learn from these experiences.

Soon, it was time for Carla to return and enjoy her new home. Eddie was comforted that she was settled and had plans to take up her career again. He moved into the apartment above the Vale Theater to run it full time while Carla relieved him two days a week. Even though the Vale was hers, she felt more comfortable with Eddie in charge while she resumed her work.

Although, Carla couldn't pinpoint why, she was uneasy about not knowing the exact whereabouts of Roy.

Chapter Thirty-two

AND THE TWAIN SHALL MEET

When Carla returned from working at the Vale on Friday, she parked inside the garage and then closed and locked the door. Saturday would be the day to clean house and do the laundry. She unlocked the inside door to go upstairs. After hanging up her coat, she went into the kitchen to make some coffee. When the pot began percolating, she turned and froze. A man was sitting in her living room.

"*Roy!*" Her yelp was sharp but not loud.

He smiled at her. "I would have called, but your number's unlisted." Roy's voice held concern, however, not enough to earn Carla's trust. "I couldn't get you out of my mind and needed to see you again. I let myself in through the patio door since it was unlocked. I'm only here to visit with you, and I didn't think you'd let me in."

Carla's head spun to see that the door wasn't closed all the way. She knew she had securely locked it that morning. Roy saw her tan slacks had turned dark from urine. She didn't know she had lost control of her bladder, so Roy assumed she was still frightened of him.

"You were supposed to be in Europe."

"I got tired of traveling. You look good, Carla. How are things going at the Vale Theater?" She knew he had been checking into her life again.

Roy started to get up but sat down again when Carla stepped backward. "Darling, please believe me, I won't cause you any trouble. Being away from you for so long gave me time to think about how horrible I was, and how I took you for granted. You're the greatest thing that ever came into my life, and I didn't deserve you. Please forgive me, Carla. I still love you very much."

She felt the chill of her wet pants and looked down. "Oh, um, excuse me, please."

Carla went into the bedroom, quietly locking the door behind her. In the silence, she quickly dialed a number.

"Is Sergeant Jim Crawford or Tom Bailey available? This is an emergency," she whispered.

"They're both out on patrol." The operator heard distress in her voice, "Can I get someone else for you?"

"No, this is Carla Martin. Please get contact them right away and say that Roy Jacobs broke into my house. He's here now, so please hurry." She silently set the receiver down and returned to the living room lest Jim called and Roy picked up the phone.

"I thought you were going to change your clothes."

Carla looked down. "Oh... I forgot." She took in a deep breath to gather her thoughts. They both knew that if she screamed, the neighbors would rush to her aid. Then again, Roy could say that she had gone berserk once more and put her back into the mental ward.

"Can I get you a drink?"

"Yes, please. Coffee will be fine."

The phone rang, so she excused herself to answer it.

"Carla, we're on our way. Are you alright?" Jim tried to sound calm.

"Yes, but I can't come over now. I have company."

"Has he hurt you in any way?"

"Not yet. I think the movie was called Run Silent, Run Deep, but I can't remember who was in it."

Although, Roy did. "That stared Burt Lancaster and Clark Gable. It's a terrific World War Two film."

"I heard that. Is the door unlocked?" Jim asked.

"Oh, yes, both of them."

"Get lost if you can. Lock yourself in the bathroom or bedroom. I'll be there in about ten minutes."

"Okay, thanks." Carla set the receiver down with relief. Turning away from Roy, she said, "I need to go change. Help yourself to the coffee. Cups are in the cabinet next to the fridge."

Carla stepped toward the entrance door, waiting to hear Roy in the kitchen. As he poured the coffee, she unlocked the main door, leaving it slightly ajar and then went into the bedroom and locked the door to wait. It was only moments before hearing a car outside.

Soon, she heard a loud thud, and then an anguished scream.

Rushing to the hallway, she saw that Jim had Roy's shoulders pinned against the wall. He slammed his knee into Jacob's crotch one, two, three times.

As Carla screeched his name, Tom raced in with his hand toward her, "Carla, stay back. *Jim*, cool it!"

There was a sudden stench as Roy lost control of his bowels. In disgust, Jim grabbed his arm and threw him down the staircase. As he charged after Roy, Tom caught him.

"That's enough! Good God, man, you don't wanna get put away for *manslaughter*."

Jim leaned against the wall as his heavy breathing subsided. Tom patted his shoulder. "You'll be okay pal, I'll go check on him."

Carla calmly called Jim's name again. When he went to her, they quietly looked at one another before embracing. Jim felt an enormous relief in her arms.

At the bottom of the stairs, Tom quipped, "That'll teach the bastard to run when a cop tells 'em to stop." Then he leaned over to feel Roy's pulse, "He's still alive, dammit." Tom opened the bottom door to release the foul air.

Going upstairs, he shook his head "Oh, man, what the hell has he been eating? Nobody can say that his shit don't stink."

Tom wrapped an arm around the former lovers. "Come on, let's sit down and get our stories straight before he comes to, then we can call it in. For one thing, Carla was hiding in the bedroom and didn't see a thing." He glanced at her, "You got that lady?"

She shrugged with a nod. "Sounds okay, I guess. I have some vodka. Would you guys like a drink? I sure would."

"You bet! Is that a police department-approved brand?" Tom joked.

For the first time, Jim saw that her slacks were wet. He looked at his partner, who nodded.

"What happened before we got here?" Tom muttered. Jim shrugged.

Setting the drinks down, Cala noticed them looking at her legs.

"Yeah, Roy just startled me, that's all. I guess I'll go change now."

"No, leave them on. When the detectives get here, they can see how much Roy frightened you," Jim said. "And we better get everything straight before he wakes up." He patted the couch for Carla to sit next to him.

"First of all, I can't be running around to rescue you all the time," he sighed. "I have a family to be with, and so do you. I want you to call Jada and tell her that you're moving down there, like sooner than you can. You'll have some great protection, and you can live a good life around them. And that's an order."

"Great idea," said Tom. "Now, we need to say that Carla called the police and asked for our help because we had been on Roy's case for some time. She was hiding from him in the bedroom and we came in with her approval ahead of time. We told Roy he was under arrest, he got scared, messed his pants, and then tried to run. He slipped on his crap, fell down the stairs, and banged his head. I checked to see that he was alright, and then we called the medics. Carla, the detectives might ask a lot of questions, so stick to those very words, and then say you don't remember anything else. Okay?"

Jim called the paramedics after Roy's weak voice called out for Carla.

Tom greeted the hurting man. "Hello, Roy Jacobs. You are under arrest for violating your restraining order, breaking and entering, assault and battery, and running from the police. You have the right to remain silent. If you give up that right..." Roy passed out again. "That's another charge — disobeying an officer."

The paramedics arrived to attend to Roy just ahead of the detectives and photographer.

One said, "My God, what was this guy eating?"

The judge looked the papers over and then set them neatly on his desk. He took his off glasses and set them on top of the documents. Then he folded his hands together and leaned across the spacious desk to look down at Roy Jacobs standing silently before him.

"Truthfully, Mr. Jacobs, I'm not sure that I want to hear your answer, but according to the law which I swore to uphold, I must ask if there is anything that you have to say in your defense."

Jacobs looked at the honorable man before him, the man who carried the weight of the gavel that was about to slam down on his head. At his father's age, he may have held that position long enough to have heard every possible defense plea, reason, and excuse that had ever been uttered. Whatever Roy Jacobs now had to say most likely didn't matter since the sentence had already pronounced, just not orally. It didn't matter now how much money Jacobs had to his name, for this judge was certainly not one to be bought.

Seated behind Jacobs was his attorney, Larry Cross, with Roy's mother, but not his father. On the bench behind them sat Sergeants Jim Crawford and Tom Bailey with Oregon State Senator Peter Nichols. Obviously absent was Ms. Carla Martin. Seated behind them were over two hundred fifty onlookers, some anxiously waiting to hear the final verdict, and then scramble to phone and call their news offices.

The judge motioned for Jacobs to begin.

"Your Honor, I feel that I must throw myself on the mercy of the court. I have no reasonable excuse for having violated that restraining order. I want to say in my defense, however, Your Honor, that I meant absolutely no harm to Carla," Roy humbly said after having practiced his humbling speech considerably.

"I still love her very much. And at that time, I had been away from her for so long that my heart was burdened to see her again. I finally realized that there is no possible way I can reconcile with her. And I swear by Almighty God in heaven that I will never try to contact her again. Thank you for hearing me out, Your Honor."

"And I'll see that you don't have that opportunity for the next three years, which you will spend in the Oregon State Correctional Facility. Case closed." He brought the gavel down.

"You can't *do* that to me!" Roy cried out.

His Honor pointed a finger at Roy with a with sharp tongue in his answer. "Another word out of your mouth, and I will make that *ten* years. In my eyes, you are one of the most disgusting, despicable, and disreputable men I have *ever* had the misfortune to have in my court. You have haunted, harassed, and humiliated this woman for several years now. When would you ever otherwise learn to stop that? It's a great wonder that this woman never put a gun to your head. And to be truthful, I would have gladly given her one to do that."

The judge turned to the bailiff. "Get this man out of my courtroom. *Now!*"

Chapter Thirty-three

THEIR NEW HOMES

The orange jumpsuit wasn't the most fashionable for Roy. However, until he was released, which wouldn't be soon enough to his liking, it was readily available to him in his exact size. Nevertheless, the word was out concerning the "newbie".

After a few more beatings, Jacobs understood that many prisoners around the yard didn't like him all that much. He made a few friends who proved to be a bit too friendly with him. But then, Roy seemed to take to their kind of friendship, so they protected him to an extent.

Larry Cross could get away for a visit periodically. However, Sam Jacobs refused to set eyes upon the disgraced son, who had brought so much humiliation to himself and his family. He regained management of his two Portland theaters, the Majestic and Regency, retaining their glory as wholesome and legitimate establishments.

Roy's mother was a loving one to her only child. She reminded Roy frequently about how he had treated her daughter-in-law, whom she loved. Through his behavior, Mrs. Jacobs lost her opportunity to be a grandmother, to have little footsteps once more in her home, to share this would-be child with her friends, and to help raise that child in the love and admonition of God. For this, she was ashamed of her son.

Although, in the Los Angeles prison, inmates had well-received David Levine as the Don Levine. They knew the possible clout that this man may still carry. Some were not sure that he had that power, although, would not question it. Fellow prisoners gave the Don gifts, who graciously thanked the giver whether or not he accepted the gift. If he felt he couldn't use that gift, he'd return it in such a way that the giver was given Levine's blessings for having offered it.

Some blatant young men thought they were the upcoming "Cock of the Walk", and tried to test Levine's Mafia virility. Even though guards watched them well within those great gray walls, they soon received word that an associate, friend, or family member had met with an "accident" on the outside. They quickly curtailed their confrontations. And when the Don received visitors such as Mr. Blum, even the prison guards were considerate in dropping an occasional "sir" his way.

Beautifully dressed, Jada Levine was often escorted in to see her husband. She brought news of how well things were on the home front, and affirmation of love for her husband.

Upon returning from a conjugal visit, there were no grins, smirks, or comments by inmates. David mentioned that Mrs. Levine enjoyed the box of chocolates or other gifts given to her on their behalf.

Stanley Fraiser visited Levine frequently and was well-received by him. "My old friend, this was a travesty. It was because some FBI upstarts wanted to feather their caps that this happened. I believe the judge who made this decision will reconsider. I promise you will not see the first year of this term served out. I'll work with your partners to see to that, and to keep contact with your loving wife as well."

Harry Philip's law firm had grown more vital now that he could devote it his full attention. Through his foresight, Harry put the Levine mansion in his name. As tension mounted with government officials, the IRS, and the FBI Phillips knew his sister would be in udder distress if she lost her husband and home to the trumped-up investigation.

Jada now had only Harry in whom she could trust. It was in his best interest to listen to any thoughts that Stanley Fraiser may have, even if they were only vague ideas, to find a flaw in a particular judge's life. And he found that flaw through his long-time friend and partner, Richard Hirsh.

When activists came out strong against wearing fashionable furs, "the skins of dead animals", Hirsh's fur salon failed to stay in business, along with most others. Through the suggestion by Jada Levine to his wife, he could make a complete turnaround by going into the cloth garment industry.

Jada asked, "Sharon, what if you use that same coat design but have Richard make it out of wool instead of mink? It's a grand style that will sell, and just about every woman could wear it."

When Sharon related this idea, Richard acted on it. "What about Jada's dressmaker? Is she busy?"

The dress designer wasn't all that busy, just enough to keep working steady and bring in a good income. She felt receptive to taking on this job since Jada referred her.

And she learned valuable information during the fitting with a lovely young lady. The gown would be paid for by a man with a name that the Hirsh, Phillips, or Levine households would never forget; Darrel Hammersmith.

Richard asked, "Say, you don't suppose that was the same judge that...?" Yes, it was. Now Hirsh held the hammer over Hammersmith.

"Sharon, we need to move on this," Richard told his wife. "You need to talk to Jada. If she can say something to Stanley

Fraiser, it will look as though we brought him into this directly instead of going around him to use his friendship with David."

"But, honey, we *are* going around him to do just that."

"Yes, but he doesn't need to know. He has the money and power to deal with the judge so he can get David out of that damned prison."

The trap was set. When the lovely lady returned for her evening gown's last adjustments, Hirsh put a tape cassette under a chair in the fitting room. It recorded her to have bragged about where she would wear the dress and who was paying for it. A cameraman photographed the gown so the picture could be put into a file, ensuring her that no one else would use this design. Interestingly enough, that same photographer was dining at the same restaurant where others saw the loving and not too discreet couple together. His camera captured their indiscretions.

Having trustworthy Blum make judgments on the judge's life, Stanley Fraiser learned of the judge's affair. Then his secretary made dinner reservations for him and Judge Hammersmith in an exclusive restaurant. When the waiter served the cocktails, Mr. Blum and his associate, "Mr. Smith", sat at the table. Blum handed Hammersmith an envelope, the contents of which Mrs. Hammersmith would be interested at a price. The price was to have David Levine released from prison sooner than possible. The judge understood the terms.

"Yes, I'll see to that right away, Mr. Fraiser." With that, the three men left His Dishonor to enjoy his cocktail and dinner, that is, if he still had an appetite for one.

David Levine was soon released from prison due to "failing health". He had developed heart troubles in that his heart was troubled for having been wrongly sent to jail in the first place.

A very chic Jada Levine stood before the steel-grated gates flanked by Harry Philips and Richard Hirsh while Blum waited by the limousine. She wanted to look her best when David walked through those gates, and for the many press cameras that would flash to see the Don emerge in the same suit he was wearing at his incarceration.

Her husband received Jada with a loving embrace. After handshakes and "manly" hugs, the two partners escorted David and his wife to the limousine, where Blum sped them away from reporters' questions

It didn't take long before Levine regained control of what remained of his empire. After consulting with Hirsh and Philips, he concluded which direction the Levine Film Corporation would take.

In a formal meeting, Levine met with Phillips, Hirsh, Blum, and the film and lighting directors. The Don disclosed his ideas.

"First, I wish to thank all of you for your support while I was... um, gone. I owe my deepest gratitude to Richard, Harry, and my dear friend of many years, Stanley Fraiser." Levine looked at the men in earnest, "Gentlemen, it turned out that not only did Hammersmith mend his ways, but he somehow convinced the FBI to return much of my illegally confiscated funds.

"While I was, well, 'on vacation', it came to my attention there are many experienced unemployed actors who want to be in our films. Of course, we will primarily use our standard actors. My two partners and I feel we can make movies that involve explicit sex but in a more sensitive and alluring manner. That will lend attraction to the love stories we will be filming," Levine announced.

"Our wives will interview these actors and, with thanks to Richard's new clothing line, we'll have our actors looking as fine as those seen in any of the top-name films on the market. This advertisement can add sales to his new line of clothing as well. And this will provide more employment in our community, so we all may prosper. Gentlemen, by working together in this new venture, we will overcome the recent setbacks. As always, we'll be making the same movies for our predominant customers who prefer showing those films. The Levine Film Corporation will once again be up and running successfully."

And, several weeks later, that proposition was noticed by an ambitious young man with aspirations. He called on David Levine.

Nona opened the door to see a large, questionable-looking man in a three-piece suit who wanted to see Mr. Levine. With him was a lean Asian man. She asked them to wait at the door while she talked to David. He hesitated before telling her to show them and Mr. Blum into his office.

"I understand that you can use some help in getting these films back into production. I have several actors ready to star in those movies," the young man announced. "I also have access to several theaters that are ready to show those films. We're prepared to make you an offer that you won't want to refuse."

The Don leaned back in his chair to look around the room. "And just how much will this service cost that you so generously offer?"

The man sat back, smiling and more at ease with this question, while his apparent bodyguard stood behind him.

"I think we can do this service for around fifty percent of the total profits," he smugly answered.

Levine coughed and then took a sip of water. He excused himself for the interruption. "My health has not been so good of late." He picked up the phone to call Donald.

"Yes, will you come into my office, please? I have two gentlemen here you will want to meet." He noticed the young man's increased smile.

When Donald entered his office, Levine introduced them. "I think you will be interested to know that we may have some new investors. If you'll excuse me, I'll let you two take charge of the matter as you see fit." With that, he left his trusted employees to discuss any final arrangements.

The limousine driver jumped out of the car as Donald opened the back door. Blum threw the mangled bodies inside, telling the driver, "They might want to go back home."

"Are they still alive?"

"That depends on how fast you can get to a hospital. You drive safely now," he grinned.

Roy Jacobs didn't fare any better than he had. Because of his exemplary behavior, the parole board planned to interview him for an early release. So, all concerned parties were notified.

Eddie Martin and his mother were sure to attend, along with the acrimonious Sergeants Crawford and Bailey. Senator Nichols sent a letter to voice his disapproval of Jacob's early release. Carla's physician would be there, along with Mr. Blum. The last to be seated was Stanley Fraiser, who returned the judge's nod.

All it took was for Jacobs to see the look of continued abhorrence and rejection on their faces to know what the court's decision would be; which was, back to the chain gang for you!

Attorney Larry Cross signed the deeds of the two Portland theaters over to their new owner, Samuel Jacobs. Cross now held the power of attorney for all of Jacob's holdings.

While counting his theater's income, he sang, "Zipity do-dah, zipity yey, plenty of money coming my way....

Chapter Thirty-four

THIS WILL ALL BE YOURS

Carla's health improved significantly. She was finally able to accept Stanley Fraiser's generous invitation to redecorate his primary home. His instruction was, "Make it so comfortable and pleasing that you'd like to be here." He also wanted her to live in the house while she worked, since he was staying in one of his smaller homes meanwhile.

She asked if he had suggestions or ideas of want he'd like.

"I would love for it to be very homey and warm. Perhaps something in an old-world theme of sorts, like the Mediterranean, Italian, or English. Which one doesn't matter, just visualize something that you would like. I'm sure I'll find your ideas extremely pleasing to me."

Fraiser's grand home provided an excellent opportunity to use the many ideas Carla had acquired during her European travels. She approached this job with eagerness.

Her thoughts fell back onto the Majestic Theater and how pleased she was with her work there. She could incorporate many of those ideas in this home. The companies from which she had previously ordered were delighted to fill the new ones, offering some at a discount.

While remodeling the Fraiser home, Carla pulled a tall stool over to one side of the dining area and sat to consider her ideas for that room and the kitchen. The grand entry, hallway, and living room were finished, which left these last rooms to remodel before starting on the upstairs bedrooms.

All the workers had gone home for the day, so she considered her theory in their absence. Carla thought by removing a short wall between the kitchen and dining room it would make the space more expansive and less formal. She knew the wall was not load-bearing, so the work wouldn't be costly.

While reaching an arm over her shoulder, Carla tried to rub some aching muscles, and then she heard Stanley's footsteps behind her.

"Everything is looking tremendous, but is the job getting to you, my dear?"

His muscular hands firmly move over her shoulders and upper back.

She sighed, "Oh-h. I'll give you a thousand years to stop that."

He felt her tension dissipate as his hands moved lower on her back and up again to her shoulders, biceps, and neck. Deft fingertips and thumbs massaged against the swollen muscles. Carla could only quietly moan as she felt the relief that his hands brought her.

Stanley felt her submission to his manipulations and smiled. He knew she needed the relaxation he gave her. His hands slipped over her neck's tender skin and onto her lower head. He smoothly ran his fingers through her long hair and over her head.

She felt warm chills and dropped her shoulders while tilting her head back in complete relaxation as his fingers moved over her tense scalp for a while longer.

Quietly, he moved in front of her. Carla felt the touch of his soft lips just below her ear, on her cheek, and then on her lips. They tasted lovely to her, and she responded to his delicious kiss. Her hand reached up to touch his face and then moved to the back of his head.

Stanley slid his hand to her waist, pulling her up to himself as she rose to her feet. While embracing ever so close to one another, their souls met for the first time.

Still holding her, Stanley turned his head next to hers as he murmured, "You can't know how many times I have tasted your lips in my dreams or held you in my arms in my sleep. But to feel those dreams come true right now, to finally hold you this close to me, is so much greater than I could have ever dreamed. Now, my dearest lady, my biggest fear that I could possibly imagine is to hear your words of rejection when I say, Carla, I love you."

Still wrapped in his arms, Carla remained silent. Then she whispered, "Oh, my Lord," but didn't move away. "Oh, heavens, Stanley, I had no idea..."

The two clung to each other, not just not wanting to part but unable to. Carla slowly drew herself away, only to look at his face and then into his eyes... into the windows of his soul.

"I cannot reject those words...." Her eyes darted over his face, noting the expression of anxiety as he awaited her next utterance. Would that be of kindness, empathy, or even outright pity?

"I cherish hearing you words and receive them into my heart." As her eyes filled with tears, she wrapped her arms around him and whispered, "I care so very much for you, and I know I can love you that much. It would be so easy."

They could only cling to one another for many moments without speaking while Stanley silently praised God for giving him the patience to wait for this moment.

As Carla sniffed and wiped her eyes, Stanley gave her his handkerchief. She tried to remove the smudged mascara. "Oh, I'm a mess."

Then he helped her. "You can never be a mess, my dear. At least it's not an eyelash," he grinned.

They talked for hours, drawing closer to each other in mind, spirit, and beliefs. Over dinner, they realized more mutual interests to share: business, travel, what he planned to build, and how she could decorate it.

The next day, Carla was anxious to tell Jada the splendid news. She was asked to come over directly.

While they were talking. Jada sat next to her young friend and held her hand. "Darling, I don't know how else to say this, and I pray that Stanley will forgive me, but that dear man has been deeply in love with you for a long time. He would give heaven and earth, if it were his to give, to see that your'e happy."

Jada looked into her eyes. "Stanley fell in love with you the day he first saw you and has loved you ever since. He has been in pain for all you went through with Roy. But he could not come between you and that man. Stanley knew you needed to make that decision for yourself. Otherwise, there could always be a doubt someplace in your mind that things might have worked out between you and Roy.

"He wants to make up for what that horrible man did in any way that he can. Let him do that for you. He wants only your best interest. Go ahead with him on that Yoat trip. I'm sure it would thrilled him if David and I joined you. His crew will be on board as well. So please, darling, let him care for you," Jada pleaded.

Carla listened intensely to her words intensely. "I didn't know he felt that deeply for me. He's always been so kind and thoughtful, and a true gentleman. I've always had a warm feeling being around Stanley, kind of like he was protecting me. Oh, dear, now I see why he said some things to me."

"Like what?"

"At your housewarming party, he said he was sorry that Senator Nichols introduced Roy to me."

Carla thought for a moment before agreeing to make that trip. She'd feel more comfortable if Jada and David joined them. And it would be good for him to get away for a while after being in that terrible prison.

This proved to be a wise decision for Carla and Stanley. It allowed him to show the woman of his heart's desire all that she had never known before. That there was a better life for her and a life more abundant.

The cruise to Mexico was thrilling, and the quaint markets sublime. Carla could laugh, live, and learn how to genuinely love. On this trip, she met the real Stanley Fraiser for the first time. And this marvelous man was not as old as she once thought him to be. The twenty years no longer separated them, as his experiences added insight to their relationship. There, Carla found freedom from the flurry of her once so troubled mind.

They came to know one another better by exchanging thoughts and sharing ideas. Their hearts blended in knowing they could achieve these goals together and as good friends that they were fast becoming, the basis of any good relationship.

While on the deck one afternoon, Carla mentioned to Stanley, "Mother said that you came to see me at the hospital, but I wasn't aware of that."

He smiled at her. "Under those circumstances, I wasn't offended that you didn't recognize me. You didn't even recognize your family."

"She told me you paid for all my bills."

"I felt it was the least I could do. I certainly didn't want Roy to pay for anything. He would have held it over your head and made you feel guilty, if not indebted to him. I couldn't possibly have let that happen."

"Well, thank you, Stanely. I do appreciate your watching over me like that. And I know mom sure appreciated your looking after me. She really hoped you cared for me."

"You can let her know her hopes came to be. A mother always wants the best for her children."

During their time together, they often shared caresses. And warm and tasty kisses became more than satisfying to them. As a true gentleman, Stanley kept complete control of his emotions, even as difficult as it sometimes seemed. He respected Carla as the lady that she was and treated her as one.

One summer's pleasant evening, as the two sat together in his garden, Stanley got down on one knee before Carla to pledge his love and ask for her hand in marriage.

She didn't hesitate before saying, "I will be honored to become your wife, Stanley."

With this positive answer he presented her with a five-carat sparkling diamond ring to signify their betrothal.

Carla couldn't wait to tell Jada the splendid news and begin making wedding plans.

Jada was honored to be her Matron of Honor, with Sharon and Marni as her bridesmaids. Marni joked that it could look like Jada was her mother, and guests would think they were her older sisters. Her smile abruptly faded when Jada shot her a look of sharp disapproval.

Marni bowed her head, "Sorry, Mom."

These three helped Carla plan her wedding. "Oh, another Christian-Jewish marriage? You definitely can't do another Unitarian ceremony, though," Sharon protested.

They also questioned where to hold the ceremony and who will marry them?

When asked, Stanley had a suggestion. "I know a Supreme Court judge. And since you don't have a church that you regularly attend, perhaps we get married in mine."

They agreed on that idea and to spare much of the "religious stuff" in the ceremony, even though Jesus was a Jew.

"That's fine with me. Besides, I think it was His Father who started all this marriage stuff in the first place," Carla laughed. "But I'd like to include some traditional Jewish things in the service. You'll have to help me with that. Do you have a preference in what color my dress should be?"

"Since you are a virgin to me, you can certainly wear white if you wish."

On this day, there could have been no prouder man than was Stanley Fraiser. To see his beautiful and beloved bride walk down the aisle was beyond his dreams. As Mendelssohn's "Wedding March" played, the congregation rose to honor this woman escorted by her father.

Carla was dressed in a pale blue, floor-length gown, trimmed in white lace with an open lace veil. Her jewelry was a double strand of pearls with matching earrings.

Sharon's youngest daughter was the flower girl, while Marni's little boy acted as the ring bearer. Bride's maids Sharon and Marni walked ahead of Jada, the Matron of Honor.

As the couple stood before the altar, a genuine blessing of peace fell over Carla and Stanley when they accepted one another in marriage by the exchanging of vows and rings.

The Levines held the flamboyant reception at their mansion, which was large enough to receive the many guests. The bride and groom surprised everyone with a gracefully executed bridal waltz that demonstrated their footwork and unity with one another.

When it was time for the newlyweds to leave, the garter was tossed to the bachelors, and then Nona helped gather all single ladies to catch the bridal bouquet.

Stanley helped his bride into the back seat of the well-decorated limousine, which headed for the Yoat for the beginning of their honeymoon cruise. On the deck they welcomed a quiet, relaxing time and a refreshing glass of the finest champagne.

After a conversation about the wedding and reception, Carla sat back to look at her groom with a touching smile.

"That was so much fun and everyone's been terrific, although, finally being here with you is so peacefull. I don't know about you, but I've had too many people around me for a quite a while. Just promise we'll never go through all of that again."

"Don't you fret, my darling, I swear we won't go through that *ever* again, cross my heart. But I do cherish the solitude of being with just you." Stanley tipped his glass to his bride. Then he tilted his head back to gaze at heaven's brightly twinkling stars and full, glowing moon. He raised his glass high.

"Thank you, Lord, for blessing us with your beautiful lights on this warm and wondrous night."

Carla raised her glass, "Amen to that. It couldn't be lovelier. And the water's so still we could almost dance on it."

"Yes. I would love to, but right now, my feet would welcome some slippers."

"Oh, my feet are swollen too," she signed. "If I take my shoes off, I wouldn't be able to get them on again."

As they looked at each other, Stanley grinned, "I'll race ya'!"

He escorted Carla to the "bridal suite". The master bedroom had softened lights, magnificent roses, and romantic music awaiting them. With a sigh of relief, they both kicked off their shoes to put their feet up on a cushioned, velvet-covered hassock. After a while,

Carla fidgeted at her waistline.

"Oh, I have got to get out of this dress. I'm too warm, and my corset is killing me."

"Me too, I mean the cummerbund," Stanley laughed. Helping Carla to her feet, "Enough formality, it's time to relax."

In the luxurious bathroom, Carla's make-up, hairbrush, perfume, and gown were laid out for her. After changing, the bride quietly stepped out to present herself to her groom. When she saw he was on his knees before the bed, she went back around the corner but could hear his quiet worrs.

"... blessing me with this marvelous woman, she was far more than well worth the wait. Lord, I ask now that you bless me to be the best husband possible to her, and in all ways possible. Amen."

Carla slipped back into the bathroom and quietly closed the door. She clasped her hands together and bowed her head in prayer.

"Father God Almighty, You blessed me deeply by giving me this man as my husband. I don't know if I can ever thank you enough. I ask that you teach me to be the wife to him that you and Stanley want me to be, and in all the ways I should be. Thank you, Lord. In the name of Jesus, amen."

When she went back into the boudoir, Stanley smiled widely to see her in the white lace peignoir over a white satin gown.

"You look far more than lovely, my dear, and your fragrance is tantalizing."

He handed her a glass of pink champagne as she admired the satin-trimmed lounging robe over his silk pajamas. They tipped the glasses together.

"To a glorious new life together," Stanley toasted.

"And a great one it will be."After taking a couple of sips of the effervescing wine, the invitingly soft strains of "I'm In the Mood for Love" filled the air. Stanley set the glasses aside to take Carla's hand, leading her into a romantic waltz. When it ended, he refilled the glasses, giving one to his bride.

They talked about the reception and their gracious hosts while sipping champagne. Then there was an awkward moment of silence between them. Carla opened her arms wide to break the subtle tension.

"I guess this the part where you pick me up, toss me on the bed, and ravish my body," she laughed.

With gracious and sweeping movements, Stanley said, "Oh, but I shall lift my blessed bride with gossamer wings, to lie thy sweet body gently down, to touch thee tenderly with my fingertips and savor thy sweet lips on mine... well, after you rub my head a little, if you will, please. I have a bit of a headache."

"Oh, darling, how selfish of me. All of this must have been a great deal of stress on you."

Carla pulled down the comforter and satin top sheet and then fluffed up the pillows. "Take your robe off and lie down, dear. Let me massage your head and rub your back."

In just his pajama bottoms, he readily obliged her. Carla removed her peignoir to lie next to him, adjusting the long gown. With strong fingers, she released much of the tension in his head and then moved on to his neck and shoulders as he softly moaned into the pillow.

"Sweetheart, your fingers are those of an angel of mercy. Oh, that feels so fantastic."

She could now closely see the fullness of his muscular biceps for the first time. His shoulders revealed the effort that he put into lifting weights and barbells. This was the body of a manly man, and she enjoyed touching it.

Stanley turned to face his bride, wrapping his arms around her. She could now see how exhausted he was. The effort he had put into the reception and the honeymoon showed in his face. As the soft strains of classical music played in the background, Carla embraced her new husband to stroke his head and neck, closing her eyes as well. They both drifted off into a peaceful slumber.

Somewhere between then and the early beginnings of dawn, Carla sensed slow movements as Stanley removed the pajama bottoms. She felt his hands on her sleepy body, his lips, and then his tongue. She purred to receive his tender touches and kisses. She responded to them and the way he helped her out of the gown as she readily untied the front bows for him.

As their hearts and bodies met in the consummation of their wedding vows, so did their souls. They became one flesh with one another in the bliss of holy matrimony. This emotion was not the passionate lust she had known before. It was love... a profound, true, and abiding love. They then lay wrapped in each other's arms to drift back into a deeper and more peaceful rest.

Carla finally found the genuine love of a good man for the first time in her life. A man she could love without compromise or condition, but with the gifts that God instilled in everyone's heart at birth; that of faith, hope, and love. The greatest of these is love.

TABLE OF CONTENTS

This story is from the author's vast imagination, although, based on actual events. Any resemblance to persons, living or dead, is entirely coincidental. Names, characters, businesses and places have been changed to protect the innocent...

and the not so innocent.

Made in the USA
Las Vegas, NV
23 January 2022